"Mallory," he said, waiting for her to look at him.

When she didn't, he repeated himself. "Mallory."

She set down the resistance bands and turned to face him with her hands on her hips. "What?"

"I am having fun and it's all your fault. Thank you for helping me get out of my head and enjoy myself for once. I really needed it."

She didn't move or speak, but her chest rose and fell with heavy breaths. Finally, she said, "You're welcome. Thank you for letting my family believe that this is the best Christmas ever, even if it's all based on a lie."

"Even if I'm not your boyfriend, it doesn't mean it can't actually be the best Christmas. The lie doesn't change the experience."

"Okay, but don't make everyone like you so much that they hate me when I have to tell them we broke up. I'm beginning to think that's a real possibility."

Dear Reader,

I am not a huge fan of the winter season (too cold in Chicago!), but I do love Christmas and being with family. Not everyone feels the same way I do, however.

In *Their Holiday Agreement*, Mallory Moore is suffering from a fear of too much family time. When Theo Seasons gives her the idea of escaping her family holiday gathering, she hatches a plan to get out of it. Her mother, however, has other ideas. If Mallory can't come to family Christmas, family will come to her.

One little problem—her mom thinks she's on vacation with her boyfriend...who doesn't exist. Thank goodness Theo agrees to be her fake boyfriend.

Relationships that start off pretend are so fun to write. The evolution of feelings and the fear that the other person might not want to venture into reality make for interesting conflicts and storylines. I hope you agree!

Welcome to the winter season at the Seasons Inn.

xoxo,

Amy Vastine

THEIR HOLIDAY AGREEMENT

AMY VASTINE

HEARTWARMING

Harlequin®
HEARTWARMING™

ISBN-13: 978-1-335-46020-2

Their Holiday Agreement

Recycling programs for this product may not exist in your area.

Harlequin Enterprises ULC
22 Adelaide St. West, 41st Floor
Toronto, Ontario M5H 4E3, Canada
www.Harlequin.com

Printed in U.S.A.

Amy Vastine has been plotting stories in her head for as long as she can remember. An eternal optimist, she studied social work, hoping to teach others how to find their silver lining. Now she enjoys creating happily-ever-afters for all to read. Amy lives outside Chicago with her high school-sweetheart husband, three teenagers who keep her on her toes and their two sweet but mischievous pups. Visit her at amyvastine.com.

Books by Amy Vastine

Harlequin Heartwarming

A Seasons Inn Romance

Her Summer to Start Over

The Blackwell Belles

A Cowgirl's Thanksgiving Kiss

Stop the Wedding!

A Marriage of Inconvenience
The Sheriff's Valentine
The Christmas Wedding Crashers
His Texas Runaway Bride

Return of the Blackwell Brothers

The Rancher's Fake Fiancée

The Blackwell Sisters

Montana Wishes

Visit the Author Profile page
at Harlequin.com for more titles.

To Ryan—I wrote this right before your
big adventure. Hoping you had the time of your life!

CHAPTER ONE

"AT LEAST LET me work on the leg press."

"You are literally six weeks post op, Theo. Using the leg press isn't something you should be doing for another six weeks. You know the routine. You've been through this before." Mallory Moore was the most frustrating physical therapist Theo Seasons had ever worked with, but she was also the assistant physical therapist for the Boston Icemen, so he was stuck with her.

Theo finished up his set of calf raises. He felt good. Mallory was right about one thing; he had done this before. Theo had an unfortunate history with knee injuries over his twelve-year professional hockey career. This time, he could tell he was going to recover quickly. He had to. Getting knocked off the roster and placed on injured reserve was not part of the plan this season. He had one year left on this contract and if he wanted to get a new one with the Icemen, he couldn't be benched for long.

"Let's try some straight leg raises," Mallory

suggested, moving over to the floor mats. "Two sets of ten to start."

"Three sets of ten," Theo replied, getting into position.

Mallory's chin tipped down. Her annoyingly pretty, big brown eyes glared at him. "Two sets of ten so I can see how bad your hip pain is this time."

How did she know he had hip pain? He hadn't been reporting it for a reason. "I don't know what you're talking about."

"Stop," she said with a roll of her eyes. "You're giving me déjà moo."

"Don't you mean déjà vu?"

"Nope, déjà *moo*," she said, tightening her ponytail. Her hair was the same warm brown as her eyes. "Meaning I'm pretty sure I've heard this bull before. Two sets of ten and we check your hip pain that you've been silent about, but I see on your face every time I ask you to do something that puts strain on it."

She was irritatingly witty and too observant. Theo tried to play it off. "If you saw anything, it was my frustration with the lameness of this workout."

"Keep telling yourself that, hotshot. If you want to get back on the ice, you need to tell me the truth and do what I say. Two sets of ten. Begin."

Mallory might have only been five foot four, but

she had clearly worked with hockey players long enough to not be intimidated by them one bit. In fact, Theo knew a couple guys on the team who were a little afraid of her.

Theo wasn't afraid of her, but he knew better than to give her any more grief. He laid down on the mat and started his leg raises and halfway through the second set there was that sharp pain that shot up from his knee to his hip. He did everything he could to not grimace.

Kneeling next to him, Mallory placed one hand on his shin and one on his hip. "Stop." She moved the hand on his shin up his leg and along the outside of his thigh, where the pain had traveled. "It's possible that you have a tight iliotibial band. That's the tendon that runs from here to here." Her hand slid from his hip to his knee again. "It also could be one of the nerves connecting your knee joint to your hip joint. It can cause pain in both the hip and the knee. Is the pain in both joints or is it running along here?" She moved her hand along the outside of his thigh again.

There was a quick internal battle over whether to tell the truth or not. Theo opted to be honest. "It shoots up from my knee to my hip along the outside of my quad."

Mallory thankfully didn't gloat about being right. "We're going to be more conscientious about stretching, focusing a bit more on this area, okay?"

Theo nodded. They continued his therapy and when they finished, she threw him a towel to wipe his forehead that had beaded up with sweat. "Did you have a good Thanksgiving?"

"I didn't really do Thanksgiving this year." Theo hadn't felt very grateful. His injury made him much less fun to be around.

Mallory did that cute thing where she scrunched up her nose and her brows pinched together. "You had nowhere to go?"

"A couple of my teammates offered to have me join them and their families, but I wasn't going to be good company for anyone. What about you?"

"I went to my parents' since the rest of my family spent Thanksgiving with their in-laws this year. It was quiet, too quiet for my mom. She's looking forward to Christmas when the whole gang will be there. I'm the boring daughter—no boyfriend, no husband, no kids. No life, my mom would say."

It was Theo's turn to furrow his brow. "You have to have a significant other and/or some kids to have a life?"

"According to Mrs. Selene Moore, one of those things or a combination of the two is the secret to a good life."

"Well, you work here. You have a *cool* life."

"Working with hockey players like you makes me cool?"

"Um, yeah," he said with a grin. "Not to mention, I have none of those things, either. I have a very full life. There are a lot of people out there who wish they were me. Maybe not me right now in recovery, but me in general."

"And still, it would break my mom's heart to know you spent Thanksgiving alone. She'd be trying to get you together with her friend's niece, so you both could settle down and find happiness."

"Your mom would try to set me up with her friend's niece instead of you, her daughter?"

Mallory began to busy herself with putting equipment back where it belonged. "Fine, she would most definitely try to throw me in your path, but we know that's not happening."

Theo could tell her face was bright red. He'd be lying if he said he didn't like having that effect. In different circumstances, he wouldn't mind spending time with someone like Mallory. Unfortunately, that was not possible, given their working relationship.

"Do you have any exciting Christmas plans since Thanksgiving was a bust?"

Christmas was coming. Theo normally didn't give much thought to the holidays since he was usually solely focused on his hockey season this time of year. He always had a day or two off at Christmas, but it never seemed like enough time to drive up north to see the family. This year was different for a couple reasons.

"I'm heading home to see my family in New Hampshire for a few days. My parents own and run an inn up there with the help of my brothers and my sister."

"Your parents own an inn?"

"The Seasons Inn up in Apple Hollow. It's on Lake Champney. It's actually a pretty big deal in those parts."

"Wow, that's cool. Do people who own an inn live at the inn? Or is that not how it works?" She didn't stop for him to answer as she cleaned the mats with some antiseptic spray and a towel. "I picture your family having its own floor or its own wing. Like is there an owner's suite or something? I would love it if my parents lived in an inn. I could have my own room and bathroom. You have no idea what it's like to go home and have to share a bathroom with three sisters and their significant others and my two nephews. It's a nightmare."

Theo had to chuckle. He liked that she had no filter sometimes. "They don't live in the inn. I grew up in a house on the property. I had to share a bathroom just like you, but when I visit these days, I do stay at the inn. I do not share a bathroom with *anyone*."

Her brows pinched together again, and she tilted her head. "Lies. You share a locker room with twenty-two other guys all the time."

He laughed and shook his head. "Okay, you're right. That's not totally the same, though. At least that space is built for all of us to use it at once."

"True. I could probably handle being home if we were sharing a locker room–sized bathroom. Or if it was an inn. Let me know if you want some extra physical therapy over the break. I'd happily accept room and board in payment for my services." She threw the dirty towels in the hamper by the door. "I'm going to make sure they prepped your ice bath. Stretching is the only thing you should be doing in here until I get back," she said as if she didn't trust him to stay away from the leg press.

Theo put his palms up. "I will only stretch. Maybe roll out with the foam roller. Is that okay, boss lady?"

There was still some suspicion in her eyes. "Rolling out is fine. But that's it."

"That's it," he repeated as she opened the door. She pretended to walk out and then opened the door like she was going to catch him on the leg press. He shook his head and laughed. He could admit it; there were worse people to be stuck with while he was on injured reserve. Mallory was tough, but she was funny. He needed a reason to laugh these days. Not much else made him smile.

Theo would personally see to it that Mallory got a huge bonus if she could get him back on the ice. That was his only goal right now. Who would he be if not Theo Seasons, center for the Boston Icemen?

Maybe having her come up north with him wouldn't be such a bad idea.

THEO SEASONS WAS his own worst enemy on his road to recovery. Of course, that was true of most professional athletes. Mallory had spent some time at the high school and college level earlier in her career, but professional, grown men were the worst when it came to taking the time they needed to do things the right way. She understood it a little. The sport they played was more than their job; it was their identity.

Even though teams could hold on to someone on long-term injured reserve, contracts came to an end, and if someone was on LTIR, they weren't often re-signed. At the same time, professional hockey players failed to realize that slowing things down a bit could help extend their careers in the long run or save them from a lifetime of unnecessary pain when they did more damage by coming back too early.

She could see how desperate Theo was to get back on the ice. He was only thirty, but in hockey that made him one of the old guys. There were eighteen-year-olds vying for Rookie of the Year these days. Mallory understood his impatience with the process, but she was also going to do everything in her power to make sure the man not only got back on the ice but was going to be able to run around with his kids and grandkids someday.

Theo didn't have any kids, but a guy like him would surely settle down someday with someone. He was right about living the kind of life other people wished they had. He was rich, ridiculously good-looking and famous. There were plenty of women who only needed those three traits in a man to fall in love.

Mallory was not one of them. Her standards were much higher, which might have been why she was still single (at least that's what her mother thought). Character meant more to Mallory than money or fame. Looks mattered only in the sense that she needed to be attracted to the man she would marry. He didn't have to look like Theo Seasons, although that wouldn't be a bad thing, either.

She walked down the hall from the strength-and-conditioning room to the athletic training room to get a tub prepared for his ice bath. Working for a professional hockey team meant being around famous, wealthy, extremely fit men all the time. These were things she had become immune to for the most part. Mallory wanted more. No one seemed to fit that bill yet.

Finn Grouch, one of Boston's star forwards, was already soaking in one of the tubs. "Mallory, Mallory. When are you going to put me out of my misery and let me buy you dinner?"

"When the Icemen trade you, I guess. You know how the front office feels about fraternizing."

Finn was full of himself. He thought every woman would fall over themselves to be with him. "They love me here. They'll never let me go. I guess you'll never know how good you could have had it."

"What a shame, Grouch. I'm sure dinner would have been delicious." The tub for Theo was ready to go, so she headed back out to get him.

"The food wasn't the part you'd be missing out on!" he shouted after her.

Mallory shook her head. *Ego.* She couldn't stand the ego on some of these guys. Where were the humble, capable-of-thinking-of-someone-else kind of guys? When she returned to the strength-and-conditioning room, Theo was on the floor rolling out his leg like he had promised. Being trustworthy was another trait Mallory couldn't always find in a guy.

"Tub's ready when you are."

Theo sighed and carefully got himself up off the ground. She noticed the way he grimaced. That hip was going to be an issue. His trying to hide that it was hurting was going to sideline him for good. Theo was still not as trustworthy as she'd like him to be.

"So, you're headed back to your parents' house for Christmas?" he asked as they walked to the tubs. "Where is that?"

"My parents live about two hours outside of Boston. It's thankfully not too far away. Hopefully, my car will make it twice in less than a month."

"Do you have to go?"

His question gave her pause. Did she have to go? That was the expectation. Did she *have* to go? She'd never really considered it before. "I would get a lot of grief. We have all this celebrating to do thanks to the engagement and the baby on the way." Celebrating that, as her mother had been sure to point out, would be nice to do for her someday if she would just settle down with a man instead of focusing on her career so much. Mallory would do just about anything to not have to listen to that anymore.

"But you don't have to go if you don't want to." Theo raised a brow.

Was he proposing another alternative? Why did she hope he was? "If you knew my mother, you would understand."

"Is she going to try to hook you up with her other friend's nephew?" he joked.

Mallory laughed through her nose. "Probably. I think she feels like she hasn't done her job as a parent until I'm married off and someone else's problem. Not that I'm a problem. I have a job, my own condo, I haven't missed a school loan payment yet. My sisters have done a better job of taking the traditional path than I have, I guess. It makes her think there's something wrong with me."

"There's nothing wrong with you, Mallory. I have three siblings who all did exactly what my parents hoped we would all do. Being the black sheep is way more fun if you ask me." He nudged her with his elbow as they entered the athletic training room.

"Well, well, if it isn't our fallen leader. How's the knee, Seasons?" Finn asked as soon as Theo walked in.

Mallory felt him bristle beside her. "It's great. I should be back in no time. I wouldn't want you to think I'm ready to give up my spot as high scorer."

"You're giving me too many weeks on the ice without you, buddy. I'm on fire this season. Even if you came back right after Christmas, you wouldn't be able to catch up."

There was no way Theo was getting back on the ice after the holidays. He'd be lucky to get back at the end of the season. Yet, there was something about Finn's ego that rubbed her the wrong way today. "I don't know, Grouch. Seasons had how many hat tricks last year? And you had how many? Seems to me that as long as you can only get one goal a game, Theo has plenty of time to catch up."

Finn stood up in his tub and snapped his fingers at the attendant to give him a towel. "If he gets back on the ice, that is. Maybe Seasons can take you out for that dinner if things don't work out the way he hopes. Although, I doubt he'd be as fun as I would be on a date." He waggled his eyebrows and Mallory had to stop herself from gagging.

"What?" Two lines appeared between Theo's brows.

Finn got out of his tub and headed for the locker room. "You wish you were me, Seasons," he called over his shoulder.

Mallory shook her head. "Ignore him. The man thinks he's irresistible when in reality he's reprehensible."

Theo let out a chuckle as he lifted his T-shirt off. "You're funny."

"My sense of humor is one of my finer traits." She did her best not to stare at his bare chest. His six pack abs and pectoral muscles were medical textbook–worthy. He was a perfect specimen. Also, off-limits for a million reasons.

He kicked off his shoes and took off his socks, then got up and sat on the edge like he was only going to soak his knee. Mallory stopped him.

"You're going all in."

"All in?" His eyes went wide like he needed to

mentally prepare for something like that and he was not ready.

"That hip needs some ice. You know it and I know it."

Theo closed his eyes and let out a huffing sigh. "Come on, Mallory."

"Come on, Theo. If you want to get back on that ice and show up Mr. Big Talk Grouch, you need to ice that hip as well."

He couldn't argue with that, so he sucked it up and sank all the way in. His face contorted as the ice-cold water most likely took his breath away.

"Fifteen minutes and you'll be done for the day," she said, patting him on the shoulder. "I'll check back in on you in ten."

Theo's teeth were already chattering. "Great."

Mallory popped into her office to catch up on emails while Theo soaked. Her phone rang before she even got to reply to the first one. Her display warned her it was her sister Erica, but she answered it anyway.

"Hello, dear sister."

"Can you please call Savannah and tell her that my engagement is a little bit of a bigger deal right now than her baby who's not coming into this world for five more months? She's got plenty of time to do a gender reveal. Not to mention she's going to have baby showers and who knows what else before this baby shows up. I only get one engagement party that should happen right after we get engaged."

Erica was the youngest in the family and hated that everyone (almost everyone) got to do things first, which meant that when it was her turn, she wanted nothing to take away from her moment.

"Well, let's not forget that you're going to have bridal showers and bachelorette parties and a wedding that is more than six months away."

"Do not take her side on this! That's exactly what she said to me." Mallory's phone beeped, alerting her to another call. She lifted the phone away to see that Savannah was calling now as well. "Looks like she must have known you were talking to me. Hang on a second." Mallory clicked over. "Were your ears burning?"

"Oh, my gosh, can you please call Erica and tell her that there's no reason Mom and Dad can't acknowledge that Greg and I are expecting our first child over Christmas? She acts like her engagement is more important than bringing a life into this world."

Mallory pinched the bridge of her nose. "I think she just wants to feel special. You and Avery got to celebrate your engagements with the family without any other event overshadowing."

"Avery was pregnant when I got engaged."

"Yeah, six months pregnant with her second kid. It was old news by then."

"So, no one is allowed to mention that I'm having a baby because Erica needs to have all the attention as usual?" Her voice was loaded with her burgeoning resentment.

This was the fun part of being one of four sisters. There was never a time that at least two of them weren't bickering over something.

"You know that Mom is not going to ignore your wonderful news. Hang on a second." Mallory clicked back over to Erica. "Listen, Savannah isn't looking to steal your thunder. She just wants you to be happy for her like she's happy for you."

"I am happy for her. Did she say she was happy for me? She's been acting like it wasn't a surprise that Hayden proposed."

It wasn't a surprise, seeing that they had been together for two years and he asked for their parents' blessing three months ago. Everyone knew this was coming. Everyone except for Erica, apparently. "We're all happy for you."

"I should call her."

"I think that's a good idea."

"Thanks, Mal. You always know how to fix things." Erica hung up and Mallory went back to her call with Savannah. "She's going to call you to make peace. Tell her you're happy for her and you are so excited about this engagement, and she will chill about the idea of Mom making it special for you, too."

"That's all I have to do?"

"That's all. And if she calls the engagement a surprise, you go with it."

"Oh, come on. It wasn't a surprise!" A beeping noise told Mallory that Savannah was getting that call right now.

"Go with it," Mallory repeated before letting her sister go.

She switched her phone to silent mode and put it in the drawer of her desk. She was not going to survive this holiday get-together. Between Avery's kids running around and Erica and Savannah wrestling for the spotlight, Mallory wouldn't even be missed if she didn't show up. Not to mention she wasn't in the mood to hear her mother go on and on about how it would be nice if Mallory would settle down one day. If Mallory wasn't so focused on her job. If she wasn't so picky. If she wasn't such a disappointment.

That was what it really felt like her mom was saying. She wasn't up for listening to how great everyone else's life was. Maybe Theo was right. Did she have to? If only she had a reason to be somewhere else. Of course, her parents would never let her miss Christmas unless...

She pulled her phone out of her desk drawer and searched for her mom's number. If she wanted out of all this holiday chaos, she had to do it now or she was going to be cutting it too close. There were exactly twenty days until Christmas. She pressed the Call button.

"Mallory, is everything okay?"

"Hi, Mom. Everything is fine." All the confidence she'd had a moment ago was fading fast now that she was actually speaking to her mom. There was no going back now. She had to say something. "I was calling because I have some news."

"News? Are you okay? Did something happen?" Her mother always assumed Mallory didn't have good news. This was good and bad.

"I didn't want to make a big deal out of it when I was home last week because this is all kind of new, but I have been seeing someone—"

"You've been seeing someone? Oh, honey! That's wonderful. You should bring him with you for Christmas. What's his name? What does he do for a living? How did you meet?"

Mallory had not thought this out enough to play twenty questions. "Mom, we would love to come home for the holidays, but he actually invited me to meet his family."

The silence on the other side of the call was not good. Finally, her mother cleared her throat. "You're going to visit his family over Christmas? *This* Christmas?"

"You're always telling me that I should be looking for those signs that a man is looking for more. Meeting the family is always a sign of more, right?"

As much as she wanted everyone home for Christmas, Mallory knew her mother was overjoyed at the possibility that her spinster daughter could be meeting the parents. "Where exactly does his family live? What do his parents do for a living?"

Again, maybe she should have thought this through before calling. This boyfriend didn't have a name, a backstory or a hometown. She decided to go with the last place she had talked about. "He's from this small town in New Hampshire. We're staying in this place called the Seasons Inn. Have you heard of it? I hear it's a big deal up there." That had to make this story sound credible. Her mom could even look the place up on the internet.

"The Seasons Inn? I'm not sure if that's the place Gina and Kyle went last summer or not. It sounds familiar. William? What was the name of that place Kyle told you he and Gina stayed at in New Hampshire last summer?" Her mother must have pulled the phone away from her face to ask her father. "Ugh, he can't remember."

"Mom, I have to get back to work. I'm sorry to spring this on you with the holidays around the corner."

"Well, wait a second—"

"Gotta go, bye." Mallory ended the call. Had she gotten herself out of Christmas chaos? She just might have. All she had to do was avoid the nine million questions that were about to come her way from everyone in her family until then. After the holidays, she and her make-believe boyfriend would break up and no one would ever be the wiser. Easy.

CHAPTER TWO

THEO WAS ABOUT to become a block of ice if he didn't get out of the tub soon. Mallory said she'd be back to check on him in ten minutes, but he was fairly certain she had been gone for ten hours.

She came bursting out of her office. "Sorry, I got caught on the phone. Let's get you out of there."

She handed him a warm towel and held out another once he got the first one around his shoulders. "I hope you were solving the world's problems in there," he said through chattering teeth.

Her face broke into the widest smile. "Maybe not the world's, but I did get myself out of going home for the holidays. I am quite possibly a genius thanks to your encouragement."

Theo checked his toes for frostbite. She was lucky he didn't have hypothermia. "Well, I'd be prouder of you if you hadn't left me to die in the ice bath to cancel your holiday plans."

She cocked her head. "I didn't leave you to die.

You were in there for fifteen minutes. Just like you were supposed to be. You're a hockey player. You love ice."

He bounced on the balls of his feet, trying to get the blood flowing through his body again. "I love skating and sweating on the ice. There's a difference."

"Well, now you can warm up. Get dressed. Go home. Sit by a fire." She was still smiling from ear to ear.

"You don't need me to be proud of you, you seem quite proud of yourself for getting out of going home."

She inhaled deeply, letting her eyes close for a moment. "You have no idea."

Maybe this was meant to be. He had thought it wasn't doable when she said she had plans, but things had changed quite quickly. "Since you suddenly have nothing to do, what if you came up north with me and kept up with my physical therapy? I would, as you suggested earlier, provide you with room and board. No money would be exchanged so you wouldn't be breaking any rules with the organization that way."

Her eyes went wide. "You want me to come home with you for the holidays?"

"I want you to come to Apple Hollow to work on my recovery so I can get back on the ice sooner than later." He wanted to be very clear this was a business proposition, nothing else.

"If I came with you, you'd get me a room at the Seasons Inn for free?"

"Yes, I will pay for your room. You'll even have a bathroom all to yourself."

She covered her mouth and then began jumping up and down. "Genius! Yes. Yes. Yes. Yes. I would love to do that. That sounds like the best plan ever."

It was a good plan. It wasn't *the best plan ever*. It certainly wasn't genius, but as long as she was on board, he was happy. "You're welcome to ride up with me or take your own transportation. I'll leave that up to you."

"My car has one-hundred-thousand miles on it and the check-engine light keeps going on and off depending on its mood. I'll grab a ride with you, if that's okay."

"Fine. I was planning to go up there the weekend before Christmas and leave the day after Christmas. Does that work for you?"

"That's when we've been given vacation. It's perfect. Tell me where to be and when you want me there and I'll be there."

Theo loved her enthusiasm. "I'll have my assistant send you an itinerary."

He grabbed his stuff, ready to get into the locker

room to put on some dry clothes. Mallory stopped him. "Hey, can I be totally honest with you?"

"I would prefer that, yes."

"I want you to know that I will do everything that I can to get you back to where you want to be, but I can't make you promises. You know that, right?"

As much as it pained him that there were no guarantees, he knew there weren't. "I know."

She put her hand on his shoulder to stop him from walking away. "And you have to be honest with me about how things are feeling. I will not help you put yourself at risk of permanent damage."

All he wanted was to be able to do his job. If he had to follow her rules to get there, he'd do it. "Got it."

Theo got changed and went home. Even after a long hot shower, the ache in his hip was still there, taunting him. He tried some of the stretches that Mallory had suggested and gave up when they didn't seem to work. They were never going to work.

No. He refused to let negative thinking take over. If he went down that rabbit hole, he wouldn't be able to find his way out. His mental toughness was as important as the physical if he was going to see the ice again. Taking a deep breath, he pushed the defeatist attitude away. It was going to take some time, but he would recover. He would skate again. He would make an epic comeback. It just couldn't take too long.

He needed to reserve a room for Mallory at the Seasons Inn. She was the key to his success. He grabbed his phone and called the number for the front desk. It was the only way to be sure Quinn would take his call. His brother rarely answered his personal cell while he was working. According to Brady, his other brother, the eldest Seasons brother was in work-mode almost 24/7 these days.

The phone only rang twice before it was answered. "Seasons Inn, this is Quinn. How may I help you?"

"I love calling you on this line just to hear your friendly voice for a couple seconds."

"What do you want, Theo?" There was the real Quinn—lacking in patience for anyone with the same last name as his own.

Theo didn't mind. He wasn't much for small talk. He felt disconnected from his family and there was little chance that was going to change because they wasted time chatting on the phone. "I'm going to need you to book me another room when I come at the end of the month."

"I'm going to have to charge you for that room. We only comp one room for family and friends."

Theo rolled his eyes. If their father had answered the phone, he would have given Theo as many rooms as he needed at no cost. Not that Theo would ever take advantage, especially since it had become clear over the last couple months that the inn couldn't afford to give away *any* rooms for free.

"I'll be paying for both my rooms, Quinn. Just don't tell Dad."

Quinn's voice softened a bit. "Okay, good. I'll add another room to your reservation. Anything else?"

"That's it."

"Okay, bye." Quinn hung up without waiting for Theo to say goodbye back. One good thing about his brother was that Quinn didn't need the details. He was a need-to-know kind of guy. If he didn't need to know, he didn't want to know. Now, if their sister had answered, it would have been a totally different story. Nora Seasons loved being in *everyone's* business.

Not that he needed to keep Mallory a secret. She was coming in a professional capacity. No big deal. Theo did not mix business with his personal life. Not only did the organization frown upon it, but Theo had enough potentially keeping him off the ice to risk it.

He leaned into the stretch for his hip flexor. A pain shot down his leg so fierce that he screamed out. This could not be happening. He had hurt his knee not his hip. Why was a new part of his body deciding to fall apart? Thank goodness Mallory had agreed to come to Apple Hollow with him. He couldn't take a break. He needed her to help him work this thing out.

TWO WEEKS LATER, he was driving the two of them to his parents' inn. This was not his favorite time of year to make the drive. The trees had lost their leaves. The gorgeous tapestry of oranges, reds and yellows was wiped away by winter's freezing temperatures and blanket of snow. Mallory was good at balancing chatting him up to help the time go by and being quiet so he could get lost in his head. She had on black leggings and a Boston Icemen sweatshirt. Her bright red goose down jacket was in the back seat. The thing was supposed to keep her warm when it was below zero as were the faux fur-lined boots she was still wearing in the climate-controlled car.

"I googled the Seasons Inn, and you were telling the truth, it is kind of a big deal up in these parts," Mallory said as she stared out the passenger window. "My parents' best friends stayed there last summer and loved it."

"I'm an honest guy. I wouldn't tell you something if it wasn't true."

She turned her gaze on him. "You would probably be shocked at how many times I've been told that only to find out the guy was very good at telling me things that were not true."

Dishonest people made things so much harder on the honest ones. "I'll just have to keep being honest until you have no choice but to trust me. Actions always speak louder than words."

"Since you're my patient and not my boyfriend, it's a little easier to have some faith in you. It's always the guys who want me to fall in love with them who stretch the truth."

That was a little more information than he was expecting. He would have thought someone like Mallory would have had no trouble attracting a decent guy. She was smart, accomplished, and her smile had this way of making the corners of his mouth curl up as well.

"I promise not to try to get you to fall in love with me. I'll just be honest."

"Good to hear," she said, turning her whole body his way. "So, on a scale of one to ten, how bad was your pain when we made that stop to stretch our legs a few minutes ago? I noticed. I always notice."

Did she have to be his physical therapist the whole time they were together? Of course, this was why he was bringing her along.

"It was a…" he shrugged "I don't know, maybe a five."

She narrowed her eyes. "Are you sure about that?"

"It was stiff. It hurts more when I've been sitting for a long time. Once I got out and got the blood flowing, things were better," he said, hoping he was convincing enough.

"So, it was a five when you got out or after you got the blood flowing?" She wasn't buying it.

"In the end, it was a five."

She nodded. "I might have you get some scans when we get back to Boston. We'll have to see how things go over the next couple days."

Scans never resulted in good news for him. Theo wanted to avoid scans at all costs. "It will be better. I am sure you are going to work your magic on me."

She faced forward in her seat. "I wish I had some magic to use on you."

So did he. So. Did. He.

MALLORY HATED THAT every time she worked with Theo there was something new to be concerned about. She didn't like that he was experiencing hip pain along with the issues related to his knee. Could he heal and get back on the ice? Other guys had done it. Was he going to have to be patient and follow her treatment plan? Absolutely. The problem was Theo had no patience. Theo wanted to be better two weeks ago. He didn't care that it would take a miracle to get what he wanted. He wanted her to deliver him a Christmas miracle. All she could do was give it her best shot. She owed it to him to try because he had brought her all the way up here to escape her family.

"Before we get to the inn, I better warn you about my family. I didn't tell my brother who you were when I got you a room. He doesn't care what I do, who I'm with or why. My sister and parents, on the other hand, are going to be very interested in you. I know you're coming up here with me to get away from your family's shenanigans, and I want to be clear, you do not have to get caught up in mine."

Mallory appreciated that he took her feelings into consideration, but she was a little flattered that his family might include her in some of the holiday festivities. As much as she couldn't bear to deal with her family drama, she had no problem watching others deal with theirs. "Are they going to want your PT to join in all the reindeer games?"

Theo chuckled and the sound made her stomach do a little flip. "When you meet my sister, you'll understand. If you're lucky, she'll only have you signed up for a million activities. If you're unlucky, she'll spend the week trying to find you your true love while you do a million activities."

"My true love?"

"My sister thinks she's some kind of matchmaker. Not for the same reasons your mom tries to hook you up. Nora just loves love."

"Is she going to introduce me to her best friend's brother instead of trying to get me to fall for her own brother?" As soon as she said it, she wanted to take it back. She shouldn't joke about the two of them getting together.

"She knows better than to mess with my love life."

Mallory nodded. "Guess it's a good thing your sister and my mother will never meet and combine forces."

Theo huffed a laugh. "Good thing."

"So, when we aren't doing therapy, I can do whatever I want, right?" she asked.

"There's going to be plenty to do. My brother has some big Seasons at the Lake event planned all day on Christmas Eve. There's going to be a lot of activity, I hear."

"What are you looking forward to doing when you're home?" she asked.

His mood soured immediately. "I love a lot of things about Apple Hollow, but thanks to my bum knee, I can't do any of it. No skiing, no skating. I don't even know if I could ride a snowmobile. Rehab and catching up with my family is about all the fun I have to look forward to."

His use of the word *fun* was not very convincing. She felt bad for him. Injuries like his changed lifestyles completely when the person was in recovery.

"You're an active guy. It's got to be hard for you to be sidelined. Aren't there any fun activities that don't require you to physically exert yourself?"

He was silent for a minute. Mallory started to think he wasn't going to answer. Finally, he said, "I do want to visit my old ice rink. Maybe catch a youth hockey game."

"That's a good idea. You must be the hometown hero. Can you imagine how exciting a visit from you would be to those kids?"

"I guess," he said, still sounding glum.

Mallory was going to see to it that Theo did at least one fun thing this week. It was the least she could do since he was giving her a free stay at his family's inn.

It wasn't much longer before he was announcing their arrival. Mallory was blown away at how gorgeous the Seasons Inn was. The internet did not do it justice. Set on a hill, overlooking a lake, it looked like something out of a movie. The gray siding with white trim and black shutters served as a charming backdrop for the festive wreaths adorned with red ribbons and pine cones that hung on each window. Garland draped around the doorway, so festive with warm white lights and winter greenery.

He put his luxury SUV into Park and popped

the back gate. Mallory felt like she had been riding in first class if there was such a thing for ground transportation. When they stepped outside, the air felt frosty. She opened the back door to get her jacket.

"Theo Seasons!" A lady came running to greet them. She had on a dark navy jacket and a Seasons Inn stocking cap. Her gray hair peeked out from underneath. "I heard you were coming home today." She threw her arms around him, and he hugged her back.

"Good to see you, Maureen. I can't believe you're still working here. Don't you want to retire and let someone carry *your* bags around?"

She let him go and started pulling their luggage from the back. "Are you kidding? This is what keeps me young. If I stop moving, I stop living."

"We're going to need two carts," Theo said, showing her which bags belonged to him. "We're in different rooms."

"Ah, you brought a lovely guest with you. Welcome to the Seasons Inn. My name is Maureen, and I am here to help you with your bags while you check in. Don't worry about a thing. I will make sure everything gets right where it belongs."

"Maureen, this is Mallory," Theo said, introducing them. "She's my physical therapist. Just like you, I believe that if I stop moving, I stop living. She's here to make sure that doesn't happen."

Her eyes shone with sympathy. "I'm so sorry about your injury. We were watching the game that night on TV, and I called your mom right away. I knew she had to be worried about you. When she told me you needed surgery, my heart broke for you. I know how much you love that game."

Mallory watched as Theo tried to control his expression. She didn't know him well, but she knew him well enough to see he hated showing weakness. "Thanks. I'm going to be fine. I'll be back on your TV screen before you know it."

Maureen patted his bulky shoulder. "If anyone can do it, it's you."

"Let's get inside where it's warm." Theo nodded toward the door. "I'll go check us in and get your room key."

"You're going to let Maureen bring all our stuff in?"

He shrugged a shoulder. "She would kick me in my good leg if I didn't let her. Trust me, let Maureen do her job. She loves it."

As they entered the lobby, Mallory felt like she was in a cozy holiday haven. She was immediately greeted with the warmth and joy of the season. The fresh scent of pine mixed with spices like cinnamon and nutmeg tickled her nose. Soft Christmas music played softly in the background.

Theo walked straight to the check-in counter,

and it was clear that everyone who worked there knew him. The young woman came out from behind it to wrap him in a hug. A man who shared similar features as Theo gave him a head nod and a slight smile.

"How was the drive, brother?" he asked Theo.

Mallory realized they didn't just know him; they were both related to him. She didn't want to intrude on their little family reunion. She wanted to take a minute to appreciate that she was here at this lovely inn and not at her own family reunion. This was the best Christmas present she could have given herself and she didn't even have to pay for it.

Several guests were milling about. A young couple took a seat in front of the crackling fireplace that was adorned with a lush evergreen garland with pine cones, red berries and warm white fairy lights woven through it. Cream stockings with gold details were hung from the mantel, while a large wreath decorated with matching accents was placed above it. There was an easel off to the side holding a poster board advertising the Seasons at the Lake celebration Theo had been talking about.

A woman entered the lobby with a tray of cookies. She offered one to each guest as she walked by, stopping in front of Mallory. "Can I interest you in a cookie, dear? I got a little carried away and made too many."

The delicious scent of vanilla and cinnamon made her mouth water. "I am incredibly interested. Thank you so much." Mallory plucked one of the still-warm sugar cookies off the tray and took a napkin from the nice lady before she went to share them with the couple on the couch.

The sweet, buttery dessert nearly melted in Mallory's mouth. It was quite possibly the best cookie she had ever tasted. She wished she had taken two. A handsome man in a blue tracksuit with the Seasons Inn logo on the back snuck up on the cookie lady and snatched a cookie before running away.

"Brady!"

"What?" he asked, turning around to face her with a smirk. "I was just getting one for my favorite brother. Did you not notice who's here?" He threw a thumb over his shoulder.

The woman glanced in the direction of the check-in. "Theo," she said in a breath, her smile bigger and brighter than before.

Cookie Lady must be his mom. Theo and his brother gave each other a man hug, clasping their hands like they were about to arm wrestle while giving each other a strong pat on the back with the other hand. Theo's mom handed the tray of cookies to her daughter and held her arms out for her own hug. Theo obliged her, lifting her feet off the ground. It was such a sweet family reunion moment Mallory couldn't look away.

As she watched the Seasons family, she heard a kid scream and another one shout, "Mom's going to be mad! Don't!"

Watching Theo's mom absolutely glow with joy and the way his brothers and sister teased him made her suddenly feel guilty she'd backed out of her own family Christmas, so much so she could almost believe the children yelling sounded exactly like her nephews. She would really miss seeing them this year. Christmas was just a tad more magical when kids were involved. As she turned, a blur of blond hair and red overalls plowed into her leg.

"Oof!" Staying on her feet, she steadied the little guy. "Are you all right, buddy?"

"Sorry, Auntie Mallory," another voice said.

Mallory looked up because why would someone be calling her Auntie Mallory? She glanced back down at the giggling monster holding her leg. Her three-year-old nephew Sebastian smiled up at her with big blue eyes and a runny nose. "Auntie!"

"Boys! I told you not to ruin the surprise." That voice was definitely Avery's, but Avery was in Evergreen with their parents, celebrating the holidays at home. Mallory's heart began to pound in her chest. She lifted her eyes and there they all were.

Not just Avery. Avery and her husband, Chance, the two boys, Erica, Hayden, Savannah, Greg, her dad and her mom. *Her mom.* Her mom was standing in the lobby of the Seasons Inn with a smile as wide as the ocean was deep.

"Surprise! We decided that maybe it was time to get together for Christmas in a place where we didn't all have to share one bathroom," Avery said, pulling little Sebastian back.

"We thought—" her mom started but her dad coughed loudly. Her mom glanced back at her dad who gave her *the look*. "Okay, *I* thought why should you be the only one to meet the family? This new boyfriend of yours could meet yours as well!" She stood in front of Mallory waiting for a hug.

Mallory was frozen in her spot. Her family was here. They were all here and they were all expecting to meet her boyfriend. The boyfriend who was not here. The boyfriend who didn't exist. It was becoming impossible to breathe. She was going to pass out if she didn't do something, say something.

"Here's your key," Theo said, breaking her out of her panic attack. He held out the key card in front of her.

Theo. Good, honest Theo. He was going to have to break that promise about being truthful because he was about to become her boyfriend for the week.

CHAPTER THREE

"Sweetheart, you're never going to believe who came to surprise us!" Mallory hugged Theo's arm. Before he could put his confusion into words, she continued, "My family is all here!" She waved at the crowd of people standing in front of them, her voice abnormally shrill.

Her family was *here*. All of them here at the Seasons Inn, where she had come to escape them. Had the shock of it made her lose her mind? He still didn't understand why she was hugging his arm and calling him sweetheart.

"Hi," he said as he waved hello with his free hand.

"Aren't you Theo Seasons from the Icemen?" a woman with a lot of blond hair asked with narrowed eyes.

He nodded. "I am. I'm Theo Seasons."

"You're dating Theo Seasons?" another woman shrieked, causing others in the lobby to take notice, including his family, who he was just about to introduce to his physical therapist.

Theo waited for Mallory to clear things up and explain they were not dating. If she didn't, then these people were playing some kind of joke on him.

"Can you please not scream in a crowded lobby? Obviously, this is why I haven't been very forthcoming about our relationship," Mallory said, attempting to keep her voice down.

Their relationship?

Suddenly, there was a barrage of introductions. Each one of Mallory's family members stepped up to shake his hand and make his acquaintance. There were her three sisters, her two brothers-in-law, her one sister's fiancé, her father and finally, her mother.

Mrs. Moore seemed like the kind of woman who made sure that she looked good morning, noon and night. Her hair and makeup were done up like she was going to a fancy event. She opened her arms, the bracelets on her wrist jangled. "I'm a hugger. We're so excited to meet you, Theo."

Theo glanced at Mallory, who gave him an apologetic grimace. She had a lot of explaining to do right after this hug.

Nora cleared her throat, helping him escape the bear hug he was receiving. "How do you know the lovely Moore family, Theo?"

Of course, his little sister knew who they were.

She had probably already signed them up for a slew of holiday activities.

"Oh, my, now it makes sense. Theo *Seasons*. The *Seasons* Inn. This must be your family!" Mrs. Moore didn't hesitate to throw her arms around his mom. "We're Mallory's family. I would have made the connection earlier if we had known Theo was the man who's stolen our Mallory's heart."

His mom looked to him to explain, but he was just as confused as she was.

Nora's right eyebrow lifted. "That's why you needed the second room? You brought your girl-friend home with you? Why didn't you mention that?" She stepped forward to give Mallory a hug. "Hi, I'm Nora, Theo's little sister."

"It's so nice to meet you. I've heard so much about you and your brothers. And you, too, Mrs. Seasons," Mallory said.

"Please, call me Laura," his mom replied.

"Would have been nice to know anything about you," Brady quipped, giving Theo the evil eye.

"Well, it seems everyone gets to be surprised this weekend!" Mrs. Moore said, her arm around Theo's mom's shoulders like they were best buddies now. "Mallory had no idea we changed our plans to join her up here. Like we said at check-in, we heard so many wonderful things about this place from our friends. I can't believe Mallory's boyfriend's fam-ily owns it!"

"Her boyfriend…" His mom was at a loss for words.

"Can I steal Mallory for just a second?" Theo tugged Mallory toward the hallway that led to the business office. "We'll be right back," he said as fourteen pairs of eyes were glued to him. Once they made it around the corner and out of sight, he did everything he could to keep his tone even. "What in the world is going on right now?"

Mallory covered her face with her hands. "I cannot believe this is happening."

"Why is your whole family here and why do they think we're together?"

She dropped her hands. "I never told them you and I were together. I told them that I was coming here to meet my new boyfriend's parents because I needed a good excuse to not go home. Telling my mother that I was missing family Christmas to be your private physical therapist would not have gone over well."

"And they followed you here?"

"Apparently," she groaned. "I had no idea they would do that, but it's important that you let them believe that we're here together as a couple and not because I was hired by you. Please, Theo. You have to help me out."

"I am not going to lie to my family, Mallory. Do you have any idea how big of a deal it would be if I brought someone home to meet them?"

She shrugged even though she had to know that he wasn't asking because it would be no big deal.

"Huge. I don't bring women home to meet my family. Ever." Never ever. Theo's family didn't need to get attached to any of the women he dated here and there. Settling down wasn't in his blood. His career was all that mattered right now. A girlfriend would only be a distraction.

"Please, Theo. I cannot tell my mom days before Christmas that I came here to escape her and the rest of them. She would be devastated and never forgive me. You have the power to save Christmas for my family."

"That's not fair."

Relentless, she grabbed his hand. "It's not. I know I am being totally unfair. I wouldn't ask you to do this if I didn't think it would ruin my family's Christmas to tell them the truth. With my whole family here, I'll be busy with them outside of your PT time. Your injury prevents you from doing anything physical, so you have the perfect excuse to not go with us. I'd only need you to make a couple appearances a day. Our fake relationship can end the moment we leave. You can blame the whole breakup on me. Tell your family that I ruined it."

As much as he wanted to say no, he wasn't about to ruin her family's Christmas even if it meant he had to bend the truth for a few days. "Fine."

Mallory squealed and hugged him around the neck. All this physical contact made him acutely aware of just how bad an idea this was. Her warmth, her scent—a mix of vanilla and something floral—was disarming, and for a moment, he believed pretending might not be as hard as he thought.

As she pulled back, her eyes sparkled with gratitude, and he felt a pang of guilt for the lies they were about to spin. "Thank you," she said softly, her voice full of relief. "You're the best."

He forced a grin, shoving his unease deep down. "I'm going to need to hear that multiple times a day while we're here."

Mallory laughed, the sound light and genuine. "Deal. Now, let's go finish meeting the family."

And just like that, he was pulled into her whirlwind, praying he could survive the holidays with his sanity intact.

MALLORY TOOK A deep breath as she and Theo reentered the lobby. She wanted to believe they could pull this off, but there were absolutely no guarantees. Mallory's relationship with Theo was completely professional. She didn't know that much about him that didn't have to do with how severe his injury had been, his current range of motion and how desperately he wanted to get well and back on the ice.

Her dad was the first to notice their return. Of everyone, she'd have to do her best acting around him. He had this sixth sense, one that told him when any of his daughters was hiding something. Maybe he had been born with it or maybe it was a skill he developed over time because he had four girls who were always hiding something.

His eyes crinkled in the corners when he smiled at her warmly. William Moore was always the calm to her mother's chaos. If Mallory eventually told the truth, she was going to need him to help her stop her mom from disowning her.

"Okay," Theo said, getting everyone's attention. "Looks like Mallory and I have some catching up to do with our own families. Maybe we can all sit down for dinner tonight and get to know everyone?"

"I'll set something up," his sister answered. "I'll make sure we can accommodate everyone."

Mallory's heart rate slowed down considerably. The fact that this professional hockey player was going to pretend to be her boyfriend in front of her entire family was unbelievable.

Everyone seemed happy with getting to know each other better over dinner. Her sisters were quick to surround her. Avery asked their parents to help Chance with the boys while the sisters went up to help Mallory get settled in her room. Their mom didn't look so happy about being left out of what was sure to be an inquisition about all things Theo Seasons, but she agreed.

The large group dispersed. As soon as the Moore sisters stepped in the elevator, the questions were fired.

"You have been hiding Theo Seasons from us for how long?" Erica asked.

"Isn't it against company rules for you to date a hockey player? I thought you told me that when you got hired," Savannah said.

"You're staying in separate rooms, so this is new, really new, huh?" Avery questioned.

Mallory's best defense was to go on the offense. "Before we talk about me, can I please see the ring?" she asked, grabbing Erica's hand. "It looks way bigger in person than it does in pictures. Holy moly."

"Doesn't it?" Erica was the easiest to divert. She moved it side to side. "Look how it glitters in the light."

"So gorgeous," Mallory fawned. "I bet you find yourself staring at it all the time."

Savannah pulled Erica's hand out of Mallory's grasp. "We're not talking about the engagement ring. We're talking about you and Theo Seasons."

Mallory went for diversion number two. "Oh, my gosh, look at your little baby bump! I am so excited to find out if it's a girl or a boy."

Like it was some kind of automatic reaction

that she couldn't control, Savannah cradled the tiny bump with her hands. "We're planning to do the gender reveal tomorrow. Greg's parents are in Phoenix visiting his brother. He's going to Face-Time them so they can find out at the same time as all of you guys."

"That's so—"

"Oh, my gosh, you two are so easily distracted! Mallory barely has to try," Avery said with a roll of her eyes.

Mallory's eldest sister was always the spoiler of all the fun. "You went with the super long extension this time, didn't you? I've never seen your hair this long." She reached over to touch Avery's hair.

"I'm not falling for your tricks." The elevator reached her floor, and they all got off, heading in the direction of Mallory's room. She used the key Theo gave her to get inside. She figured she'd try one more time to keep them off the topic of her pretend boyfriend.

"Little Sebastian is getting so big. It took me a minute to realize it was him hugging my legs. And Xavier is so handsome. I bet all the little girls in his kindergarten class are in love with him."

Avery wasn't fooling around. "Start talking about Theo or I'm going to text Mom to come up here."

"You wouldn't dare," Mallory said, knowing she

had delayed the inevitable as long as she could. "I'll talk."

"How long has this been going on and why didn't you tell any of us?" Avery asked.

"It hasn't been long, and I didn't tell anyone because like Savannah pointed out, we aren't allowed to date. If the Icemen found out, there could be some major consequences for both of us."

"Why would you risk everything you've been working for to date a guy who's off-limits? That's not like you." Savannah knew Mallory the best out of all her sisters. Only a year apart in age, people often mistook them for twins growing up.

Never in a million years would she risk her job for some guy. She had worked for the Icemen for a few years now and never been tempted. Hockey players liked to be flirtatious, but she knew it was a silly game to them, so it was easy to not take any of them seriously.

"I can't explain it. I can only say that Theo isn't like anyone I've ever met before. We've spent a lot of time together during his rehab and he opened up to me and showed me a side of him that I don't think he shows many people. You know how I feel about guys who allow themselves to be vulnerable."

It was true that she had a thing for men who were willing to let their guard down and be real with her. Unfortunately, Theo Seasons did not enjoy being vulnerable. *At all*. He literally did everything in his power to hide any tiny bit of vulnerability that tried to slip out. Hopefully, that particular lie wouldn't come back to bite her.

"His injury is bad, isn't it? Is that why you're daring to do this? He's not going to be playing?" Erica asked her questions in rapid succession. Of course, she knew about his injury. Hayden was a huge hockey fan. She was surprised at how well he'd kept his composure when he realized who was standing in front of him when they met.

Mallory shook her head. She was not going to jinx his recovery by pretending there was no hope for his return to the ice. She couldn't have that mindset if she was going to help him. "No, that's not what's happening, and don't go spreading that rumor. Don't even voice it again, okay?"

Her little sister raised her hand, palms facing outward to show she meant no harm. "Geez, I won't even think it. You sure are defensive about your boyfriend's ability to bounce back from his injury. This is serious."

"Theo's working extremely hard to get back in the lineup. He hates being sidelined. He needs to keep his spirits up if he's going to overcome this."

Avery and Erica exchanged gleeful glances. "She's in love!"

Love? Oh, goodness, she didn't want them to think things had gone that far. She wasn't going to pretend it was love already. Her intentions were to play this off as very new and a secret that will most likely be the excuse for why they have to break up. She'd tell them she couldn't be with someone who she couldn't date openly.

"She is not in love," Savannah said. She was still suspicious.

"Well, not yet, at least," Mallory shot back.

"This is exactly what Mom was hoping for. She's got Avery married with kids, Savannah married and expecting, me engaged and Mallory falling in love for the first time in forever," Erica said with a toothy smile. "Christmas magic is in the air."

If Christmas magic existed, Mallory would be sitting by that fire in the lobby eating Mrs. Seasons's delicious sugar cookies, and her family would be back in Massachusetts celebrating the holiday without her.

Avery laughed. "Mom must have been really nice this year."

Mallory's mom always seemed to get what she wanted somehow some way. "Can I just say that as mad as you are about me not telling you that I am dating Theo, I am equally not happy with all three of you letting Mom plan a sneak attack."

"She swore us to secrecy. You know how she is," Erica said, using the excuse Mallory would have probably used if she had been in her sister's shoes.

Avery clearly had no regrets. "She offered us a free vacation at a charming inn with a million activities for Chance and I and the boys. How was I supposed to say no?"

Savannah's expression was somber. "I wrote and erased probably a dozen texts to warn you, but part of me was mad at you for ditching us for some guy. It hurt my feelings that you weren't going to be there for the gender reveal."

A new reason for feeling guilty twisted Mallory's gut. She hadn't put much thought into how Savannah would feel about her skipping out on Christmas this year. She hugged her. "I'm sorry, Sav. I really am so excited for you. You will always be important to me. Until I meet the man I want to spend the rest of my life with, I will always put my family before some boyfriend."

"Does that mean Theo could be the man you want to spend the rest of your life with since you did choose him over your family?" Erica questioned.

Theo had nothing to do with why she had tried to escape this year's family gathering. That would probably break Savannah's heart more than the lie. "Stop trying to marry me off. If I remember correctly, you didn't want to share the family spotlight with anyone this Christmas. If Theo proposes, we will have to have a joint engagement dinner. Is that what you want?"

Erica's eyes bulged and her hands squeezed into

fists. "Don't you dare get engaged this week, Mallory. I will never forgive you."

"Oh, my gosh, that would be hilarious," Savannah said with a laugh. "I think I'll ask Theo what his intentions with my sister are and see if I can get him to consider it."

"You are so annoying, you know that?" Erica put her hands on her hips. "You're lucky you're pregnant. I am too nice of a person to shove a pregnant woman."

"No, you're not. You just know I'd swing you around this room by that big ol' braid of yours." Savannah gave Erica's plait a tug.

"Please stop," Avery said in her best parenting voice. "My three-year-old and five-year-old don't fight as much as you two do. Can you at least try to pretend you're mature women?"

"You're not the boss of us," Erica quipped.

"So, that's a no for being mature?" Avery crossed her arms over her chest. She was used to being in control. She stayed home with her two boys and ran a successful small business venture. Avery was the definition of a girl boss.

Mallory couldn't help but laugh. There was no escaping them. At least they were entertaining. Hopefully, Theo would feel the same. If her fake boyfriend didn't already regret extending the invite for her to join him, he might once he got to spend some time with the bickering Moore sisters.

CHAPTER FOUR

NORA MAY HAVE been chomping at the bit to get the details on Theo and Mallory's unexpected relationship status, but he managed to escape with his mom. He wanted to see his father, who was helping set up in the Four Seasons Room for a private party that was being hosted there tonight.

"Your dad has been excited for you to get here." She moved quickly down the hall, leading the way with an urgency that could only be related to her being knocked sideways by his little announcement.

"I'm excited to see him."

"He would probably appreciate it if you led with the fact that you've brought your girlfriend with you. We've been trying hard not to spring things on him after that scare with his heart."

Theo took a deep breath. She was talking about the heart attack they *thought* he'd had this past summer. Only, it was an anxiety attack not a heart attack. "I'm sorry I didn't tell you, Mom. I didn't mention she was coming with me because I didn't want to answer a million questions."

That was the honest truth. He hadn't mentioned Mallory was joining him because he knew they would ask him a million questions about his injury. Why did he need to bring his physical therapist? Were things really that bad that he couldn't do some exercises on his own over the holidays? What were the chances he'd be back on the ice?

The best thing about this fake relationship was that the questions they would have for him now would be about everything *but* his stupid knee. Theo was going to let Mallory answer all those questions since this was her lie. He was simply not refuting it. At least that was what he told himself.

His mom stopped short of the Four Seasons Room, causing him to almost run her over. She turned to face him. "I wouldn't have asked you a million questions," she asserted. "I may have asked a couple of questions, which I think is reasonable when your son is coming home with a girlfriend for the first time ever."

He gently grabbed her upper arms and gave them a rub. "I'm sorry, Mom. You know that you're not the one I was worried about bombarding me. I'm shocked Nora let you drag me away before she got half a million questions in."

She reached up and touched his cheek. "We love you. If this young lady is special enough to bring home, do you blame us for wanting to know something about her?"

The guilt of not being completely honest with his mother was almost as bad as the pain he felt the night of his injury. "I get it. I'll do better next time."

"Next time? The next time you and Mallory come home, I won't have a million questions!"

Maybe this was worse than the injury. The next time he came home, there would be no Mallory. Hopefully, she wouldn't make too much of an impression this week. He didn't want his mother to get too attached to his fake girlfriend. "You know what I mean."

"I'm happy for you. Although, I saw your face when you realized her family had come to surprise her. I hope you two aren't moving too fast. Meeting the parents is a big step."

They were definitely moving too fast. So fast that it would be over before it began. One week. He could do this for one week. "Mallory was actually looking forward to a little breathing room from her family this year, but she's taking their Christmas crashing in stride."

His mother's brow furrowed. "Is she not close with her family?"

He didn't want to give his mom the wrong impression of Mallory for some reason. The woman was a good person, but even he could tell her family was a lot to handle in the few minutes he had spent with them. No one should hold it against her that she wanted a bit of space this one time.

"She's very close. I think they're so close it can be kind of suffocating at times, if that makes sense."

His mom nodded knowingly. "Ah, well, we're just going to have to keep them all busy so you two can have some time together. Come on, let's go see what your father is doing. He's going to be so happy to see your face," she said, giving his cheek a pinch.

She opened the doors to the Four Seasons Room, and it was like he was walking into some kind of gingerbread-man land. The tables were adorned with gingerbread-inspired centerpieces. There were edible-looking cookie trees and gingerbread men and some gingerbread women smiling gleefully beside them. The tablecloths were a vibrant candy cane red, with napkins rolled to resemble candy swirls.

In the center of the room was a colossal gingerbread house made out of something that remarkably resembled real gingerbread. If it wasn't for his dad squirting construction spray foam to look like icing along the roofline, Theo may have been tempted to take a bite. The house was complete with candy cane–striped columns, gumdrop accents and two giant lollipops on either side of the front door.

"Honey, this looks amazing!" Theo's dad immediately turned at the sound of his wife's voice. It only took a second for his eyes to land on Theo.

"Look who's finally here!" His dad handed the other guy the spray foam and hustled over to his family with arms wide open.

Theo gave his dad a heartfelt hug. Even though he fully understood that the episode last summer was due to anxiety and not heart failure, Theo still felt extra grateful this year to have this opportunity to wrap his arms around his dad.

"Good to see you, old man. What are you going to do next year when you're not in charge of this place anymore? Make Quinn let you work whenever you want to?"

His dad chuckled. "You know me too well, Theo." He pulled back to give his son a once-over. "You look good. How are you feeling? How's the knee?"

These were the questions he expected to field all along. "It's good. I feel good. I should be back on the ice in no time."

"He has some extra help this time," his mom added. "A special physical therapist."

His dad's gaze turned curious. "What does that mean?"

The lying was not getting any easier. He hoped it wouldn't always be this awkward. "I surprised everyone by bringing a special friend home with me for Christmas. She also happens to be my physical therapist."

His dad glanced at his mom, probably hoping she would better explain.

"Theo brought a lady friend home for Christmas."

"Theo brought a lady friend home for Christmas?" his dad repeated.

"He did. I didn't get to talk to her much yet. She kind of got surprised by her family, who knew she was coming here even though your son failed to tell us she was coming here."

"To be fair, I did tell Quinn I was bringing a guest and needed an extra room."

"You told Quinn, and he didn't tell us?" His mom had a new target for her disappointment. Theo felt zero regret passing some of that on to his older brother. Growing up, Quinn had gotten both Theo and Brady in plenty of trouble with their parents. Payback.

"I can't believe he didn't mention it to any of you. You would have thought he would find that to be interesting information to pass along."

"Unbelievable." His mom shook her head. "That boy acts like nothing is ever a big deal unless it has to do with the finances or bookings. Where did he come from? You know your sister would have gotten all the details and announced that over the loudspeakers."

That was exactly why he had called Quinn and not Nora.

"Something tells me your middle child knew that all too well, Laura," his dad said with a wink and a pat on the shoulder. "Theo has a girlfriend. When do I get to meet her?"

Well, there was no time like the present, but Mallory had gone to be interrogated by her sisters. There was no way the four of them would emerge any time soon. "We were hoping we could use one of the smaller private dining rooms so we all could have dinner together tonight. You can meet Mallory and her entire family."

The twinkle in his dad's eye at the thought of Theo having a girlfriend and her family here almost made this lie worth it. He knew his parents couldn't wait for him and his siblings to settle down and start their own families. They had made it clear that the two of them weren't getting any younger and they wanted to be grandparents. Theo had no plans for any of that, in reality, but in this gingerbread fantasyland, maybe he'd let them believe it was a possibility.

What's the plan? Mallory texted Theo. She had entertained most of her sisters' questions and taken a tour of the inn led by her nephews. Since her family had arrived before she did, they had already done some exploring and knew exactly where to go.

The inn was so charming. There was a large dining room decorated so festively for the holidays. Mallory and her nephews had counted six Christmas trees during their tour, but the real fir tree in the dining room was Mallory's favorite. The towering tree was covered in twinkling white lights and cranberry garland. The ornaments reminded her of the ones that used to hang on her grandparents' tree when she was little. Glass baubles in different colors hung from the branches.

"Look at the angel," Xavier said, pointing to the top of the tree. The blond-haired angel topper held candles in her hands that lit up. "She looks like Mom."

Where are you? Theo texted back.

Mallory, her mom, sisters and nephews were sitting at a table in the dining room, enjoying some hot cocoa. Avery scooped some of the ice out of her water glass and stirred it into Sebastian's mug of cocoa.

"You think the angel looks like me? That's so sweet, honey."

I'm in the main dining room.

The dancing three dots told her he was composing his reply, but nothing was delivered. The dots disappeared.

"Can we eat these?" Xavier, who was sitting on his knees, tried to pull a candy cane from the centerpiece on the table.

"No, no, sweetheart. That's for decoration not for eating," Mallory's mom said, grabbing him by the wrist. Mallory understood why he thought it was a snack. The centerpiece was bright and festive, with a clear vase wrapped in candy canes all the way around. White flowers and fresh evergreen sprigs were arranged with shiny red ornaments and a few pine cones poked out the top. Sparkly red branches stood tall, and mini candy canes were wired to them.

Sebastian, also on his knees, didn't bother asking and snatched one of the snowman-shaped salt and pepper shakers. They didn't have to wait long to find out what it was holding as salt poured out of the black hat while he pretended the snowman could fly. Mallory forgot that sitting at a table with tiny humans required all the adults to give them their full attention.

With your family here, I'm not sure how to ask for my PT time

The whole reason she was here was to provide him with the PT that he wouldn't have gotten otherwise. There was no way she could renege on the promise she'd made him. Explaining that to her mom and sisters was going to be harder than she wanted it to be.

"I need to meet up with Theo," Mallory said, pushing back from the table. She stood up and slipped her phone into her back pocket. "Once I know what the dinner plans are, I'll text you guys."

"Why doesn't Theo come here? We won't bite," her mom said. "I, for one, would love to get to know him a little bit."

"You will have plenty of opportunities to get to know him, but you're not going to overwhelm him on day one. He invited *me* to his family's Christmas, not my whole family. I think you need to remember that."

Her mom clearly didn't think about how intrusive she was being by showing up here unannounced with the entire family to boot. Fortunately for her, the Seasons owned the inn and therefore had to treat them as guests.

"Go find your boyfriend. We'll wait to hear from you," Savannah said before blowing on her hot cocoa and taking a sip.

Mallory could hear her mother complaining about being called out as she walked away. She had to remind herself that it was because her mother loved her so much that she didn't want to be away from her on Christmas. She also still had her own bathroom even if they were all together. All was not lost.

She texted Theo. Where are you? We can do some PT right now, if you want. Don't worry—we will stick to the schedule.

Mallory cut through the lobby, trying to get to the elevators, but got intercepted by Nora. "I'm so glad I caught you. I made a list of the activities that are going on this week, so you and your family can make some plans." She handed her a very comprehensive typed list.

"Thank you so much. I will share this with everyone. I can't believe how much you have going on around here. My mom is going to love that there's antique hunting in town and the boys will love snow tubing."

"Apple Hollow has so much to offer this time of year. Your family picked a perfect time to visit."

She was so kind, but this was far from the perfect time for her family to be here. "I just hope your brother doesn't feel like this is some kind of invasion. When he invited me, he wasn't expecting my whole family."

Nora smiled. "If Theo likes you enough to bring you here to meet us, there's no way he's going to let something like your excited family mess things up. I think it's sweet that they all wanted to be here. I know I would have been jealous if he had gone to meet your family first."

Mallory's shoulders felt too tight. His sister was so sweet and understanding. Lying to her felt so shameful. "I appreciate that." Her phone pinged with a text from Theo, inviting her to his room. She held up her phone to show Nora who was texting. "We'll see if you're right. Thanks again for this list."

"You're welcome, but you don't need to thank me. This is my job. Oh, and I have a private room for dinner tonight. Six thirty. Do you think that works for everyone?"

"That's amazing. Thank you so much for that, too."

Mallory texted her family about dinner on the ride up the elevator. She stood in front of Theo's door and took a cleansing breath before knocking. Theo answered the door without a shirt on, causing her heart to race after she had just attempted to center herself.

"Do you always answer the door half naked?"

Theo slipped the T-shirt over his head that he had been holding in his hand. "Do you always gawk at your clients? My eyes are up here," he said, pointing at them like she wasn't looking at his face.

She folded her arms across her chest. "You're hilarious. Are we doing this or not?"

Theo stepped back and gestured for her to come in. Theo wasn't in a guest room; he was in some kind of suite. This place was big enough to host her whole family for drinks before dinner. He had pushed the furniture against the wall and had some basic equipment like resistance bands and weights. He had a BOSU ball to work on balance and an exercise bike in the corner.

As if reading her mind, he said, "If I had known your family was going to be here, I would have offered them this suite. They could have all shared the one bathroom."

Mallory couldn't stop herself from laughing. "I think my sisters are happy they all got their own rooms and bathrooms, but we could have one heck of a party in here. Is this where you always stay when you come home, in this giant suite all by yourself?"

"No, I usually get a regular guest room, but I figured I could do my therapy up here instead of the inn's gym," he explained. "I don't need to be stretching in front of Richard from Long Island while he's on the treadmill and wants to know if I'm Theo Seasons from the Icemen. This gives me privacy."

"Richard from Long Island. Is that a real person?"

"I mean, he could be." Theo shrugged.

Mallory's cheeks were hurting from smiling so hard. "Well, I don't blame you for that. I do need to warn you that my soon-to-be brother-in-law Hayden is a huge hockey fan and will probably be unable to refrain from fanboying at some point this week."

"Noted. Can we get started?"

He was Mr. No-Nonsense. "We can, and I promise we will stick to the original agenda even though my family is here. There's enough of them that they won't miss me a few hours every day."

"I appreciate that. I wasn't sure how to navigate all this now that we're doing this...you know." He waved his hand around.

"This?"

"*This.* This dating thing."

Mallory nodded as she tried to contain her smile. She had to admit, it was kind of nice to know she could rattle the Theo Seasons. He was usually cold as ice. "This *fake* dating thing."

"Right. That's what I meant."

"Well, as your fake girlfriend, I am totally going to come in here and use your exercise bike in the mornings. As your PT, you will not be using that BOSU ball while we're here, so we can take that back to the gym."

Theo cocked his head to the side. "Come on. I think I'm ready to start working on my strength and flexibility."

"When you have regained sufficient strength and range of motion to safely handle the added instability, you can use the BOSU ball. That will be later in your recovery. Doing anything on there before your knee is ready will set you back, not move you forward." She'd seen it too many times. Athletes who wanted to speed up their recovery did the opposite when they tried to skip the proper steps.

"I think I like the fake girlfriend better than the PT."

Mallory's phone buzzed again as they started the session, and she glanced down at her sister's text: Mom says your boyfriend better be ready for family game night tonight. She's picking teams.

Theo raised an eyebrow. "Problem?"

"Not unless you're bad at charades," she muttered, slipping the phone into her pocket.

"Charades? Seriously?"

Mallory rubbed her forehead; she definitely had a headache coming on. "My mom is determined to make you dislike your fake girlfriend."

Theo let out a low groan. "You better try harder to make me feel like I'm making progress with my knee or your fake boyfriend is going to fake an injury to get out of game night." Theo smirked as he reached for the resistance band.

Mallory rolled her eyes. "You already have an injury, genius."

"Yeah, but this one's real. I'm thinking something dramatic, maybe clutching my shoulder and collapsing during charades."

He thought he was so clever. "If you're going to act like that, you might as well play. My mom will love it. You'll be her favorite."

"Great," Theo said dryly, stretching the band. "Just what I need. Your soon-to-be brother-in-law *and* your mom in love with me."

Mallory laughed, but as she met his gaze, her heart fluttered. No, she wouldn't let her body betray her like that. No one in her family was falling in love with Theo. No one. Especially her.

CHAPTER FIVE

THEO WAS BEGINNING to think Mallory was trying to torture him. Not the Mallory who was his PT, but his fake girlfriend Mallory, who was forcing him to play nice at a family dinner with a million people. At least it felt like there were a million people here. There was so much going on around the table he wasn't sure how anyone could keep it all straight. On top of his head spinning, his knee was throbbing. If Mallory knew he hadn't listened to her when she said to ice it for the next hour, she would never let him hear the end of it.

"So, you have to tell me, how long did it take the team to embrace Coach Randall as the head coach? Most of you guys had been so loyal to Coach Kennedy, I heard there were some issues in the locker room and at practice after he got fired. I heard it was hard for Coach Randall to earn everyone's respect. Is that true?" Mallory's soon-to-be brother-in-law could no longer refrain from fanboying just as she had anticipated. He now wanted to know everything about everything that had ever been speculated about on a sports podcast or in internet comment sections.

"Brian Randall is our coach. We're professionals. We all understand the Icemen organization decided to part ways with Coach Kennedy and that's the way the business works." That was as much as he was going to say about it. It was the PR statement they had all been told to repeat in interviews.

He glanced at Mallory, who somehow got seated across from him instead of next to him. She managed to catch his vibe even though Nora was talking her ear off about the breakfast with Santa in the morning and how her nephews were going to love it.

"Hayden, can you—" she gave him a pointed look and a swift swipe of her hand under her chin, clearly gesturing to him to stop "—not?"

Her sister, the one he was sure wasn't named Avery but was maybe something that started with an *E*, patted her husband or maybe fiancé on the back. "You know how you hate it when people talk about work when you're on vacation. You have to remember hockey is Theo's job, honey. He doesn't want to talk about it when he's on vacation."

"Oh, sorry, man. I'm just so excited to meet you. I've been such a fan for so long."

Theo wanted to discourage the questions but also didn't want the guy to be begging for his forgiveness all night, either. "We're cool, man. Your fiancée is right, though. I am on vacation. Let's save the work talk for when I'm back on the job."

"You got it, man. Hey, if you and Mallory stay together, we could be spending lots more time together."

Theo's face must have blanched. This was getting messy, and they had barely begun this ruse.

"Honey, maybe we should switch seats. I don't know if you can handle being next to this man. Mallory doesn't usually date people in general. Let's not scare the famous one away."

Mallory choked on her water. "Wow, thanks for that, Erica."

Erica. He knew it started with an *E*.

The three-year-old started crying. Something about his hot dog touching his corn. He was not happy about it.

Theo pushed back from the table. "I'll be right back." He couldn't get out of that room fast enough. In the hallway, he could at least breathe. What had he gotten himself into and why was he allowing it to go on? They should come clean now while the lie was still young.

"Hey, you okay?" Mallory seemed to appear out of nowhere. "You were limping when you walked out. Did you take the anti-inflammatory I left for you?"

He should have, just like he should have iced his knee the second twenty minutes. He couldn't bear to see the disappointment in her eyes if he told her that. "We need to tell them the truth. I don't think I can do family dinners like this all week. It's too much."

Mallory shook her head. Her eyes were wide and panicked instead of disappointed. That wasn't much better. "We don't have to do any more family dinners. This can be the first and last, but please don't drop out on me. I need you to stay in this with me. Please."

Theo scrubbed his face with both hands. "It's a lot of people to keep straight and a lot of questions and I'm trying to remember how I'm supposed to answer the ones about us. And your soon-to-be brother-in-law is trying to get the team gossip. I just—"

"I will make sure you never are cornered by Hayden again. He's done. You're doing so well. Everyone likes you; I can tell."

"Do I want everyone to like me? What happens when this week is over, and you tell them we broke up?"

She reached for his hand and a strange tingle ran up his arm. She wore her hair down for dinner. The soft curl in it made him want to touch it to see if it was as soft as it looked.

"Don't worry about what happens after. I promise to make this easier than it's been. Please."

Mallory's eyes shifted over his shoulder and then back to his face. Before he could say anything, she wrapped her arms around his neck and pressed her lips to his. He was so caught off guard he didn't have control over himself. His automatic reaction was to grip her waist and kiss her back. She was an excellent kisser and that was the only encouragement he needed.

She pulled back, her expression impossible to read. She leaned to the left. "Can I not have one minute alone to make out with my boyfriend?" she snipped at someone behind him.

Theo turned to find Mallory's other sister, also not named Avery but maybe something starting with an *S*. She looked embarrassed and apologized, ducking back into the room.

"Sorry about that. I panicked when I saw Savannah open the door."

Savannah. The one expecting the baby. The one who Mallory gets along with best. "We need to talk about boundaries when there aren't so many eyes and ears nearby, but I'll let that one slide since you're quite the kisser."

Her cheeks bloomed red. In all the time he had worked with her and listened to other players shamelessly flirt with her, he'd never seen her blush. He was sort of proud of himself for being the first one to do it.

"You're not too bad yourself, Seasons. Must be from all the practice you've had with your adoring female fans."

"I don't kiss the fans, Mallory. I mean, they might become fans after they kiss me—"

She swatted him on the arm before he could finish. "Do you think your ego can follow me back through the door or do you need me to get your brother over here to deflate it first?"

Theo chuckled. "I'm good. I think I'll fit."

She started for the door but stopped short. "Are we good? I know I'm asking a lot. This is as painful as it's going to get."

"We're good. At least until family game time. I might have to fake that injury if it's really bad." After kissing her, he couldn't stop himself from brushing back some of her hair from her face. Resisting the urge to touch her was impossible now that he knew what her lips felt like against his.

Her cheeks darkened again as she took a step back. "Oh, it will be that bad. My mom puts a lot of effort into these games. Don't say I didn't warn you."

Given the predicament they were in, something told him Mallory's mom wasn't the only one who knew how to play a game well. Theo hoped he wouldn't lose too much when this game of boyfriend and girlfriend came to an end.

MALLORY DID HER best to pretend she wasn't thinking about the kiss she'd shared with Theo in the hall, but it was pretty much the only thing she could focus on.

"Mallory, it's your turn," Avery said with a nudge of her elbow.

After they had all finished eating and the table was cleared, her mom had assumed the role of game show host. She had brought with her several items that were needed for her silly Christmas games. She did this every year. A couple years ago, they all had put cookies on their forehead and without using their hands had to shimmy the cookie down their faces and into their mouths. The first one to accomplish this without dropping or touching the cookie won.

Last year, they had unwrapped a giant ball of cellophane that was filled with candy and lottery scratch tickets. If the next person in line rolled doubles with the dice, you had to hand it over to them even if you could see the next prize was right there. Mallory actually won a hundred dollars. That one hadn't been so bad.

This year, her mom was overjoyed to include the Seasons family in the nonsense. Instead of playing Seasons against Moore, her mom had decided it would be men versus women. Tonight's first game was Snowball Shovel. Her mother had placed giant marshmallows all over the table. One player from each team would be blindfolded and handed a spatula. With the spatula, they had sixty seconds to place as many marshmallows as they could in a bowl. The team with the most marshmallows at the end won. Avery and Chance had gone first. Nora and Quinn had gone next. It was now Mallory versus Theo. The men were currently winning by five marshmallows.

"You got this, Theo. It's just like flicking the puck into the net," Brady said, cheering his brother on.

"His hockey skills are not going to help him," Nora said with a laugh. "Think more like flipping pancakes, Mallory. You've got this."

Theo stood on the opposite side of the table, spatula in hand. "Don't be too mad when I put the guys ahead by double. I'm a professional athlete. Losing to me is nothing to be ashamed of." He winked at her before Quinn helped him with his blindfold.

"Whatever you say, Seasons. I have a feeling you underestimate how many times my mother has made me play weird games blindfolded."

She heard him laugh as the blindfold was put over her eyes. He was so cocky and such a darn good kisser. It was annoying.

"Ready, set, go!" her mom announced.

Mallory started doing what she thought was flicking marshmallows into the bowl, but based on the way Savannah was directing her to lighten her touch, she might not have been as successful as she hoped. Brady's girlfriend, Alexa, was so sweet. She kept telling Mallory she was awesome.

"Have you ever made pancakes in your life?" someone asked Theo. Mallory guessed it was Quinn. "Hold the spatula flat!" Maybe he wasn't doing as well as he'd thought he was going to do.

"And…times up! Spatulas down!" her mom shouted.

When Mallory pulled down her blindfold, she could see that Theo had done a great job clearing the spot in front of him of marshmallows, but it didn't look like many got in his bowl. Hers on the other hand was brimming with giant blobs of marshmallow goodness.

"You actually hit Mallory's dad with a marshmallow and he's standing all the way over there," Brady teased Theo, pointing to her dad at the far end of the enormous table.

"Mallory got twelve marshmallows and Theo got two. The ladies are now in the lead by three marshmallows. Good job, sweetheart."

"Twelve to two? Ouch, Seasons. Don't worry about it, though. I'm practically a professional Christmas game player. You shouldn't feel bad losing to me."

Theo shook his head, trying but failing to look mad. He couldn't stop his mouth—that perfect mouth—from curving into a smile. "The night is young. There are more games to be played and more chances for me to redeem myself."

Was Theo Seasons having fun playing games with her family? Mallory was sure that he was, and something about that made her feel warm in the center of her chest.

He was right. There were more games to be played, and Mallory took some losses. He won Flip Cup Tic Tac Toe, she beat him during a very close game of Candy Cane Carry Over and she lost badly in the Bow Toss.

By the end of the night, everyone had laughed and cheered on their teammates until they were exhausted. At the start of the final game, the men and women were tied two games to two. Santa on a Roll would decide the grand champions.

"For the last game, each team will nominate one player from their team to represent them," her mom said.

Greg groaned. He hated sitting out.

"It's better we don't waste so much toilet paper, Gregory. Deal with it."

Savannah had already announced her early retirement. She was sitting with her feet up. "If they pick Greg to play, does that mean I have to play or can we choose whoever we want?"

"I'm out," Quinn said. "I need to go check on the event down the hall."

"I can do it," his dad offered. "You stay."

"I got it, Dad. You're passing the torch, remember. Let me handle it."

Gavin paused then nodded, letting Quinn represent the inn at the other event. Laura patted him on the back when he sat back down as if to acknowledge she was proud of him for stepping aside.

Mallory had forgotten that Theo's parents were retiring. It appeared his brother would be taking the helm once that happened.

"I think it should be Theo versus Mallory. They're the reason we're all here. It should come down to Seasons against Moore for the final," Avery suggested. She was also down for the count or at least Sebastian was. She sat next to Savannah with Sebastian fast asleep in her arms.

"Is your team good with that?" Mallory asked Theo. She was more than willing to be the last woman standing. "I mean, I would have voted for Alexa because she is probably the most competitive person in this room."

"I am not going against Alexa anymore tonight. I can't take another loss," Brady said, coming around to the ladies' side of the table and wrapping his arms around Alexa. "This is why I like being on your team, not against you."

She gave him a peck on the cheek. "Thank you for saying that."

They were too cute together. Mallory learned that Alexa had been a guest at the inn last summer and that's how she and Brady met. They said it was almost love at first sight. She loved that for them. Mallory wasn't sure if she had ever been in love for real. There were times she'd thought she was but quickly realized what she'd had was far from love.

"I am more than happy to take on Mallory in this final battle. I think I have proven that I am a worthy adversary to our practically professional Christmas game player."

They were also tied two to two in the individual competitions. The final game was going to be a tiebreaker for them as well. Mallory wasn't one to back down from a challenge. "Let's do this."

Her mom pulled out two rolls of what had to be the cheapest toilet paper sold in the United States. One-ply generic brand torture paper is what Mallory would call it. Standing at the head of the table, she explained, "You each get a roll of toilet paper. You will roll it out, starting on this side of the table and ending at the opposite end. You two will sit there with the roll and on this end of the paper will be chocolate Santas." She pulled the two little chocolate Santas wrapped in foil from her bag. "You will attempt to carefully reroll your toilet paper until the Santa gets all the way to you down there."

"That doesn't sound too hard," Theo said, taking his seat at the end of the table.

"Oh, but the catch is that if you break the toilet paper at any point, you have to start all over. The Santa must get to you on an unbroken strip."

Theo's brow furrowed. "Okay, that sounds hard."

"Your teammates can help you by being the ones that reset your Santa if the paper breaks," her mom added.

Mallory glanced at Avery and Savannah. They were done for the night and would be no help. She was going to have to rely on Theo's family to help her win.

"Are you ready?" her mom asked. Mallory and Theo both nodded. "Go!"

Mallory could tell that slow and steady was going to win the race. She also learned quickly that this toilet paper was a nightmare to work with. Hers ripped a few seconds into it. Alexa was quick to help her reset.

Theo also tried the slow method, but it didn't take long for the cheap paper to snap. He had several eager helpers on his side of the table. His brothers and her brothers-in-law worked together quite nicely.

"You look a little flustered there, Mallory. You know that's going to work against you," Theo said, pulling his Santa closer and closer.

Her paper had ripped three times in a row after one simple tug. Of course, she was flustered. This was her mom's game. She had to win. It was destiny.

Theo's Santa was a foot away when his paper separated. Hayden snatched the Santa up, running it back down to the other end of the table while Greg helped unroll a new length of paper.

Mallory was just about to give him a hard time when her paper broke apart. Alexa had gone to use the bathroom, and Nora was talking to Savannah and Avery. Erica was too busy cheering on Hayden to notice Mallory needed the same help. That left her mom and poor Mrs. Seasons to do the work. They were laughing it up and getting along way too well. There was no sense of urgency from them. Theo was already reeling his Santa back in.

"Mom! Come on. Let's go."

Theo was steady as a rock. He was completely calm and unbothered. He gently spun his roll, pulling the Santa to him. Mallory could feel the sweat on her neck. She was losing patience, and without patience, she was destined to lose.

Theo rolled his paper until the Santa was standing proudly in front of him. "We win!" Greg shouted. Hayden and Brady high-fived. Quinn and Chance shook hands like they had done something to help them win. Her dad and Theo's dad were sitting together having a drink and probably talking about sports, oblivious to their win.

"The men have won it," her mom announced. "You did a good job, sweetheart. Maybe Theo can teach you a thing or two about staying calm under pressure. I can tell you compete for a living, Theo. You were laser focused and cool as a cucumber."

Mallory couldn't look at him because she knew he was going to smile and drive her insane by silently rubbing it in that he had won.

"You did an amazing job putting this all together, Mrs. Moore. I think I can speak for my whole family when I say it was a very fun evening."

Mallory wanted to crawl under the table. He was going to have her mother eating out of the palm of his hand any second. This was too much.

His whole family chimed in that they'd had a wonderful time. Even her own family started carrying on about how that had been the best Christmas game night in history.

She ventured a glance in Theo's direction. He was grinning. "What can I say, when you invite excellence into your circle, you get excellence. I really think I delivered tonight. What do you think?"

Clearly, the rubbing-it-in was not going to be silent. "I think you're going to be invited to Christmas every year from now on. I hope you're happy."

His smile faltered for a second and then he started to laugh. "There are worse things, Mallory. There are worse things."

CHAPTER SIX

"Do FIVE MORE and then you can get on the bike for twenty minutes, but no more than twenty. Deal?"

"Deal," Theo replied, getting to work.

Theo was beginning to think he was starting to like both PT Mallory and fake girlfriend Mallory. Last night had ended up being the most fun he'd had in a long time. He went from having a panic attack to being the grand champion of their family game night. He wasn't the only one who'd had a good time, either. His family was texting about it in the family group chat this morning.

Maybe playing along with this charade wouldn't be as bad as he feared. Mallory's family was entertaining. There was something about having some fun that made this morning's workout that much easier. Maybe his sour mood had been what was holding him back when he was in Boston.

"My sister's doing the gender reveal at lunch today. She was wondering if you would be joining us. I told her I wasn't sure in case you've had enough of my family after last night and want to skip it."

Was she offering up another chance to play? He didn't want her to feel so nervous about inviting him out. "I'll come. Are we betting on if it's a boy or a girl? What do I win when I'm right?"

Mallory rolled her eyes. "Win one family game night and you think you're the Christmas MVP. You need to work on your humbleness, my friend. This exaggerated sense of self is too much."

Theo pressed a hand to his chest. "I have an exaggerated sense of self? Wow, someone is super sad this morning that she lost last night. You claimed to be a professional Christmas game player, but I think you're a professional sore loser."

She clicked her tongue. "Sore loser? I am not a sore loser. You're a sore winner."

Shaking his head, Theo got up off the floor and started toward the bike. "That's not even a real thing."

"Fine, let's bet. I think my sister is having a girl."

"I think she's having a girl, too."

"You can't pick a girl. I picked a girl."

He got on the bike and slid his feet into the pedals. He loved bantering with her. Probably more than he should. "You don't get to decide what I vote for by voting first. I don't have to vote opposite of you when I know girl is going to win."

"Well, who wins if we vote the same way?"

Theo kind of loved seeing her so flustered. "Um, we both do. Could you handle it if we *both* won?"

"Something must be wrong with you. You're having too much fun." She busied herself with cleaning up the equipment they'd used today. Was it wrong to be having a good time? Last night, she had begged him to keep up the ruse, promising it wouldn't be as bad as he feared. Now, she was stressed because he believed her. This was a good thing. He'd been down in the dumps for too long.

"Mallory," he said, waiting for her to look at him. When she didn't, he repeated himself. "Mallory."

She set down the resistance bands and turned to face him with her hands on her hips. "What?"

"I am having fun and it's all your fault. Thank you for helping me get out of my head and enjoy myself for once. I really needed it."

She didn't move or speak, but her chest rose and fell with heavy breaths. Finally, she said, "You're welcome. Thank you for letting my family believe that this is the best Christmas ever even if it's all based on a lie."

"Even if I'm not your boyfriend, it doesn't mean it can't actually be the best Christmas. The lie doesn't change the experience."

"Okay, but don't make everyone like you so

much that they hate me when I have to tell them we broke up. I'm beginning to think that's a real possibility."

Theo didn't mean to laugh at her, but she couldn't be serious. "Your family would never choose me over you. I see the way they love you, Mallory. I get that it can be annoying that your mom wants you to find someone so badly, but I also heard the way she talked about you to my parents. She told my mom about how you graduated at the top of your class and how they weren't hockey people until you started working for the team. That your dad wears Icemen stuff all the time and brags to everyone that his daughter works for them. They are extremely proud of you."

Her eyes turned glassy, welling with tears. Theo was so confused. Mallory ran out of the room and into the bathroom before he could ask her what was wrong.

He got off the exercise bike and stood in front of the closed bathroom door. "What did I say? I was trying to cheer you up."

He could hear her blowing her nose. "I'm fine. Go finish your workout!"

He needed to know what was going on. What made her so upset? Was she mad? He truly meant everything he'd said. "Open the door, please."

After a couple seconds, the door opened and Mallory bit down on her bottom lip. He was not good with tears. Crying women tended to scare him off, but for some reason instead of running away, he wanted to move closer and wrap his arms around her. He felt oddly protective of her.

"What did I do wrong?" he asked.

"Nothing. I have a complicated relationship with my family. Sometimes I don't feel like I'm as successful in life as my sisters based on my mother's standards for success. What you said you heard means more to me than I can say."

"Like I told you before, you are awesome just the way you are, but they do think the world of you. I can tell."

"You are way better at this than I thought you would be," she said in a quiet voice.

"Way better at what?"

"Being a supportive fake boyfriend, I guess," she said with a shrug of her shoulder.

"I am an overachiever. Just look at my stats on the ice. I've been this way my whole life when given a challenge."

She laughed and wiped her face. "Sorry. I just can't believe you were paying attention to things like what my mom was saying to your mom. I'm also glad that you had fun last night. I know this is so weird. You should hate me, but instead you've been smiling and joking around all morning. I should be happy about that because it means I'm not torturing you."

"But?" Clearly there was a but in there.

"But I can't like you this much, Theo. In a week, we'll go back to Boston, and it will be like none of this ever happened. I need to keep it real when we're in here. The lines are already blurry enough when we step outside this room. I need you to be Theo Seasons, the hockey player who needs therapy. Not some good-looking, charismatic guy telling me sweet things and making me feel like we're connecting on a different level. There can't be levels."

Good-looking and charismatic? He was flattered. She liked him. She liked him too much, though. If he was honest with her, he would admit that he liked her, too. He probably liked her more than he should because she was right. It was odd to think in a few short days they'd go back to barely knowing each other. They certainly couldn't like each other beyond a friendly working relationship in Boston. They had to keep this professional.

"We will keep it real in here when we're doing therapy. I don't want there to be any mixed signals. You're my physical therapist. We can be friends, but there's only one level. We like each other, but we don't *like* each other."

"Exactly."

It was good they were on the same page about things. It didn't change the fact that he still wanted to grab her and pull her close. He wanted to reach up and wipe that tear she'd missed. He wasn't sure what that meant, but he knew he had to be better-disciplined. He couldn't let his feelings get out of control.

"I'm going to ride the bike for twenty minutes, so you're free to go. Let me know what time you all are meeting for lunch. I'll make my appearance and then I was going to head over to the rink. You can have the rest of the day to spend with your family."

"Sounds good. I'll text you." Mallory pulled herself together and left him alone to finish his workout.

Fun. This could be fun. Fun was the opposite of serious. Theo could not have serious feelings for Mallory. It would be bad for both of them. They could have fun and get through the holidays without complicating things. That's what he told himself, anyway, as he pedaled in place, staring out the window at the snow falling over Apple Hollow.

Theo needed to view her as PT Mallory. PT Mallory had boundaries. But even as he tried to focus on the rhythm of the bike and not the ache in his knee or the tightness in his chest, he couldn't shake the image of her teary-eyed smile.

He liked her laugh, her sarcasm, her determination. And that terrified him. Because it wasn't PT Mallory who made him want to memorize the way she tilted her head when she was annoyed or how she bit her lip when she was nervous. PT Mallory didn't make him think back to that kiss she gave him last night and wish they could do it again. Fake girlfriend Mallory had him tied up in all kinds of knots.

He had to keep things in check. Because if he didn't, he wasn't sure how either of them would recover.

MALLORY CURSED HERSELF the whole way back to her room. She was catching feelings for Theo Seasons one day after begging him to pretend to be her boyfriend. What kind of person would ask someone to do that and then let themselves fall head over heels knowing that it could never be a real relationship? She was hopeless. They were going to go back to Boston, and she'd have to work to uncatch these dumb feelings while he went on with his life like it was no big deal.

All this so she didn't hurt her mom's feelings. Maybe this was karma for trying to skip out on Christmas.

Theo was funny. He was charming. He was thoughtful even though she was sure he was like every other hockey player she worked with—hung up on themselves and unaware that people like her had a life outside the Icemen training facility.

Theo saw the real her. He met her whole messy family, and he still liked her. He'd had *fun*.

She didn't want him to be a jerk, but did he have to be so…perfect? Her entire family thought he was amazing. It was all they'd talked about at breakfast this morning. They were definitely going to be mad at her for "blowing it" when she told them she and Theo broke up after Christmas. She didn't have the heart to make him the bad guy, so they'd feel sorry for her. She'd have to take the blame.

Savannah stood outside Mallory's room when she got there. "Oh, there you are. I was just about to text you," her sister said, slipping her phone back in her pocket.

"What's up?" Mallory unlocked her door and held it open for Savannah.

"Were you working out? We're on vacation, please tell me you weren't working out. You're going to make me feel like a bad person."

Mallory laughed. Savannah had run the Boston marathon twice. She was very fit, but when she was on vacation, she allowed herself to be a total slug. "I was not working out. I was doing some PT with Theo."

Savannah's expression changed. "What do you mean? You were working? You can't work while you're on vacation, Mallory."

"I told him that I would supervise his workouts to make sure he did what he was supposed to do.

He needs to stay on track if he's going to get back on the ice."

"You're here as his girlfriend, not his physical therapist. There should be boundaries."

Mallory wanted to laugh at that word. The boundaries of their relationship were very strange at the moment. "It's fine."

"He's taking advantage. This is probably why the organization has a no fraternizing policy. He has the power because he's the superstar. I like Theo, but I hate this situation you two have gotten yourselves in. The only one truly risking something is you. That's not right."

Always the protective one, Savannah had a point—*if* they were in a real dating relationship, but they weren't. Since Mallory couldn't explain why there was nothing to worry about, she tried to change the subject.

"I love that you worry about me, but you don't need to. Can I just say I'm so excited about finding out if we are finally going to break the boy streak this family has been on the last few years. How are you planning to reveal if it's a boy or a girl? Cake? Balloon? Party popper?"

"We're not done talking about you and Theo, but I can tell you're not ready to listen to me yet, so I'll back off. For now."

That was a relief. Hopefully, there would be too much Christmas chaos for them to find time to revisit the topic. Mallory wanted to stick to safer subjects. "Well, what's it going to be? Cake?"

"Didn't you hear us talking to Theo's parents about it last night?"

"There was a lot going on, I could only pay attention to the conversations I was in."

"We're doing a gingerbread theme. What am I baking—gingerbread boy or gingerbread girl?" she said as she rubbed her belly.

"That's adorable."

"Theo's dad offered to let us have it in the room where they had some private event last night that just happened to be gingerbread-themed. He said the decorations are amazing. I wanted to see if you were available to go see it with me before we start making the arrangements."

"Um, yes. I would love to go check it out with you. Are we going right now?"

"If you're up for it. Or we can stay here and talk about Theo some more."

Mallory linked arms with her sister and dragged her back to the door. "Nope. Let's go."

Nora was more than happy to show them the Four Seasons Room. Theo's dad was not wrong. The decorations were incredible. It was like walking into some kind of storybook fantasyland. There were gumdrops the size of watermelons and lollipops as tall as Mallory. She might have been considered short for a person, but lollipops her size were gigantic. Then there was the life-size gingerbread house in the center of the room.

Savannah was in complete awe. "I can't believe this exists at the same time that I planned to use gingerbread to reveal the sex of my baby. This is the luckiest baby ever. Thank you so much for letting us have lunch in here. It's like someone knew exactly what I wanted but didn't know was possible."

"It's no problem," Nora said. "We were planning on leaving this set up for the Seasons at the Lake celebration on Wednesday. My dad was so excited when he heard you could benefit from it as well."

"Xavier and Sebastian are going to freak out when they see this," Mallory said, carefully touching the house to see if she could tell what it was really made of.

"True, but Erica is going to have a meltdown."

Mallory grimaced and Nora gasped. "Why would she have a meltdown?" Nora asked.

There was no way to sugarcoat this. "Let's just say our baby sister doesn't like not being the center of attention when she thinks she should be the center of attention and since she got engaged very recently, she believes that her engagement should be center stage."

"Oh. That's…problematic."

Savannah giggled. "You can say that again. This is over the top and out of this world. I don't know what

Mom had planned for their engagement celebration, but there isn't anything that's going to top this."

"We're not going to worry about Erica," Mallory said. "You didn't ask for the room to be decorated like this. It just happened to be this way. It was a fortunate coincidence. We will all make sure to be very happy for her when we celebrate her engagement."

"Just not as happy as I am going to be when we decorate the little gingerbread cookies Laura is making and take a million pictures in front of that backdrop over there and in front of the house and by that Christmas tree." Savannah was over the moon, and it made Mallory feel so much better.

"We also have some leftover gingerbread houses you all could decorate if you want. Or is that too much? I don't want your younger sister to get so upset that it ruins everyone's lunch." Nora looked so concerned.

Savannah and Mallory shared a look. There was no way Mallory would let Erica spoil the gender reveal.

"No, that would be awesome," Savannah said. "We could make it a contest and we'll tell everyone to vote for Erica's house even if it's not the best."

Mallory was all for it even though she knew Erica would not be satisfied. At least this would take everyone's mind off her and Theo. Thank goodness for huge favors.

THERE WAS NO way lunch was going to disappoint. The whole family was speechless for a solid minute when they walked in the room. Her mom cried. Erica wanted to cry but somehow held it together. Mallory had warned her that someone had spent a lot of money to have a very extravagant party last night and Savannah was merely the fortunate beneficiary of their exceptional party planning.

"What in the world?" Xavier exclaimed over and over as he ran around the room, exploring everything it had to offer. Sebastian tried to keep up.

Theo came up from behind and leaned down to whisper in her ear, "I think he likes the decorations."

His proximity made her get the stomach flutters. She had to push back on those kinds of feelings. She could not let her body try to trick her into thinking her relationship with Theo was real.

"What in the world?" Xavier screamed again. "Dad, did you see this?"

Mallory smiled at the pure joy on Xavier's face as Avery took a picture of him and Chance standing in front of a giant gingerbread man holding an even taller candy cane. Her mom picked up Sebastian so he could get a better view of the gingerbread house. His eyes lit up when she showed him the candy details around the windows.

"It's magical," Mallory said in a happy sigh. "I'm actually ecstatic that they're here to see this. I was so freaked out to see them yesterday, but this makes it worth all that anxiety I felt."

"People always tell me things happen for a reason. Maybe this is why they had to crash your Christmas."

They did crash her Christmas, but as much as she wished she didn't have to be dishonest about why she was here, she was grateful that they'd been given an opportunity to experience something this amazing.

"Hey, you two, get together for a picture," Avery said, holding up her phone in their direction.

Instead of leaning closer or wrapping an arm around her shoulders, Theo stepped farther away. "We can't do pictures," he said, walking toward Avery. "But I'd be happy to get one of you and Mallory. Maybe we should get a picture of the whole family in front of the gingerbread house."

Avery's face scrunched up in confusion. "Why can't you take a picture?"

"It's just better there aren't pictures of us floating around. We're not allowed to go public right now."

It wasn't a lie. If this was a real relationship, they would not be able to go public. Mallory couldn't help but wonder if the actual reason he didn't want pictures was because he knew this wasn't real. They weren't a happy couple. There was no need to memorialize the moment.

"You could just ask me to not post it on my socials. I understand you two are on the down-low."

Theo played it off. "Yeah, I know, I'm just super cautious. When you're a professional athlete, you can never be too careful. It's just easier to not take the picture than worry about it getting out. I don't think you'd do anything on purpose, I just know things happen."

"Oh." Avery didn't seem to be too thrilled with that answer, but got everyone's attention and had them get together by the gingerbread house.

She gave Theo her phone and he took pictures of Mallory and her family. She plastered on a smile even though it stung he wouldn't take a picture with her. It was a dumb reason to let her feelings get hurt. Why would she want a reminder of this when it was all over? Avery would definitely delete all pictures of him when Mallory "broke up" with him in a week. That was what good sisters did. They got rid of any evidence that their sister had been in a bad relationship.

"Got it," Theo said, handing Avery back her phone so she could review the shots he'd taken.

Theo's dad had seen to it that a table was set up for them and waitstaff were sent in to take their lunch orders. Savannah and Greg had given Theo's mom the envelope with the sex of the baby in it. She was the one at the inn who made all the delicious desserts. She was kind enough to make a gingerbread man or woman for the reveal.

Once they finished eating, everyone was given a cookie. Bags of icing and bowls of candies were placed in the center of the table.

"We invite everyone to decorate their gingerbread person as a girl or boy based on what you think the baby is," Savannah said. "Once everyone has made their guess, we will reveal the baby gingerbread person."

Theo kept checking his phone while everyone else got started. Mallory sensed that cookie decorating wasn't his thing. He was only here because it made them look like they were together. It didn't mean he wanted to be there. This maybe wasn't as fun as game night. Again, she tried not to let his disconnectedness hurt her feelings. He wasn't her real boyfriend, she reminded herself.

Xavier had decided Savannah was having a boy, so he plopped a blob of baby blue icing on his cookie. Erica also went with blue, but Hayden chose pink. Avery and their mom were helping Sebastian make a pink gingerbread person with blue sprinkles. He was undecided if it was going to be a boy cousin or a girl cousin.

"What do you think it's going to be, honey?" her dad asked. He had taken the seat next to her and hadn't reached for a bag of icing yet.

"Girl. I'm feeling eighty-eight percent sure."

She grabbed a pink icing bag and began outlining a dress on her gingerbread person.

"Eighty-eight percent?" He chuckled. "Not a hundred, huh?"

"I'm a hundred percent it's a girl," Theo chimed in. "That way when it's a girl, I win by twelve percent."

Mallory stopped what she was doing and set her bag down. She turned to look at him. "Excuse me?"

"I figured out how we can tell who wins when we both vote for the same thing. We can use confidence level as the deciding point. If it's a boy, you win because I had zero percent confidence, and you had twelve."

He was so strange. One minute it seemed he couldn't care less about this and the next minute he was claiming his confidence level made him more right. She would accept these terms, but he had to fully commit. "You can't win if you don't vote via cookie design."

He set his phone down and that was when she noticed he had pulled up a picture of a cookie decorated like a hockey player. "Who said I'm not voting? I needed to find the perfect design. I'm making mine play hockey."

Mallory was stunned into silence. Her dad leaned over to take a peek at Theo's inspiration. "That's a fun idea. You're very creative, Theo."

"Thanks, Will."

Will? People did not call her dad Will. He was William to everyone she knew. Sometimes her mom would call him that, but she was the only exception. "You're giving my dad nicknames now?"

"I asked him if I could call him Will and he said sure. Do people not call you Will, Will?"

Mallory's head whipped back over to her dad. "No one calls you Will."

"I don't have an issue with it. It can be mine and Theo's thing," her dad replied. He squeezed the blue icing onto his cookie.

Her dad and Theo were going to have a thing. A nickname thing. What was happening?

CHAPTER SEVEN

THEO HAD A new appreciation for the work his mother did. She baked and decorated all the goodies at the inn, and it was not easy based on the fact that his hockey playing gingerbread girl looked like a pink and white blob. He had tried to put his number on its chest, but the one and the seven sort of smeared together.

"I mean, you tried," Mallory said when he finally gave up. Hers had on a pink icing dress with a white crown on her head that Mallory made sparkle with some sugar sprinkles.

"Good thing we're not determining a winner based on the best decorated cookie."

"Oh!" Mallory perked up. "That's a much better idea than your idea of judging who won based on confidence level. Let's do that."

"No, no, no. You can't change the rules after they've been established," Theo argued.

"The rules you made up on the fly? I feel like those are debatable."

"They're not. But nice try." Theo stood and

picked up the plate his cookie was on. "Would you like me to take yours over to the guessing table?"

She scowled at him as she handed over her plate. "Thank you," she grumbled.

Theo had to tamp down the feelings that her adorableness flared up. He wasn't supposed to think about her that way. She was his physical therapist, not his girlfriend.

He placed their plates on the girl side of the table. There was an even split—five for boy, five for girl. Avery and her mom hadn't finished theirs yet, but it was obvious who they were voting for. Savannah's excitement was also evident. She moved around the room, chatting with her family, stopping to sit next to Mallory.

The two women leaned in close, whispering and laughing as though sharing secrets. Theo couldn't help but watch them from across the room, his gaze lingering on Mallory longer than it should have. She had that effortless charm, the kind that made people want to be around her. He could imagine her getting along with almost anyone in his life. That thought was unsettling in a way he couldn't quite articulate.

"They're a lot, but this is one of the best families around. I feel like I was in your position not too long ago," Savannah's husband's voice snapped him out of his thoughts. Greg stood beside him, arms crossed and a sly grin plastered on his face.

"At least I knew I was meeting them all and could prepare. I give you so much credit for managing all this with no warning."

"They aren't so bad," Theo replied, just as Sebastian screamed at the top of his lungs as Xavier took a bite of his cookie. Chance took the cookie away from Xavier, who began to cry as well.

"You were saying?" Greg raised an eyebrow.

As much as Theo hated seeing a woman cry, he disliked children crying even more. "They're loud. That's for sure. You should be paying attention. You're going to have to quiet crying kids down soon enough."

"You're not wrong," Greg said with a concerned expression. He ran a shaky hand through his hair. "I hope I'm ready for this. I mean, I don't have a choice, right?"

Theo chuckled. "Yeah, I think you're past the point of no return."

"Whose cookie is this?" Erica came up behind them, squinting at the pink and white blob.

"That would be mine," Theo admitted. "It's a hockey gingerbread woman."

Mallory's youngest sister pressed her lips together and nodded. She patted him on the shoulder. "Good thing you're better at skating than you are at cookie decorating."

"Wow, thanks a lot. You're not even going to pretend it was a good try?"

Greg and Erica laughed. "Nobody is safe in this family. Everyone is fair game, even famous hockey players," Erica said with a wink.

Across the room, Savannah stood up, pulling Mallory with her. "All right, everyone, it's time for the big reveal!" she called out, her excitement infectious.

Theo watched as Mallory caught his eye, giving him a small smile and a quick wink. His heart did something it shouldn't have, something he refused to acknowledge. He couldn't afford distractions, not from his recovery and definitely not because of her. But as Mallory joined the crowd around the guessing table, Theo couldn't shake the feeling that this fake relationship might be just that— a distraction.

Greg made a video call to his family as they were going to participate virtually. Once Greg's family entered their votes, baby boy was in the lead. Theo shook his head. He had no doubt it was a girl.

The gingerbread person his mom had decorated for the reveal was in a box with a light blue and pink ribbon sticking out on each side. Greg and Savannah each held one of the ribbons and lifted the lid to reveal quite possibly the sweetest gingerbread person anyone had ever seen. The cookie had a light pink dress with darker pink polka dots and white ruffled sleeves. There was a bow around her waist covered in glittery sugar that matched the one on her head.

Savannah and Greg hugged as the family in front of them and on the phone cheered. Theo held up his hand for a high-five and Mallory slapped it. He knew they had been right.

Mallory's mom was in tears, hugging everyone she could get her hands on. She hadn't been kidding when she said she was a hugger. Mallory congratulated her sister and brother-in-law before coming back to stand beside Theo.

"If you want to duck out now, you can. I'll tell them you needed to go," she whispered as Avery took pictures of Savannah, Greg and their cookie.

Theo was taken aback by the offer. He had been having a good time, why would she think he wanted to leave? Maybe it wasn't about how he felt. Maybe she wanted him to leave. Maybe she was tired of pretending for the afternoon.

He leaned down, so no one else could hear him. "I don't mind staying, but I can go if you want me to."

"I don't—I just mean, I don't want to keep you from the things you want to do."

It was still hard to tell if she meant it or not. "I was going to stop by the ice rink later this afternoon."

"Oh, good. I know you were looking forward to that." Mallory shifted her weight and fidgeted with her hands.

"Mallory, Erica, let's get a sister picture. Everyone else stand by, we'll do a whole family picture next."

Family pictures—Theo would offer to take those. There was no way he should be in any of the photos. It wouldn't be right to taint this memory with the man Mallory tricked her family into thinking she was dating. Someday, when she had a real boyfriend, someone she could marry and truly make part of her family, she'd confess to her family she had lied to them that one Christmas they surprised her in New Hampshire. His knee ached right along with his heart at that thought.

He shook his head at himself. There was no reason for that to make him feel sad. Mallory deserved to be happy and to come clean with her family.

As soon as he noticed they were done with the sister picture, he stepped up. "I can take the whole group photos."

Hayden was about to hand him the phone, but Avery stopped him. "We can get someone else to take it, so you can be in it."

"I don't—"

She eyed him with way more suspicion than he liked. "You don't want to take a picture with the family?"

"I think we talked about this earlier."

Avery waved over one of the staff who was

clearing the dining table. She was not going to take no for an answer. "It's not going to be just you and Mallory."

"Avery, don't bully my boyfriend," Mallory said, stepping in as Avery asked the waitress to take the picture.

"You're serious enough to spend Christmas with his family but not serious enough to be in a picture together?" Avery challenged. "There's something off about that."

Theo had no choice. If they continued to argue with Avery, they would attract the attention of the rest of Mallory's family. If they started to question this relationship, they would be doomed. "It's fine. I'll be in the picture."

"You don't—" Mallory started.

He took her by the hand, pulling her toward the group. "It's cool. All good."

"I know you don't want to."

Maybe she was more worried about making him do things he didn't want to do than not wanting him to be there. "If anyone asks why I'm in it, you can explain you were at my family's inn. I don't think anyone in the main office is going to question that."

MALLORY COULD FEEL the weight of Theo's hand on her shoulder as she smiled for the pictures with her family. She knew it was silly, but part of her was kind of happy he would be included in this memory. Even though there wasn't a chance for her relationship with Theo to be anything other than a working one when they got back to Boston, they would always mean a little bit more to each other than therapist and patient.

"So, what do you two have planned for the rest of the day?" Hayden asked Theo when the pictures were done being taken.

Theo and Mallory exchanged a look. They hadn't talked about what they were going to say.

"What are you guys doing?" Mallory deflected.

"Erica heard about some sleigh ride around town and then she signed us up for the ornament-making event. I'm down for the carriage ride, I'm not so sure about the ornament making. If you want to take my place, Mallory, just let me know."

"I don't know about that. I think I used up all my creativity for the day with the cookie decorating, but if I change my mind, I'll let you know."

"I lacked creativity before the cookie decorating, so ornament making is definitely not for me," Theo said.

"You were very creative with your cookie. It was the execution that was the issue," Mallory said, wanting him to know she appreciated his efforts.

"Your cookie was the best out of all of them."

His compliment made her blush. "Your mom's

was the best. That cookie was incredible. I have a feeling she's going to be missed around here when she retires."

Theo smiled conspiratorially. "You're lucky she's my mom. We can get desserts from her whether she works here or not."

"You two are so great together," Hayden said, drawing Mallory's attention away from Theo. He was right; Theo was the most perfect fake boyfriend in town. It was so easy to get lost in his warm brown eyes and his easy smile. She wanted to touch the short, cropped beard, knowing it was soft and not scratchy like she had first assumed. It hadn't bothered her when she kissed him yesterday.

"What are you guys talking about?" Erica turned to join their conversation.

Mallory felt her cheeks warm again. How could she let herself keep falling down this rabbit hole of attraction? Theo was not that guy.

"Your sister and Theo are totally in the ooeygooey stage of the relationship. I know I haven't been part of this family for long and this is the first time I have seen Mallory in a relationship, but it's nice to see you so happy. Before Theo, you used to…"

Mallory's curiosity spiked as Hayden trailed off. "Before Theo, I used to…what?"

"You used to third-wheel without hiding the fact

that you hated every minute of it," Erica answered for him. "It is nice to see you with someone who makes you smile."

"Well, no more third-wheeling for her," Theo said smoothly, sliding his hand from her shoulder to her lower back in a way that made her skin tingle.

Erica gave an approving nod. "Glad to hear it, Theo. Don't get me wrong, it's completely unfair that she's dating one of the best hockey players of our generation and doesn't even know the basic rules of the game, but she does deserve to be happy, and you seem to have a part in that."

Mallory couldn't believe her ears. Was her usually jealous younger sister showing signs of emotional growth? First, no meltdown at Savannah's over-the-top gender reveal party and now she was happy that Mallory was faking being happy?

"You don't know the rules of hockey?" Theo asked, stuck on something Mallory hadn't even considered a big deal.

"Why do I need to know the rules of hockey?"

"You work for a hockey team. You work with hockey players. Don't you think you should have at least a little knowledge of the game?"

"I have a little knowledge. You hit a puck into a net. The team that does that the most wins."

Theo scrubbed his face in what appeared to be disbelief. Mallory laughed at how rattled this had him. "I'm bringing you to the rink with me. We cannot allow you to be unaware of the basics."

"What rink?" Erica asked, raising an eyebrow.

"It's the ice rink in town. It's been a while since I've been there. I used to spend hours playing hockey there when I was a kid, it was like my home away from home. Figured it'd be nice to drop by, say hi to some old friends and check out the kids who are falling in love with the game like I did."

"That's so cool. Those are some lucky kids to have you show up at their rink today. I would have freaked out if one of my favorite players showed up at my practice when I was a kid." Hayden was dangerously close to fanboying again.

"We should probably head out to the rink if that's what you want to do," Mallory said to Theo. "We'll catch you guys later. Have fun on the sleigh ride."

Her mom, who was nearby chatting with Savannah and their dad, caught the tail end of the conversation and jumped in, determined not to lose them to Theo's plans. "The rink? Oh, no, no. You can't just sneak off, you two. We've got a full day planned! Don't you want to do the sleigh rides? I was hoping you'd both join us for hot cocoa and carols by the fire after dinner."

Mallory pressed her lips together, struggling to

find an out. "Mom, it's just for a little while. I'll catch up with you for the evening stuff, I promise."

Her mom's expression wavered between disappointment and determination. "What about Theo? I know it's Christmas time and that means family time, but you're welcome to come sit by the fire with us, too."

"That's very sweet of you. I will see what I can do. I love a good hot chocolate and listening to Mallory sing."

Mallory elbowed him in the ribs. "Liar, you've never heard me sing. Don't make fun until you hear me. Maybe I'm talented."

"She's not talented," Erica said, refusing to play along with Mallory's little white lie.

"If I'm not talented, then you are totally tone deaf. Were you planning to come to carols by the fire because I will suggest Theo get some earplugs if you are."

Erica's jaw dropped. Those were fighting words. "He'll need earplugs and noise-cancellation headphones to survive your singing."

"Oh, you two," their mom scolded. "Stop it. It's almost Christmas. You know it's my rule that there's no fighting during Christmas week."

Both sisters laughed. There was always fighting when the Moore sisters were together. It was inevitable.

"We should head out if we're going to be back in time for all this family fun," Mallory said.

"Well, I suppose." Her mom finally accepted her fate. "But don't let him hog you all day, Mallory."

"I'll make sure to return her before anyone starts singing," Theo promised, flashing a grin that could disarm even the most persistent Moore matriarch.

"Thank you, Theo. You are so far my favorite of all Mallory's boyfriends."

"Good to know," he replied, seemingly amused.

Mallory laughed softly, shaking her head as they left the party room. There was no way to avoid being embarrassed by her family at this point. "You know, you're way too good at that."

His brow furrowed. "At what?"

"Winning people over."

Theo leaned down slightly, his voice low and teasing. "Guess that makes two of us, huh?"

The casual remark made her heart skip, but Mallory ignored it, focusing on his invite to the rink. "Are you sure about this?" she asked, following him to the elevators. "Bringing me to such a public place?"

Theo shrugged, his easy smile drawing her in again. "It's not like I'm going to let you make out with me again."

If he was attempting to embarrass her, he was

succeeding. "I did not make out with you. It was one quick kiss to scare my sister away."

"That was a quick one, huh?"

There had been nothing quick about it. It had been a lot harder to stop kissing him once she'd started. She hadn't intended for it to be that way, but she hadn't known how electric kissing Theo could be.

"I'm kidding," he said, letting her off the hook. "We can go into town as hockey player and physical therapist. We don't have to pretend outside of the inn as long as both our families aren't out with us. Plus, the ice rink is important to me, and I'd like you to see it."

How could she say no when that was his reasoning for inviting her along? "All right," she said with a small smile. "Show me where the great Theo Seasons began."

CHAPTER EIGHT

THE APPLE HOLLOW ICE ARENA was where Theo had spent most of his time when he was a kid. If he wasn't at school, he was at the rink. During the summer, he opted to work at the rink part-time instead of the inn—that was how much of a love he had for it.

He was so blessed to have the support of his parents and the hockey community in Apple Hollow. If it hadn't been for them, he might not have reached the level of success he had.

"Oh, my goodness," Mallory said as they pulled into the parking lot. "They love you."

A weatherworn banner hung from the side of the arena that read, "BIRTHPLACE OF NHL SUPERSTAR THEO SEASONS." This arena had been around decades before Theo had set foot in it and would be around long after he was gone hopefully. It meant a lot that they felt his years spent there were worth memorializing.

"Coming back here makes me realize how far I've gone. Sometimes I can't believe I get to play hockey for a living. So many people who love the sport aren't lucky enough to get that opportunity."

"You are very fortunate," Mallory agreed. "But you worked hard and you have a talent that not everyone has. That's not luck."

As they exited the car, a gust of wind reminded him that winter was in full effect up here. The temperatures had dropped and the snow that had fallen the last couple days was crunchy under their feet. Mallory pulled the zipper of her jacket farther up toward her chin as they trudged to the front doors.

Inside, the cold still tingled his nose. The faint aroma of old wood and the familiar sounds of skates cutting across the ice and the hollow thud of a puck slamming against the board hit that part of Theo's brain that told him he was home.

"Tell me I'm dreaming! I can't believe it. Theo Seasons, is that you?" Hank Vermeer hadn't changed since the last time Theo had seen him. His bright blue eyes gleamed with a kindness that was shared with everyone who entered the rink.

"You're not dreaming. It's me." Theo approached the old man with his arms wide open.

Hank didn't hesitate to give him a hug and a big pat on the back. When Theo was a kid, he'd thought Hank was a giant. Time made Theo older, taller and stronger but Hank stayed the same. He was still tall and solid, but age had given him a slight stoop to his shoulders. He no longer seemed larger than life.

"I was hoping you were coming home for the holidays. I'm glad you decided to take some time to see your biggest fan."

Theo pulled back. "I know I don't usually get to stay long enough to venture out of the inn, but my knee had other plans this year."

"You have no idea how sorry I am to hear about all you've been through this season. I've been praying for you and your recovery."

He hated that when he finally made it back to the rink, it had to be when he was injured. "I appreciate that. I can use all the good vibes anyone wants to send my way."

"You got it," Hank replied, running a hand through his white hair. He raised one of those bushy eyebrows that were a shade darker than the hair on his head and the neatly trimmed beard on his face. "And who is this? You brought a friend?"

Theo turned and motioned for Mallory to step forward. "Hank, this is Mallory. Mallory is my physical therapist. I don't leave home without her these days."

"You're forcing this poor woman to follow you around over Christmas? I sure hope he's paying you well."

Mallory's face was alight with her smile. She seemed so much more relaxed since there was no need to pretend here. "My family is staying at the inn, so it worked out perfectly. I get to celebrate with my family and make sure he stays on track with his therapy sessions."

"That worked out for everyone. It's nice to meet you, Mallory. We've got a game starting in a few minutes. I know the teams will go wild when they find out Theo is here. You want to drop the first puck? The kids would go absolutely berserk if you did that."

Theo was hoping to stay a bit more under the radar, but hearing the excitement in Hank's voice, made him feel like he had to say yes. "I don't want to make too much of a big deal out of myself."

"He lies, he loves making a big deal out of himself," Mallory said. "I vote for getting him out there."

Hank's laughter shook his belly. "You've got his number. This one used to do all this hotshot stuff when he was playing here as a kid. He'd try to get people's attention by spraying ice during warm-up when he stopped by certain fans along the glass or show off puck skills. Everyone else would be running their warm-up drills and this guy would be flipping the puck up and catching it with the blade of his stick or spinning it on the ice."

"Oh, he was a little bit of a show-off, was he?" Mallory asked, giving Theo a teasing grin.

"There was never a time Theo did anything little," Hank replied. "He was always about doing more. Taking more shots, bodychecking more opponents, scoring more goals."

"Okay, okay, okay. You two have had your fun. I came here to watch some hockey, not listen to what an obnoxious kid I was."

"You weren't obnoxious. You were amazing. We all knew you were destined for bigger and better things and look at you now. We couldn't be prouder of you," Hank said, placing his hand on Theo's shoulder and giving it a squeeze.

Theo patted his hand. There was a lump in his throat that made it hard to speak. He cleared his throat and tried again. "I have this place and people like you to thank for believing in me."

It was moments like this that made having an injury so much harder. He had people counting on him. People who had dedicated years and years of their lives to helping him find success in his. They knew him as Theo Seasons, hockey player. If he wasn't playing hockey, who was he?

"Well, we put our faith in the right person now, didn't we? Let's get you out there on the ice so your hockey community can celebrate your return."

They followed Hank past the skate rental and into the arena. It carried a heavy sense of nostalgia, though its age was impossible to ignore. The arched ceiling, made of exposed wooden beams, was adorned with faded banners celebrating past championships. The penalty boxes and benches were scuffed and dented. The boards and warped plastic wall around the ice had seen their fair share of shoves and collisions over the years.

Theo couldn't get over how much hadn't changed. It was like walking back through time. The old scoreboard hung on the far wall. The fluorescent lights up above buzzed and some of them weren't fully functional, leaving a dim area in one of the corners of the rink.

"Why don't you find your friend a seat in the stands, and I'll let the coaches know you're here and willing to make an appearance on the ice before the game," Hank said before shuffling off in a different direction.

Theo led Mallory to the bleachers. The weathered wooden planks creaked under their feet. Theo wondered if some of the seats still had initials, dates and crude drawings that had been carved into them back when he was a teenager. Despite its flaws, the arena still had its undeniable charm. The imperfections told the stories of players who had come and gone, leaving their mark on this place that had been loved by so many.

"I know this isn't the Icemen's arena, but hopefully you won't judge it too harshly," Theo said as they found a spot to sit that wasn't filled with people or didn't look like it was about to fall apart.

Mallory scrunched up her nose. "I wasn't going

to judge. I love this place. This looks exactly like the setting of a 1980s movie where a bunch of riff-raff kids band together to make a championship-winning team by the end."

Theo laughed. "I think you're correct in assuming that this place hasn't been remodeled since the '80s. It needs a little work. I think I just found my next pet project."

The Icemen required players to give back to the Boston community every year, and Theo didn't mind that, but maybe it was time for him to give back to the community he had left to make it big in Boston. A generous monetary gift could go a long way at this place. Hopefully that would assuage the guilt he felt for not coming back here sooner to see how it had fallen into disrepair. It was long overdue for a facelift.

Mallory put her hand on his good knee. "I think that's a great idea. I think Hank would appreciate that."

Her affirmation felt almost as good as her touch. He rubbed his bearded chin with his knuckles. He couldn't let himself get caught up in that feeling. Not if they were going to keep their romance fake.

"Would you like some hot chocolate? They used to have a little concession stand over there." He stood up to get a better look. Since nothing else had changed, it was sure to still be there.

"Yes, please," she replied, rubbing her hands

on her thighs as if they needed warming up. Hot chocolate would do the trick.

MALLORY WATCHED AS Theo went to get her some hot chocolate and tried to stop the tingles she got from touching him. Rubbing her hands on her own legs did the trick. Seeing him take a step back in time was clouding her judgment. She could tell he was struggling with a myriad of emotions and wasn't sure what to do with them all. That little bit of vulnerability was all it took to send her heart fluttering.

Heart flutters weren't going to be helpful in the end. She needed to keep her wits about her. It helped that Theo had introduced her as his physical therapist and not as his girlfriend. They didn't have to put on a show for anyone. They could simply be themselves, and they were two people who worked for the same organization. An organization that did not support people who worked there being personally involved with one another. So that was what they would be—two people not personally involved.

It was so hard when he was so cute and kind and funny and hurting. She tried to focus on something, anything else.

Voices echoed in the cavernous space. Coaches shouted at kids who were goofing around and called for everyone to line up. There was constant chatter from the people in the stands. She could see Hank talking with someone on the ice. When the guy's eyes went wide, she knew he had just learned that Theo was here. She had a feeling there was going to be a lot of excited people very soon.

Theo came back with two cups in his hands. Mallory noticed that some women sitting a section away from them had their heads together but kept looking over their shoulders in her and Theo's direction. One of them took their phone out and clearly took a picture.

"I think you've been spotted," she said, taking one of the hot chocolates from him. She placed her feet on the bleacher in front of her and rested her arms on her knees. Keeping her eyes on the ice, she let him know where to find his admirers. "Two o'clock. Black jacket and white sweater. They definitely took a picture of you."

"Oh, great. Maybe if I go out there and do the puck drop, they'll get their fill of pictures and let us watch the game in peace."

Mallory tried to hold back her grin by taking a sip of cocoa. "That's wishful thinking for someone I thought was aware of how popular he was, especially with hockey moms. Oh, boy."

"You think the hockey moms love me the most?"

She tilted her face in his direction and caught

that twinkle in his eye. "You know they do. Don't lie. I thought you were all about honesty."

"You're a bad influence on me. You asked me to lie and now I can't stop."

She shook her head and laughed through her nose. Hank made his way to them. Thank goodness he was going to take Theo away. She was doing a terrible job not becoming more infatuated with this man. She was no better than the hockey moms, wanting to ogle him and flirt.

Theo gasped as he got to his feet. The sound caused Mallory to jump to her feet. "Are you okay?"

He had a hand on his bad hip. "I must have stood up too fast. That was unpleasant."

"Shooting pain down your leg?" she asked, setting her cup down. She stepped down one bleacher and stood in front of him. "How bad one to ten?"

Theo's eyes were closed and he took a deep breath through his nose and out his mouth. Mallory knew that meant it hurt a lot. She placed a hand on his hip.

"What happened? Is it his knee?" Hank asked, looking as alarmed as Mallory felt.

"He'll be okay." At least okay enough to move in a minute, but she was beginning to worry that there was something else going on that was going to make truly being okay less and less likely. "Can you try to cross your right leg over your left and bend away from the side that hurts?"

She took a step up and put her arms around his neck. Theo's eyes opened. She could see the disappointment and frustration. "Just pretend we're hugging," she said. "Put your arms around me and lean this way." She guided him through the stretch.

The tension in his jaw eased. She could tell he was feeling better. "Stand straight and then one more good stretch before I let you go."

"I'm good."

"One more," she demanded.

"I think you just like being this close to me," he teased. His face inches from hers. He was feeling much better.

She pulled him to the right to stretch that iliotibial band and bit down on her lower lip as the heat of his gaze made her own knees weak. She brought him back to center and released her hold on him. It took him a second to let her go, his eyes dropping to her lips and back up to her eyes.

"Thanks," he said, his voice a little rough. "It's all good. Let's go drop the puck, Hank." He stepped around Mallory, not breaking eye contact until he'd have to turn his head to see her.

She blew out a breath and rubbed the nape of her neck. Her body temperature had skyrocketed. She shrugged out of her jacket and sat back down. The hockey moms were whispering back and forth with a renewed fervor. Lord only knew what they thought that was about. She had been trying to disguise his pain but probably caused a whole bunch of new questions for curious onlookers to ponder.

Mallory couldn't worry about that right now. She knew Theo was going to need scans done of his hip when they got back to Boston. There was a good chance that his injured knee had set off a series of issues that weren't going to get resolved easily.

Someone unrolled a red carpet on the ice. The two teams lined up on opposite sides of it, the boys doing a terrible job of hiding their excitement about who was going to be walking that carpet soon.

Hank tapped his fingers on a microphone. "Does this thing work?" he asked into it. His voice went in and out. He fiddled with it for a minute. "How's this?"

The person who had unrolled the carpet gave him a thumbs-up.

"Ladies and gentlemen, boys and girls, welcome to tonight's game here at the Apple Hollow Ice Arena! Before we drop the puck on what's sure to be an exciting match, we have a very special moment to share with all of you. It's not every day that we get to welcome home a local legend, but tonight, we're honored to have one of our own back on this very ice. He still holds the title of the highest-scoring player ever to play in our league."

Mallory could hear it in Hank's voice—the pride and admiration. She knew Theo needed this. If he was going to be able to keep fighting the good fight to play again, he needed some positive motivation.

Hank continued, "But his success didn't end here. He took his talent to Boston, where he made a name for himself as one of the greatest Icemen that town has ever drafted. Through it all, he never forgot where he came from. So tonight, we're thrilled to have him back where it all began. Please join me in giving a warm Apple Hollow welcome to the pride of this rink and an inspiration to every young player out there, Theo Seasons!"

The crowd went wild as Theo walked out on the carpeted ice. It didn't matter which team they were here to root for, everyone was thrilled to see him. Mallory cupped her hands around her mouth and cheered right along with them.

Theo waved to the adoring crowd. He seemed to move easily, his hip and knee not bothering him thankfully. Hank called over the captains from each team. Those lucky boys skated to the center of the rink. Pictures were taken and Theo shook hands with each boy. He held the puck in his hand and dropped it on the ice.

The arena shook with the applause and cheers. Everyone had their phones out, capturing the moment so they'd never forget it. Mallory took out her own phone and took a video of the crowd and excited players on the ice, hoping it would help Theo to never forget, either.

CHAPTER NINE

"OKAY, SO YOU can't cross the blue line before the puck or you're offside, right?" Mallory was a fast learner. By the end of the first period, she had the basics down.

"Don't forget that *both* skates have to cross," Theo reminded her.

"Right. Do they have instant replay in hockey like they do other sports? I feel like offside would be hard to call."

"Not in youth league, but in professional hockey, yes. They usually only use it when there's a close call on a goal. When it comes to offside calls, if someone scores and the other team challenges, they'd use instant replay."

She nodded and turned her focus back on the ice. The two teams were equally matched, the score tied one-one. The Apple Hollow Howlers were on the offensive. They wanted another goal. The coach was yelling at the right wing even though he was the hardest working kid out there.

"If the center would pass the puck off to the

right wing earlier, he'd actually have a decent chance at getting a shot off," Theo said aloud but to no one in particular.

"I thought the wingers were supposed to set the center up for shots," Mallory said.

He had told her that was one of their responsibilities. "Yes, usually it's the center's main objective to shoot, but he can pass it off to the wing for a shot as well. That kid is talented. He should be given more opportunities or moved to center. I don't know what the coach is thinking."

Hank climbed the bleachers and took a seat next to Theo. "This is a close one. I think both teams are playing their hearts out knowing you're in the stands watching."

"The Howlers' coach needs to swap his center and right wing. Number forty-four is their best player."

"Ah, these poor kids haven't had a coach for a month now. They've got parents filling in until I find someone permanent. I just don't have anyone right now. The guy helping out today is the center's dad."

Well, that made sense. No wonder he was positioning that boy in the wrong spot. He was hoping it would give him all the glory. Something told Theo he was usually a defenseman.

"You can tell him that Theo Seasons says if he wants to win this game, he'll put his kid on defense, shift the right wing to center and put number twenty-five back in as the new right wing. They'll score two more before the period ends."

Hank squinted as he watched the kids play. "You think so?"

"I'll guarantee it."

Mallory clapped as the Howlers' goalie stopped a shot on goal. "I love it. Please, go tell him Theo said that. I have to know if he's right."

"If you say so, I'll suggest it." Hank got to his feet and hitched up his jeans by his belt. "You want to come down there and help coach?"

Theo shook his head. "I don't need to be a coach. I'll just be a distraction."

"Probably right. All right, let's see if he'll listen to you. This particular guy doesn't do much listening, he likes to do the talking."

"I hope he listens to you. I can see how frustrated number forty-four is getting."

"You noticed that from up here?" he asked her, intrigued by how interested she was in this game for not being a fan of the sport.

"I notice things." She gave him a small smile that felt too apologetic.

They hadn't spoken about what happened with his hip even though he knew she was thinking about it just as much as he was. Another complication could be the end of everything. Sitting in the place where his dream began was not where he wanted to accept that dream could be ending.

The game was a welcomed distraction. It gave him something to talk to Mallory about and his mind to focus on. Hank went down to the bench and called over the parent helping out. He passed on Theo's message and the guy immediately searched the stands for him. When their eyes connected, Theo gave a wave and a nod. With a strained smile, the parent waved back. He and Hank exchanged a few more words before Hank made his way back to Theo and Mallory.

"He's not going to listen to you?" Mallory said, watching with rapt attention.

"Give him a second to think about what's best for the team. He'll do the right thing." Theo had faith. This guy clearly knew enough about hockey to know that his son wasn't going to win this game for them no matter how much he wanted him to be the star.

As soon as Hank made it back to them, time-out was called. When the team got back on the ice, number forty-four was center, twenty-five was right wing and the volunteer coach's son was back at left defense.

"Here we go," Theo said, clapping his hands together and leaning forward with his elbows on his knees.

Number forty-four won the face-off at center

ice. The puck went to number twenty-five who was quick and had great control. He skated behind the net and passed the puck off to the center waiting patiently right where he should have waited. With a flick of his stick, he hit the puck into the upper right-hand corner of the net for a goal.

Mallory was on her feet, cheering and celebrating. Her excitement was endearing her to him more and more. Something selfish inside him wanted to see her in the stands at the Icemen's arena, cheering for him when he scored. He could imagine skating past her and raising his stick, pointing it in her direction like some of the other guys did with their wives and girlfriends.

She wasn't his girlfriend, though. She was his fake girlfriend but only for a couple more days. He needed to purge that idea from his brain as quickly as possible.

The Howlers were up by one with two minutes left. The other team tried to make an offensive strike but ended up getting the puck stolen by none other than the former center. He passed it up to the right wing, who passed it to the center, who made an incredible move to slip the puck between the defenseman's skates and took a shot that the goalie never saw coming. And just like that, they were up by two.

"I can't believe you were right!" Mallory said, back on her feet. "That was insane!"

With less than a minute left, Theo knew this game was over. "Let's start making our way down to the ground level so I can congratulate the team and we can head out before we get swamped by all the parents."

People had been pretty respectful of Theo's privacy, leaving him and Mallory alone as they watched the game, but he knew all bets would be off when the game was over.

Theo cautiously stood up, mindful of his knee and hip. The last thing he wanted was a repeat of the last time he got to his feet.

"You good?" Mallory asked, making him wonder if he had grimaced out of fear that the pain would resurface.

"I'm fine." He offered his hand to help steady her as she maneuvered toward the steps.

As soon as her hand was in his, that tingly feeling was back. As they left the stands and headed toward the bench, Mallory was grinning. "Okay, I'll admit. I will never doubt you when you're certain of something. You know your stuff. I guess I can see why you were such a big deal around here."

"*Big deal*, huh?" Theo teased, glancing down at her. "Don't undersell it. I'm pretty sure you saw that banner outside with my name on it."

She laughed, rolling her eyes. "Oh, I did. And I bet you helped the Howlers win a couple of those banners hanging from the rafters up there." She pointed to the ceiling.

Theo smirked. "More than a couple."

"Well, you definitely helped this team believe they might raise a banner someday," Mallory said, bumping him lightly with her shoulder. "You know how to read the game."

"Reading the game's one thing," Theo said, his voice dropping slightly. "Playing it is another."

The weight of his words hung in the air between them as they went to congratulate the team on their big win. The kids were piled on top of each other at center ice in celebration of their victory. The excitement reminded him of the joy hockey used to bring him before the weight of injuries and expectations. How he hoped he'd feel that again as a player.

MALLORY COULD SENSE that Theo wasn't as happy as he tried to pretend to be. He was proud of the kids for the win, but his injury flaring up had set him back psychologically.

They waited by the bench for the kids to come off the ice. Mallory watched as number forty-four took off his helmet and it became clear *he* was a *she*. Number forty-four was a girl! For some reason that made Mallory even more excited for the win.

Theo exchanged a look with Mallory that told her he noticed the same thing at the same time.

He appeared equally as shocked but impressed. He was kind enough to give each player a high-five and commented on something he saw them do out there on the ice to let them know he had been paying attention to everyone.

When he got to number forty-four, he let her know exactly how he felt about her play. "You were incredible out there. Keep skating like that, and you'll be unstoppable."

The parent coach stepped forward with a sheepish grin. "Thank you for helping us out. That lineup change made all the difference."

"Sometimes it takes some fresh eyes to look at things from a different perspective. I'm glad it worked out."

"You should be our coach for our next game," the girl wearing number forty-four said. "We play our rivals, the Snow Tigers, the hardest team in the division. We need a good coach or we're going to lose."

Theo stood there speechless. Mallory nudged him to make sure he realized he needed to answer.

"I'm just visiting for Christmas. I won't be around for your next game. Sorry."

"You can't stay one day past Christmas?" she replied, unwilling to give up. This little girl was tenacious on and off the ice.

Mallory pressed her lips together to keep from laughing. He didn't have a good excuse to say no other than he was a professional hockey player not a coach for some middle school team. There was no way he would act like he was too good to coach them since he was one of them almost twenty years ago.

Hank stepped in. "Mr. Seasons was a special guest today. He's not here to stay."

"Do you guys have practice before you play again?" Theo asked even though Hank had given him an out.

"We have one Monday night," the dad who had coached today said.

"Since I can't be here for your game, how about I come to practice on Monday and help get you ready for the big game?"

Mallory couldn't believe it. He was going to compromise with a twelve-year-old. The excitement she felt was unexpected. She was also proud of him for stepping up and giving back in a way that wasn't as easy as writing a check.

Hank seemed just as surprised as Mallory. "Are you sure about this? You must have things to do back at the inn."

"A couple afternoons on the ice isn't going to get in the way. In fact, it's like old times—everyone else in the family running the inn and me running off to play hockey at the rink. I'll tell my family that someone has to come to the game so they can FaceTime me when I'm back in Boston."

Hank patted him on the back. "This is a Christmas miracle. What do you think, kids, how do you feel about Theo Seasons coaching you to beat the Snow Tigers?"

The group of kids whooped and hollered. The parents joined in, too. Mallory applauded him as well.

When they walked to the car after they made all the arrangements, Theo wore an unreadable expression. Mallory stuffed her hands in her jacket pockets to keep them warm. "You okay?" she asked.

"I'm fine. Did I just agree to coach a youth hockey team while I'm in town?"

Mallory laughed, her breath visible in the cold air. "You did. And you made about twenty kids even happier than Santa is going to make them in a few days."

Theo groaned, though the corners of his mouth twitched upward. "My brother Brady is going to think this is hilarious. I don't even know how to coach. I can tell you who should play where based on their talent, but what do I know about coaching?"

"Oh, please," Mallory teased, bumping his arm lightly. "You're Theo Seasons. You'll be fine. Besides, it's middle school hockey. You just need to tell them to skate fast, pass the puck and have fun."

His head fell back as he barked a laugh. "I

know you think you're an expert after watching *one* game, but it's a little more complicated than that, Coach Mallory."

"Well, you're the professional. I'm just here for moral support and to point out how much better you are at coaching than decorating cookies," she shot back, grinning.

"You are right about that," he said, unlocking the car and opening her door for her. He was always a gentleman. Another reason it was getting harder and harder to ignore the way her heart skipped a beat when he looked at her.

When he slid into the driver's seat, she noticed the pain flash across his face. He reined it in quick. They needed to have a conversation about his knee, but it didn't have to be tonight. Mallory could tell he wasn't ready to face the realities that were beginning to make themselves loud and clear.

"I think I'm going to pass on the carols by the fire tonight. I should spend some time with my family," he said, starting the car. "My sister is going to be mad at me for taking this on. She had a bunch of plans for me the next few days. I need to make it up to her."

The disappointment that hit her was more surprising than anything. It made total sense that he would want to have some time with his family. Thus far, his time had mostly been monopolized by her relatives. It was unfair, given that their being here was not part of the plan. Still, she enjoyed his company. Having him around made being with her family easier for her.

"No worries. If there was one activity I could miss, it would be caroling by the fire. I don't know where my mom came up with that one."

"You're welcome to come hang out with me and my family tonight, if you want. I don't know what the plans are, but I'm sure they could include you."

The unexpected invite flipped her mood from down to up in an instant. Maybe he was enjoying their time together as much as she was. "What if I make an appearance at carols by the fire and then you text me about fifteen minutes in, and I have to excuse myself to go meet up with my boyfriend? My mom will be happy that I showed up at all and I will be happy to get out of there before Erica tries to sing a solo."

"She's that bad?"

Mallory nodded. "That bad. When she was in middle school, the lady who volunteered to sponsor the school's talent show had to call my mom and politely ask her to encourage Erica to do a different talent than singing. The poor woman basically said that she feared Erica would get bullied if she sang in front of the school, seeing as how middle schoolers *never* speak before thinking and are *always* kind to one another."

"Oh, yeah. That age group is known for their respectful behavior for sure. Did your mom talk her out of it or did she get blasted by every twelve-year-old in attendance that day?"

"Mom begged one of her friends to convince her daughter to ask Erica to be part of their group that was doing a dance routine together. Mom convinced Erica that she had heard they were afraid they were going to flop if she didn't join them. Erica couldn't resist coming to their rescue, and the talent show was a success."

"Your mom saved the talent show and helped Erica save face. It was a win-win," Theo said, pulling out of the hockey arena parking lot.

Mallory always thought her mom should have told Erica the truth, but her mom had her reasons for handling it the way she did. There was one thing Mallory strongly believed about her mom— her intentions were always good even if her methods were occasionally questionable. She loved her family and did what she could to keep her girls happy and safe.

Mallory felt like a hypocrite for judging her mom for lying to Erica all those years ago. Had she not lied to keep her mom from getting her feelings hurt? She was lying to her entire family because she didn't want them to be mad or sad. Her mom had been trying to save Erica from herself.

Mallory was only trying to keep herself in everyone's good graces.

"Are you okay?" Theo asked, pulling her from her thoughts.

"Yeah," she said, shaking her head not in response to his question but to clear her mind. The truth was she was beginning to lose sight of the truth. She had asked Theo to lie. They lied to his entire family. At this point, she was lying to him as well. She kept telling him that this was all pretend, but the feelings she had for him were beginning to feel all too real.

CHAPTER TEN

"You're doing what?" Theo's dad exclaimed as he passed the bowl of mashed potatoes to Brady.

"I agreed to coach one of the youth hockey teams while I'm here. They don't have a coach right now and the parents have been trying to help, but these kids have talent. They could use some help from someone who knows what they're doing. At least give them some tips before their big game against the Snow Tigers the day after Christmas."

"You know what you're doing?" Brady snickered. "Since when do you know how to coach a bunch of middle schoolers?"

It was dinnertime at the Seasonses' home. His mom and dad had a house on the same property as the inn. It was where he and his siblings had grown up. Everyone except Theo still lived under the same roof. He had fond memories of growing up here, but he had known at a young age that he would move on to bigger and better things thanks to hockey.

Brady and Nora were home for dinner. Brady told Theo that Quinn tended to stay at the inn, working nonstop. The inn was his whole life.

"Which town are the Snow Tigers from again?" his mom asked, filling everyone's water glass. The kitchen table at the house seemed much smaller now that they were all adults.

"Belmont. Remember, they're our rivals. Apple Hollow always plays their best when it's against Belmont."

"What days are you going to be at the rink? I had you signed up to go snowshoeing around the lake with Mallory on Monday," Nora said with a frown.

"I don't know if I can snowshoe, Nora. I need to be careful about what I do during this recovery period."

"How are things coming along in your injury recovery?" his dad asked. "We haven't talked about it with everything going on and Mallory and her family being here."

Theo was shocked that it had taken this long for them to broach the subject with him. Mallory and her family had helped keep it from being the center of every conversation like he had feared it would be. It was finally time to answer their questions.

"I told you the surgeon said things went well. He was worried about this being the second time

I've torn the ligaments in this knee. He warned me that the recovery time would probably be longer than the first time."

"But you'll be able to get back on the ice, right?" Brady asked with his mouth full.

"That's the hope. That's what I'm doing all the therapy for."

"And it's coming along? Mallory's helping you make the progress you want?" His mom sounded worried. He didn't want her to worry.

"Mallory is doing a great job keeping me on track, making sure I don't overdo things like I sometimes want to. She reads me really well, knows when I'm not being totally honest with her about how things feel. She's been good for me."

"She got you to fall for her by not putting up with any of your baloney. She's smart, I'll give her that," Brady said, reaching for his water glass.

"I'm confused, though." Nora pushed her peas to the side of her plate. "I can understand why you fell for Mallory. She's great, I like her a lot. But how do you continue to build your relationship if you both work for the Icemen? I thought that wasn't allowed."

"Can we not talk about his boring love life and get back to the fact that he's going to attempt coaching a bunch of kids?" Brady interrupted. "I want to come just to watch the mayhem."

"Why would we want to talk about that over the

predicament he has gotten himself in with someone who works for the Icemen?" Nora argued.

"Predicament? Who talks like that?" Brady
asked.

"Someone who paid attention in school," Nora
quipped, causing Brady to throw some teasing
remarks her way.

"Okay, you two, that's enough," their mom said,
attempting to put an end to the bickering.

"I was just trying to stop Nora from meddling
in Theo's relationship," Brady said in his defense.

Nora was quick to retort, "I was simply asking a question because he's my brother and I care
about him."

"I think we need to let Theo and Mallory figure
things out by themselves. They don't need to hear
from any of us on the topic," his dad said. "Can
someone pass the potatoes?"

Theo was happy to do anything other than field
questions about his fake relationship or his unfortunately very real injury. He handed his dad the
bowl of mashed potatoes.

"Brady, I'd ask you to be my assistant coach,
but I know you have too much going on with planning your big event on Wednesday."

"It's going to be awesome. I can't wait to see it
all come together. Alexa and Ivy have gone above
and beyond to help me with the last-minute details."

Ivy worked for the inn and Alexa was Brady's

girlfriend. Theo had gotten to talk to her at the Moore's family game night. She seemed like a nice person and very much in love with Brady. She was the one who had helped him develop the idea for Seasons at the Lake. Christmas Eve was going to be a day celebrating winter and all that Apple Hollow had to offer this time of year.

"Mallory likes Alexa. She thought she was a lot of fun," Theo shared.

Brady's smile widened. "She's the best. I am a very lucky guy. I was going to go over to her place tonight to hang out. You and Mallory should come."

"I'm not invited?" Nora complained.

Brady sighed. "You're always invited. You know Alexa loves you."

One side of Nora's mouth curled up. There wasn't anyone Theo could think of who wouldn't love Nora. His sister had such a good heart. Sometimes, she tended to meddle in people's love lives, but it was always with the best of intentions. She wanted to see people happy, and she was a true believer in the idea that everyone had a soulmate.

Theo wasn't so sure about that. Soulmate seemed a little too extreme to be real. He knew that strong relationships were possible, though. His parents were excellent role models for how to have a successful marriage. They complemented each other's personalities—his dad was outgoing and loved being out and about, talking to guests and making everyone feel welcome. His mom was a bit more reserved; she loved being in the kitchen and whipping up some incredible pastries that everyone at the inn would enjoy.

"She can only come if she promises not to interrogate Mallory or bring up the issue of us both working for the Icemen," Theo said.

Nora stuck out her tongue at him. "But she's so much more cooperative than you are."

Theo shook his head. Mallory had asked him to rescue her from caroling, and part of him was excited for her to spend some time with his family without the distraction of hers. Maybe that was the opposite of what he should want, but there wasn't anything he could do to change the way he felt. As much as he tried to keep her at an arm's length, the desire to hold her close kept getting stronger.

After dinner, Theo helped his dad clean up. Theo's job was to dry the dishes as his dad washed them.

"I think it's nice that you're helping out the junior league. Those kids can benefit from having a role model like you. They get to see that hard work pays off."

"It's one practice. I don't know that I'll have much of an impact."

"The fact that someone in your position is willing to do that much shows them that they matter.

Feeling seen can have a huge impact on a child."
His dad handed him a pan to dry.

"I'm going to donate to the arena, too. I was
a little surprised that it didn't look like they've
made any improvements since I left. It's not in
good shape."

"Hank has had a tough time keeping that place
running. I think he'd love to retire, but he has no
idea what would happen to that place if he wasn't
around."

"That sounds like someone else I know," Theo
said, giving his dad the side-eye.

"At least I know I have your brothers and sister
ready and willing to take over when I step down.
I know it's going to be hard to step away, but I
don't worry they won't maintain my standards for
this place. Hank doesn't have that."

Theo felt bad for Hank. He didn't have any kids
to take over the business for him. He and his wife
had spent their lives providing a space for other
people's children to have fun. His wife managed
the figure skating lessons while Hank's focus was
hockey. Apple Hollow was lucky to have them.

"Well, maybe I can find a way to generate some
more donations. A new and improved arena will
make finding someone to take over much easier.
He'll probably have several people vying to buy it."

"That's good thinking, and kind of you, son. I

know whatever you do will be more than appreciated."

Theo's phone buzzed in his pocket. He pulled it out to find a text from Mallory, letting him know that caroling was beginning in a couple minutes and she was going to need that rescue as soon as possible.

He texted her back that she shouldn't fear. He was coming to get her and they were going to go somewhere her family couldn't find her.

I know that was meant to be reassuring but if anyone other than you had said that, I would think I was being kidnapped.

He laughed at her interpretation of his message. He wasn't a kidnapper but being alone with Mallory didn't sound so bad.

MALLORY KNEW SHE shouldn't be so excited about hanging out with Theo tonight, but that didn't stop her heart from beating a little faster when she saw his name pop up on her phone.

Would you like to go to my brother's girlfriend's house with me? They would really like you to come.

She knew he was only saying that to help her get out of this painfully awkward activity with her family. She tried to stay rational about it, but her emotions had other plans.

"What is making you smile so hard at your phone?" Savannah asked. She leaned over to read the text. "Ah, your hot hockey-playing boyfriend."

"I think I need to go. I mean, I came here to get to know his family and all I've done is hang out with mine."

"You were with him almost the whole afternoon. Of course, Mom is going to tell you to go because she's so excited that you have a boyfriend."

It was not going to be hard to convince her mom that she had to leave. It was the reason this plan in particular was so perfect. But even more than trying to get out of caroling, she wanted to spend more time with Theo. It was probably a mistake to let that feeling take root, but she couldn't stop herself.

She typed her reply, agreeing to join him. "I better tell her I have to go. I'll see you tomorrow morning for Breakfast with Santa?"

"I'll be there. Have fun." Savannah gave her a wink.

"Okay, let's get started," her mom said, getting everyone's attention. "I have taken all your suggestions into consideration and made a song list for us to work off of."

Mallory stood up. "I hate to do this, but I have

to go. Theo invited me to hang out with his brother and Alexa. I will see you all in the morning. Someone better video all these carols so I can watch your performances later."

"You're leaving? Is that an option for the rest of us?" Avery asked.

Her mother shook her head. "You're married. You and your husband are staying."

"I'm not married," Hayden said, raising his hand like he was in school. "Does that mean I can leave?"

"Are you serious? You don't want to at least listen to me sing?" Erica looked absolutely heart-broken.

"No, no, no." Hayden's eyes went wide as he realized his mistake in asking. "That's not what I meant. I love listening to you sing."

That was Mallory's cue to leave. She needed to go upstairs and get her jacket, and if she stayed one more second, she'd get sucked into watching Hayden trying to dig himself out of the hole he'd just buried himself in.

She kissed her dad on the cheek and made a break for the elevators. Ten minutes later, she was in Theo's car headed to Alexa's.

"I thought Erica was going to have a total melt-down. Poor Hayden did not see that coming."

"How did he not?" Theo said with a tut of disapproval. "Even I could have told him that it would have made her upset if he asked to leave."

Mallory nodded, agreeing with him wholeheartedly. Erica was pretty transparent. "He's still figuring it out. I think he loves her so much that he forgets she needs him to show it in the little ways as well as the big ones."

"Relationships are so complicated. I want someone in my life that gets that I'm going to mess up sometimes. Heck, I might even mess up a lot, but I need to know I'll be shown some grace. I'll happily return the favor. I don't hold a grudge."

"Good to know," Mallory said without thinking about how that sounded. She felt like Hayden, struggling to backtrack. "Not that I would be the person who needs to know that. I just mean, it's good to know that people want that in a relationship. I should probably try to be that way with whoever I end up with someday."

"You're not one of those women. You're easygoing. I don't see you giving anyone a hard time about anything."

"I'm easygoing to a point. I don't think it's good to let everything slide. Sometimes people need to be held accountable, so they're motivated to make real changes that are needed for everyone to feel good about their situation."

Theo grinned. "That is true about you, too. I like that you can set boundaries."

Good thing he couldn't read her mind at the moment because she had knocked all the boundaries over that she had drawn around her feelings for him. They were leaping over the boundary and zooming all over the place.

"I like that you like that about me."

They soon arrived at their destination, a little house on the west side of the same lake the inn was on. Alexa greeted them each with a glass of wine and a hug. She was tall and blonde. She reminded Mallory of her sister Avery in appearance and attitude. She had a boss-lady vibe to her. "I was so excited when Brady said you were going to join us tonight."

Nora was also there, waiting for her chance to say hello.

"I hope you don't mind, but we do need to get a little business out of the way first," Alexa said. "I told Brady to text Theo, but he didn't. I'm sorry."

Mallory waved her off and took a seat on the couch. "It's fine. What business are we discussing?"

"We need to talk about the surprise retirement celebration we're going to pull off during Seasons at the Lake," Brady replied. "I think we have it figured out, but I wanted to see what Alexa thinks."

"Oh, I didn't realize it was going to be a surprise. How fun! You don't think your parents have any idea that you're up to something?" Mallory asked.

"Usually it would be impossible to surprise our dad because he always knows everything that's happening at the inn, but with the Seasons at the Lake, winter edition, going on, we can invite the whole town of Apple Hollow and Dad won't be any the wiser that they are there to celebrate him and Mom," Nora explained.

"That was good thinking," Theo said, taking a seat next to Mallory. "Dad is hard to keep in the dark."

Nora joined the two of them on the couch, causing Theo to move closer. Their legs were touching and he threw his arm behind her to make more room. Mallory knew no one would think anything of them cuddling, given that they all thought the two of them were dating, but the reality of him being in such close proximity caused the butterflies in her stomach to make an appearance.

The Seasonses talked about the logistics of getting their parents in the same place at the same time as well as a quick review of the guest list. Mallory had no idea who anyone was, but it was fun to watch Theo's face light up when they mentioned someone who he had a connection with back in the day.

Theo's brother and sister were so devoted to their parents. Mallory could see how desperate they were to make this retirement celebration memorable for them.

As the Seasons siblings wrapped up their plans, Alexa opened another bottle of wine so she could refresh everyone's glasses. Theo shifted on the couch. His hand briefly pressed against her thigh. Mallory caught the faint wince that flickered across his face and placed a gentle hand on his arm.

"You okay?" Mallory asked under her breath, leaning closer.

"I'm fine," he muttered, but the tension in his jaw told a different story.

"Do you need to stand up? Maybe you need to stretch."

"I said I'm fine." His tone got a little gruffer.

"What's the matter?" Brady asked, taking notice. "Is it your knee?"

"It's nothing. I moved wrong and it let me know it didn't like that. It's fine now." He played it off, but Mallory knew it was more than that. He wasn't going to be honest with his brother just like he wasn't being honest with himself.

Brady turned his attention to Mallory. "Is it weird being his physical therapist and his girlfriend? When I hurt my shoulder a couple years ago and had to do PT, I hated my therapist. That guy made me miserable some days. Theo's got to get cranky sometimes, which has to be hard as his girlfriend."

Mallory had to think about how to answer that question since it wasn't a real issue. Well, Theo could get cranky during therapy sessions—she had dealt with that on more than one occasion. She hadn't had the experience of taking it personal because of being his girlfriend, however.

"He's a very good patient. Sometimes he wants to push himself further than I would like him to, but he's always nice to me."

Brady and Nora exchanged a look and both started laughing. Theo reached over Mallory and grabbed the throw pillow on the other side of her. He promptly threw it at his brother's head. "Don't laugh."

Brady deflected the pillow. "He's cranky when he's not in pain. There's no way he doesn't get cranky when he's in physical therapy."

Alexa came back in the room and picked up the pillow. "What did I miss? Is Brady behaving himself?"

"I need to know," Nora said, leaning forward, "how long have you two even been a couple? This seems very new. Like so new you haven't even seen the real Theo yet."

The room fell silent. Mallory's heart thudded in her chest as all eyes in the room turned toward them.

Theo chuckled, the sound light but forced. "What's that supposed to mean?"

"I'm just saying," Nora continued, her gaze narrowing as she ignored the awkward laughs from

Brady and Alexa. "She says you're always nice. People are *always* nice when they're in a brand-new relationship. I'm just wondering how long you have been in this relationship? A couple weeks? A month?"

Mallory froze, this wasn't something they had nailed down. They had agreed to keep it vague. They'd been working together since he'd had surgery, which was two months ago.

"Maybe when you finally meet the right person, you're nice all the time no matter how long you've been together," Theo said smoothly, flashing Nora a grin that didn't quite reach his eyes.

"There is something to be said for meeting the right person," Alexa said, sitting on the arm of the love seat Brady was on. "When I met Brady, it was different from every relationship I had had before that."

Brady smiled up at her and rubbed her back. "Love changes people for the better."

Mallory was used to being around happy couples. Her sisters were all in loving relationships, but something about the way Brady and Alexa looked at each other made her feel jealous. Maybe it was because they were talking about their real experience and what she had with Theo was make believe. Would she have the same thing as Brady and Alexa if she was actually dating Theo instead of pretending? She'd most likely never know.

CHAPTER ELEVEN

BREAKFAST WITH SANTA was a core memory for Theo. When he was little, it was one of his favorite things to do during the holiday season. It meant a delicious meal and he got to talk to Santa himself about exactly what he wanted for Christmas. No letter, no trip to the mall to see a fake Santa who would pass on the message. His parents sent Santa himself an invite to breakfast, and he'd actually show.

The Icemen had a game tonight. If he hadn't been on injured reserve, he would have been back in Boston getting ready to head over to the arena later that afternoon. He wouldn't have made it up to Apple Hollow and only had the three-day holiday break that the league took. That was how the last dozen years had gone.

Today, he was here and Mallory's family was going to Breakfast with Santa, and Theo was playing the role of doting boyfriend to his fake girlfriend. The fake girlfriend who in just a few short days had found her way under his skin. He went to bed thinking about her and if she'd had a good time hanging out with him. He woke up wondering if she had slept well and was looking forward to hanging out with him again.

There was a nagging fear under all that. Did she regret asking him to pretend to be her boyfriend? Was she tired of acting like she enjoyed his company so no one would question them? Last night, Nora had pushed for answers about their relationship. After that, Mallory seemed a little off. He thought he had deflected pretty well; Brady had definitely believed it.

Nora could tell something wasn't right. She knew there was no way Theo would bring someone home to meet his family if he wasn't super serious about her. It wasn't making sense that he had just started dating Mallory and was willing to introduce her to the family so quickly. She wasn't wrong. If he had really been dating Mallory, there was no way she would have come up north with him.

Nora was thinking about this rationally. Why would he risk getting in trouble at work? Why would Mallory? Nora was protective of Theo. She had met one woman he dated back in Boston a few years ago and knew immediately that the only thing she wanted out of that relationship was the prestige of dating a professional hockey player. Nora hadn't hesitated to tell Theo he deserved better.

If she thought for a second that Mallory was in a relationship with him for the wrong reasons, she would call it out immediately. Theo considered telling her the truth to get her off his back, but they had dug in pretty deep. Nora would want him to come clean with everyone in the family, and he wasn't up for explaining to his mom and dad that Mallory was not who they thought she was.

"Look at you all dressed up. Santa's going to be very impressed," Nora said when he walked over to the concierge counter Sunday morning. He was dressed in black slacks and a festive red sweater.

"I'm not sure if I made the nice list this year, so I thought I better try to make a last-minute good impression," he joked.

"Good luck with that, brother. Have you seen Brady this morning? He's supposed to be taking Alexa to Breakfast with Santa."

Theo shook his head. He hadn't seen either one of those two since yesterday.

"I saw him talking to Maureen not too long ago," Quinn answered from the front desk.

Theo lifted his chin in his brother's direction. "We missed you at dinner last night, Quinn. Don't you come home for dinner anymore?"

"It's Christmas week," he replied as if that was a complete answer. When Theo stared blankly back at him, he sighed in frustration. "There are a million things going on here—private events, Brady's Seasons at the Lake prep, Mom and Dad's retirement party, plumbing problems on the second floor, and there's a big snowstorm coming that we need to make sure we're prepared for. We're almost fully booked for Christmas Day with guests arriving at all times of the day between now and then. I don't have time for dinner."

Sometimes Theo felt guilty for being the only one who didn't help out at the inn. He provided what he could financially, but that was it. When his parents retired, they wanted to leave the inn to all four siblings, and he knew that made Quinn the most frustrated. He didn't think Theo deserved a piece of something he didn't care about, and to Quinn, the only way he could show he cared about it was by working there like him.

"You have your hands full. I know Dad appreciates all that you do around here. He told me that he knows this place is in good hands when he steps away."

"Well, someone has to do it."

This was why Theo avoided interacting with Quinn. Even when Theo made an effort to be nice, Quinn was always snippy. Not everyone wanted to be Dad. Theo wasn't going to apologize for choosing a different life. When their parents first told them about retiring and the financial burden the inn had become, Theo's knee-jerk reaction was practical. He had thought they should sell it. None of his siblings had been on board with that idea. Once he looked at it from their perspectives, he realized he couldn't imagine the Seasons Inn not being owned by the family, either.

Just because he didn't want to work here, didn't mean Theo didn't want to help. Alexa had been the one to devise a plan to alleviate some of the financial strain. She had fallen in love with Brady and decided to do a little pro bono consulting. First, she suggested Theo take out a loan in his name to pay off the one that was about to put the inn out of business. With Theo's financial portfolio, banks were more than willing to work with him, offering interest rates a lot lower than their dad was able to get.

When Theo was drafted into the NHL, his parents made it very clear that he was not responsible for funding anyone's life other than his own. His dad flat-out refused to take money from him. Alexa convinced both his parents that her plan wouldn't include taking money from Theo; it would simply be using his name to make their debt more manageable.

For example, Alexa encouraged Theo to seek out some specific endorsement deals. One such deal was with a heating and cooling company that had franchises all over New England. They were happy to pay him with products, including brand-new HVAC systems for the Seasons Inn that were installed this past fall. Another deal was with a roofing company that replaced the entire roof on the inn. All Theo had to do was make a few television commercials and pose for some ad photos. It was a win-win. The inn got a few of the upgrades it needed and Theo didn't pay a dime of his own money. How could his dad refuse?

Quinn should have seen his value, but his older brother was determined to act like the martyr in the family. "Well, I'll be sure to remind Santa that you should once again be on top of the nice list. We wouldn't want you to not get all the things you asked for this Christmas."

"You're funny," Quinn said as his fingers tapped on the keyboard in front of him. "Why don't you take your sense of humor somewhere it will be more appreciated?"

Theo didn't need to be asked twice. Having breakfast with Mallory, her family and Santa sounded a lot more fun than hanging out with his overworked brother. He said goodbye to Nora and headed to the dining room, where Mallory said she would meet him.

The dining room was buzzing with holiday energy. Kids in their Sunday best ran between tables, their laughter mixing with the warm sounds of clinking silverware and the quiet Christmas music playing over the speakers. The scent of syrup and bacon hung in the air. Theo's mouth was already watering at the thought of all the goodies his mom had prepared for this breakfast feast.

He scanned the room, his eyes landing on Mallory near the far corner. She was standing by her family's table, smiling down at Xavier, who was patiently waiting for her to unwrap the candy cane he must have gotten from the hostess who was handing them out to all the children as they entered.

Mallory was dressed in a forest green sweater dress that fit her perfectly, highlighting her figure without trying too hard. The two of them would make the perfect Christmas pair. Once again, her hair was loose and fell in soft waves over her shoulders. He wondered if he'd ever be able to convince her to wear her hair down during PT when they were back in Boston. The thought of only seeing her in a ponytail once this trip was over made him sad.

As he got closer, he noticed that unlike the fresh-faced physical therapist he spent every day with, his fake girlfriend was glammed up. The sparkle in her eye makeup caught the light when she tilted her head and laughed at something her sister said. A warmth spread through his chest that had nothing to do with the temperature in the room. Mallory was beautiful on a normal day.

Seeing her like this made him forget why they were pretending to be a couple. At the moment, he didn't feel like he needed to pretend.

Mallory glanced up and saw him approaching. Her smile grew, and she walked over to him instead of waiting for him to make it all the way to the table. "You made it."

Theo's heart did an unfamiliar little lurch. "This is my favorite Christmas tradition at the inn," he said, his voice soft.

"It is?" Her eyes shined in a way that made his chest tighten. "Did you do Breakfast with Santa when you were little?"

"Every year. I think I was more excited for this than actual Christmas."

"Seriously?" she asked with a giggle.

"Seriously. I actually got to meet Santa at breakfast. On Christmas, he came and went while I was asleep. I was always so bummed he didn't wake me up to say hi since we had just had breakfast together."

She shook her head at him, amused. "You are funny."

Before he could overthink it, Theo leaned down and kissed her on the cheek, his lips brushing against her skin for just a second longer than necessary. He'd tell her it was part of the act if she asked about it later, but he'd done it because he wanted to kiss her.

Mallory stilled for a heartbeat, her cheeks turning a soft pink. "Come say hi to my family before I do something I promised I was not going to do because we agreed on clear boundaries."

Theo straightened, his pulse thrumming. He had forgotten about those dumb boundaries they established. There wasn't supposed to be kissing. He wanted to apologize, but his words caught in his throat. The kiss had been innocent enough, but now he couldn't shake the thought of what would happen if he kissed her again, boundaries be damned. They wouldn't need boundaries if they liked each other for real.

"Theo! We're so glad you could join us," her dad said, as he followed Mallory to the table instead of dragging her out of there and making out with her somewhere a little more private.

Theo walked over and shook Will's hand. "Good morning, Will. You look lovely, Selene," Theo said, forcing himself to focus on something other than these unexpected feelings that were developing for Mallory. Speaking to the whole table, he asked, "Is everyone looking forward to a visit from Santa this morning?"

Xavier and Sebastian shouted out that they were. Theo couldn't wait to see their faces when the Santa his parents hired showed up in a real sleigh pulled by some horses. Santa had always explained the reindeer were for Christmas Eve deliveries only.

"Will Mrs. Claus be making an appearance?" Selene asked. "You know she's often overlooked."

"I don't think Mrs. Claus is making it to breakfast. At least, when I was growing up, she didn't attend."

"That's a shame," Selene said with a frown. "Why is it that the wife is always left at home while the man is adored and revered? I'll have you know that I played Mrs. Claus at our neighborhood Christmas party the last couple years. Our friend Mitchell plays S-A-N-T-A," she said, spelling out the name and glancing at her grandsons to see if they were paying attention. "He owns the costume, but his wife doesn't look good in red, so she refuses to be the Mrs. I stepped in and was such a hit, they've asked me back every year since."

"How do I not know this?" Mallory said. "Did you guys know this?" She looked to her sisters.

Savannah nodded. "She posts pictures on social media. How do you not know?"

"Who clicks through all the pictures?" Mallory mumbled quietly so only Theo heard her.

Mallory led Theo to their seats in between Savannah and Erica. Theo couldn't help but wonder if Mallory had any idea how attached he was getting to her and her family. Her sisters and brothers-in-law were starting to feel like this strange extension of his own siblings. He had never experienced anything like that with anyone he had ever dated.

MALLORY WATCHED AS Theo played tic-tac-toe for the second time with Xavier, who had somehow ended up sitting on her fake boyfriend's lap when he finished eating even though Theo still had a plate of pastries and baked goods left to eat.

Theo used the red crayon to make an *O* in the upper right-hand corner of the board they had drawn on the paper place mat in front of him. Xavier held the green crayon tightly as he contemplated his next move.

"You always want to take the center square if you can, buddy," Chance said from across the table. He had no qualms coaching his son even though Theo was trying his very hardest to let Xavier win.

The little boy followed his father's instructions and drew his *X* in the center square that Theo had so clearly left open on purpose. Theo drew an *O* that in the bottom center space, giving himself no advantage. They went back and forth until Xavier won. Mallory's heart skipped a beat as Theo gave her nephew a high-five. He was so good with kids. That was a pleasant surprise.

Erica returned to the table after visiting the ladies room. She didn't sit down next to Theo; instead she ran around the table and whispered something to Avery. Mallory wouldn't have thought anything of it if Avery's facial expression hadn't registered such surprise.

"Are you sure?" she asked.

Erica nodded.

"Sure about what?" Mallory wanted to know the secret.

"Nothing. Don't worry about it," Avery said, getting to her feet. "Savannah, can you come with us to get some more cookies? No one will question why a pregnant woman is getting another plate."

"What if I want more cookies?"

"You don't. Can you watch the boys while I'm gone?"

Mallory motioned in the direction of Chance. Was their father not capable of watching them?

"You can have some of my cookies," Theo offered her, pushing his plate closer to her. He was too sweet. Her gossiping sisters could go gossip. She would stay with her fake boyfriend and enjoy it.

"What time is Santa supposed to arrive?" her mom asked Theo since he was the Breakfast with Santa expert.

"He should be here—" Theo checked his watch "—in about ten minutes. They'll announce that all the kids should come look out the windows overlooking the lawn."

"It's not actually Breakfast *with* Santa. More

like Breakfast *then* Santa," Hayden said, putting his napkin on top of his empty plate.

"No one is stopping us from continuing to eat once he gets here," Greg pointed out, leaning back in his chair and patting his belly.

Mallory glanced over her shoulder at her sisters congregated by the dessert table. No one was putting cookies on a plate. They were too busy talking and freaking out about something.

Erica came back to the table and tugged their dad out of his seat. "We need your advice about what cookies to get," she said, clearly lying.

"I'm happy to help you choose," Mallory said, pushing back her chair.

"Don't be rude and leave your boyfriend alone with Mom," Erica said sternly. "Dad can help us."

"I want to know what's going on, too," their mom said, also aware that this was not about cookies.

"No, Mom, stay. This is about Christmas presents, okay? A Christmas present." Erica glanced at Theo and quickly looked away. He was too busy trying to lose at tic-tac-toe again to notice.

Was this about Theo? Were they trying to come up with a gift for him? Why wouldn't they ask Mallory? Shouldn't they think she was the expert on what to get him?

It hit her that she didn't have a gift for Theo. He probably didn't have one for her, either. They drove up here with the intention of working together and that was it. She figured she'd spend Christmas Day enjoying the peace and quiet.

"What's the matter?" Theo was staring at her and pressed his finger on the spot above her nose. His touch caused her mind to go blank. "You're stressing about something."

She blinked a couple times as she tried to remember what the problem was.

"Are you okay, Auntie Mallory?" Xavier asked. "Are you worried Santa isn't going to bring you presents? Mommy said Daddy isn't going to get any if he doesn't get his act together."

Chance sat up a little straighter, his neck turning a splotchy red. "Mommy was just kidding, buddy. She didn't mean that. She was just annoyed with my snoring," he explained to the adults at the table.

Theo raised an eyebrow and the corners of his mouth curved upward as well. She loved his little conspiratorial looks. It was like they could communicate without words like a real couple. Her eyes briefly widened as she gave him a tight smile. From the mouths of babes.

"You should get that checked out," Greg said, pointing at Chance. "You're a young, fit guy. You shouldn't be snoring up a storm yet. As soon as Savannah told me I snored, I went to the doctor.

Found out I had a deviated septum. They fixed that right up. No more snoring."

"What about you, Theo?" Mallory tilted her head to the side. "Do you snore?"

"I don't know. I'm sure I have a deviated septum. My nose has been broken more times than I can count."

"Are those your real teeth?" Hayden asked. "I've been wondering all weekend. You hockey guys usually don't have all your teeth."

Theo pressed his lips together. Mallory leaned in, full of anticipation for his answer. She had never thought about this before.

He smiled and said, "Not all these babies are mine, but I'll never confess which ones are real and which are fake. The fake ones have been with me so long I have accepted them as my own."

If he hadn't made her laugh, she would have been disappointed not to know. Someday she'd get it out of him.

Her dad and sisters returned to the table. Without any cookies.

Mallory glared at Savannah. She was the best bet to tell her what was going on. "Did you guys eat all your cookies right at the buffet table?"

Savannah picked up her water glass. "Yep."

Mallory decided to pretend she didn't care what they were talking about. Whatever it was, they didn't want her to know.

"All right, boys and girls. Can I have your attention, please." Theo's dad was at the front of the dining room, microphone in hand. His mom and Nora were there, too. "We've been told Santa is on the property! If you turn your attention to the back lawn, you can see him arrive."

Xavier jumped off Theo's lap. "Come on, Sebastian. Let's go see Santa!"

Avery and Chance, along with Mallory's mom, took the boys to look outside. Nora made her way over to the Moores' table. "Good morning, everyone. I hope you all enjoyed your breakfast."

Everyone raved about the food, but Nora seemed to only be half listening. As soon as there was a lull, she jumped back in. "Do you mind if I steal my brother away for a second? I need his help with something."

Theo seemed confused but went with his sister. Mallory's sisters waited until Theo and Nora were far enough away to freak out again. "Dad, you have to say something."

"I don't know. What would I even say?" Dad asked, looking a little pale. The muffled sound of sleigh bells came from outside. The children in the dining room all cheered. Santa must have been spotted.

"You need to say exactly what we talked about. You got this, Dad. He'll listen to you."

"You think I should say something before he actually does it?"

"Yes!" Erica and Savannah said in unison.

Mallory had had enough. "Okay, what in the world are you talking about? And don't tell me it's about cookies or a present."

Savannah and Erica looked at each other before each taking one of Mallory's hands.

Savannah finally spoke. "Erica overheard Nora talking to some of the people who work here. She was trying to be quiet about it, but you know Erica, she's nosy so she eavesdropped anyway."

"I am not nosy! She was quiet about it, but I couldn't help but hear what she was saying. I wasn't trying to listen, it just happened."

Mallory's patience was nonexistent. "Why is Nora's secret making you all secretive?"

Erica glanced around, making sure no one else was listening. "She told the girl that she was excited about Breakfast with Santa because something big was happening this year."

"Okay…"

Savannah squeezed Mallory's hand. "She told the girl that her brother was going to propose to his girlfriend. And the girl said, 'But they just started dating!' And Nora said, 'I know, but he's never been surer about anything.' Mallory, Theo is going to propose today during Santa's visit."

"No, he's not." Her dad brought his fist down on

the table, making all the dinnerware rattle. He got to his feet. "I'm going to tell him that this is too soon. And that all my other sons-in-law showed me the respect of getting my blessing before asking for my daughter's hand in marriage."

He took off before Mallory could get any words out. "Dad, no!" She pushed back her chair and tried to get up.

Erica pushed her back down. "I know you might think that you're in love with this guy, Mallory, but you barely know him."

"We know you're not out of your mind enough to say yes," Savannah said. "We're also trying to help him save face. Let Dad talk to him. You can act like you were never the wiser."

"You guys." Mallory got them both to stop touching her so she could stand up. Her lie had somehow gotten them into a very big mess. Her dad was about to humiliate her in front of Theo.

"Mallory, it makes sense. You two haven't known each other long, but it's obvious he's obsessed with you. This is how he plans to get around the policy at work. If you're married, what can they do about it?" Erica's reasoning was totally flawed.

"Theo is not going to propose to me. Trust me on this."

She scanned the room to find her dad or Theo. She had to get to one of them before they ran

into each other. Before she spotted them, Brady
and Alexa captured her attention, sitting at a table
for two. That was when it hit her. Nora's brother
was proposing to his girlfriend, someone who he
hadn't known long but was madly in love with.
That brother wasn't Theo, and Mallory wasn't that
girlfriend.

CHAPTER TWELVE

THE CHILDREN SQUEALED with excitement, their laughter mixing with the faint jingling of Santa's sleigh bells. Theo followed Nora toward their parents, who were practically glowing with anticipation. Santa was a big deal, but they did this every year. Theo didn't understand why they seemed extra giddy this time.

"You guys are jazzed Santa's here, huh?" he asked. "Do you need me to help with something?"

His mom's grin stretched from ear to ear. "We just wanted to give you a heads-up."

"Your brother is planning to propose to Alexa," his dad revealed.

Theo blinked. "Wait, Brady is proposing *right now*? How come no one told me?"

"Because you're the secret spiller," Nora said flatly, crossing her arms like she had been waiting years to share that bit of judgment. "You always have been. There isn't one secret that you've been told that you didn't intentionally or accidentally spill."

He was taken aback by her attack. "Whoa, that is not true."

"It's a little bit true," his dad admitted with a shrug.

"More true than not true," his mom added. The apologetic pat on the arm she gave him must have been to soften the blow. "I do think that it's usually accidental. At least, I hope so."

Theo was wounded by these accusations. Was this the shared opinion of the entire family? If they only knew. He was keeping a massive secret right now about him and Mallory and no one suspected a thing. For a second, he wanted to blurt out the truth just to prove his point, but that would confirm their theory.

"Well, what's the plan? I must not be able to ruin it if you're telling me now."

Nora leaned in. "We need to get the ring to Santa before Brady takes Alexa up for a picture. Santa's going to hand it to her as a *special gift*. Brady thought it would be cute, and she'd never see it coming."

Theo nodded, loving this plan. "I'll give it to Santa. I can go up with Mallory's nephews. No one will notice."

"Are you sure?" his dad asked, pulling the small black box from his suit coat pocket.

"I got this." Theo felt confident he could accomplish the task and slipped the box into his own pocket.

Santa's entrance into the dining room was met with enthusiastic cheers and the inevitable tears from the toddlers who weren't so sure about the bearded stranger. The Seasons Inn Santa was legit, though. His posh red suit, real white beard, wire-rimmed glasses and polished leather boots made him as authentic as they came. It was easy for anyone to believe they were meeting the real Santa.

"I'm going to go introduce Santa and explain the meet-and-greet process," his dad said, grabbing his microphone and weaving through the tables to reach Santa's chair.

"Okay, I know everyone's excited to see Santa. Mr. Claus, it's so good to see you again," his dad said, shaking Santa's hand.

The jolly old man let out a hearty, "Ho, ho, ho."

"We're going to do this in an orderly fashion."

Everyone was ushered back to their tables so groups could be called up one at a time to take pictures and get a gift from Santa.

Theo stopped at Brady and Alexa's table. He kept his tone casual, determined not to let anything slip. "Hey, you two. Excited to get your picture with Santa, Alexa?"

"I don't think I have had a picture with Santa since I was like five years old. I am kind of excited." She smiled across the table at Brady. She truly was in love. Theo couldn't help but be happy for his brother.

"You should be excited," Theo said, his grin widening. "I'm going to go up with Mallory's nephews. We'll probably go up before you do. I'll put in a good word for you with Santa. You've both done a lot to help Mom and Dad. Santa's sure to give you exactly what you deserve this year."

He gave Brady a wink. That was good. There was no way Alexa would know what was really happening.

Brady's eyes went wide, his voice tight. "That's great, Theo. Maybe you should head to your table so you don't miss your turn with the boys." He mouthed the word *go*.

Theo froze. Had he said too much? He was not going to be the secret spiller today. No way.

Before he could analyze it further, Mallory's dad appeared beside him, his expression serious. "Theo, I need to talk to you."

"Hey, Will," Theo said, playing it cool. "You remember my brother Brady and his girlfriend, Alexa."

"Hi," Will said distractedly before turning back to Theo. "I need to talk to you about my daughter and your intentions."

Theo blinked. "My what?"

"Erica overheard your sister talking about what

you were planning to do here today, and I think it's best that—"

"Dad! Stop." Mallory came flying out of nowhere, grabbing her father's arm and practically dragging him toward the exit. "Don't say another word, please."

Theo watched them disappear into the hallway. Before he could follow, Alexa's curious voice broke the silence. "What surprise is Theo planning?"

"Nothing!" Theo and Brady said in unison.

Theo felt the urge to get as far away from Alexa as possible before he spilled any secrets. "I don't know what he was talking about, but maybe I should go find out."

"Okay, but make sure you get to see Santa before I get to see Santa," Brady said, but he really meant to say Theo better not ruin his entire plan.

"I'll be right back. I promise."

Theo made a beeline for the hallway, where Mallory and her dad were locked in a hushed argument. "What is going on?" Theo asked, stepping in. "For a second there, I thought you were going to ruin the surprise, Will."

"So, you are planning a surprise?" Will waved his hands around. "See, I told you," he said to Mallory.

"Whatever surprise he's planning, it's not the surprise you think it is, Dad. Please believe me."

"What are your intentions with my daughter, Theo? I think I have a right to know."

Mallory groaned and covered her face with her hands. "Oh, my gosh, someone beam me up and take me as far away from here as possible."

"It's a reasonable question. I can prove it. Theo, what's in your pocket?"

Why Mallory's dad was so interested in the plot to get Brady engaged was beyond him. Theo pulled out the little black box and Mallory gasped. Her face paled.

Will clapped his hands together. "See!" he said triumphantly.

"Theo?" The way Mallory said his name turned all the lights on in his brain.

They thought that the box in his hand belonged to him. "Oh, no." He started to laugh. "This isn't mine. This is for Alexa. *Brady* is proposing to Alexa."

"What?" a voice gasped from behind him. Theo spun around to see Alexa standing there. Her mouth fell open as her eyes darted between him and the ring box.

"Oh, great," Theo muttered. "I *am* the secret spiller."

Brady rushed out of the dining room with Nora hot on his heels. As soon as he saw Alexa's stunned face, he groaned. "I knew this would happen. I should have made sure they weren't out here."

"This is unbelievable," Nora said with a hand pressed to her forehead.

Theo held up his hands. "This was not my fault."

"It was all my fault," Mallory said.

"No, this was my fault," Will said, placing a hand on his chest in a gesture of apology. "I shouldn't have listened to my daughters."

Nora shook her head. "It was my fault for letting Theo know what was happening."

Before anyone else could take the blame, Brady dropped to one knee, taking the box from Theo. "Alexa Fox, you walked into my life only a few short months ago, but I cannot imagine spending the rest of my life without you in it. I had a plan, but it looks like the universe had a better one."

Alexa covered her mouth with her hand. "Brady," she said with tears filling her eyes.

"Would you make me the happiest man alive and do me the honor of marrying me?" He popped the lid and presented her with a gorgeous diamond engagement ring.

The tears fell down Alexa's cheeks as she nodded yes. "Yes, I'll marry you."

Brady sprang to his feet and wrapped his arms around the love of his life. It was the first time Theo had ever seen someone get engaged in real life. It was beautiful. Brady slid the ring onto her finger and kissed her.

Alexa was crying, Nora and Mallory were crying, and Will looked mighty relieved. He put his hand on Theo's shoulder. "They heard Nora's brother was going to propose to his girlfriend. They missed the part where she meant Nora's and *your* brother."

Theo nodded.

Nora nudged him and wiped her face. "You're lucky this ended the way it did, secret spiller."

Mallory looked at him, remorse and amusement battling in her expression. He didn't want her to feel bad. He reached for her hand and gave it a reassuring squeeze. There were worse things than messing up a proposal that still ended with the happy couple engaged.

MALLORY WANTED TO scream at her sisters when she got back to the table. How could they go straight to their dad about what they had overheard instead of coming to her? She could have helped them sort everything out in a matter of seconds. Instead, they turned what should have been a sweet, thoughtful gesture into an awkward mess of assumptions.

Brady and Alexa seemed happy enough now, showing off the ring to Brady's parents. Still, it bothered her that a completely different, more personal moment had been planned, and her family ruined it with their misguided fear.

She had almost come clean about the fake relationship with Theo just to emphasize how wrong they had been. None of that would change the fact that Alexa's proposal was hijacked by her father's interference. Her cheeks burned with embarrassment.

Unexpectedly, Theo's hand came to rest just above her knee. He gave her leg a gentle squeeze, unaware that he had her full attention. "You're quiet."

"I'm embarrassed," she admitted, wanting to avoid his gaze but unable to look away.

He shook his head, his expression soft. "Don't be."

She sighed. "Easier said than done."

He leaned in slightly, but close enough that she could smell the faint scent of his cologne. It was probably meant to reassure her, but his proximity was anything but calming.

"You wanna get out of here or did you have your heart set on meeting Santa?" he asked quietly so she was the only one who heard.

The warmth of his breath sent a shiver down her spine, and she narrowed her eyes at him, unsure if he was serious. "We can leave?"

Theo didn't bother answering, he simply slid his hand into hers and stood, tugging her up from her seat. The contact sent a jolt through her, but he didn't seem to notice. He led her out of the dining room, headed for the exit.

When they made it to the elevators, Mallory's pulse had gone from fluttering to racing. Theo pressed the up-arrow button on the wall.

"I think we've had enough family time today," he said with a lopsided grin. "What do you think?"

"I am pretty familied out," she admitted with a small laugh.

"Good answer. If I promise to let you hide out with me the rest of the day, can we do some work on my knee?" he asked.

Her hand was still in his, making it hard for her to focus on his words and not on the way the contact sent heat radiating up her arm. "Sure," she managed to reply.

The elevator arrived with a soft ding that must have broken the spell. Theo let go of her hand, getting in and pressing the button for her floor and his. She stood next to him, trying to keep from making a bigger fool of herself in front of him.

She wasn't sure what hiding out with him the rest of the day would entail, but getting his physical therapy out of the way first felt like a good plan.

They got to her floor and he asked, "Meet in my room in fifteen minutes?"

She nodded, stepping out when the doors opened. As she walked to her room, Mallory shook her head, determined to snap out of the haze he had her under. Nothing was happening between her and Theo. There was no whirlwind romance, no secret connection they'd been ignoring. They were spending too much time together, and that was all this was. Nothing more.

After changing into comfortable clothes and pulling her hair into a ponytail, her phone chimed repeatedly. She glanced at the screen, seeing what must have been a dozen text notifications from her sisters. Each one was apologetic, remorseful and desperate to make amends for their part in the proposal fiasco. She sighed and put her phone down. She'd deal with them later. For now, she would get back to the reason she was in Apple Hollow—rehabbing Theo's knee and escaping her chaotic family.

When she knocked on Theo's door a few minutes later, she braced herself. She'd spent the walk over repeating to herself that nothing was happening between them. But when Theo opened the door, her confidence in that being true vanished.

He stood there in a fitted T-shirt and sweats. He gave her an easy smile as he leaned casually against the doorframe. "Right on time," he said, his voice warm and inviting.

Her stomach fluttered as the air between them seemed to shift. For a moment, it felt like the rest of the world had faded away. If he got down on his knee like his brother had earlier, she would have a hard time telling him no. What was this man doing to her?

Mallory forced herself to smile, even as her heart thudded in her chest. She was his physical therapist when she came to his room. She needed to make sure she acted like it.

"Ready to work?" she asked, her voice steadier than she felt.

"Always," he replied, stepping aside to let her in.

Mallory entered his suite, acutely aware of how close she brushed past him. She silently repeated her mantra. *Nothing is happening between us. Nothing at all.*

The way her pulse quickened with every step she took into the room made her wonder how much longer she could keep believing it. The work helped. Focusing on the therapy, having him do specific stretches, and checking his range of motion was safe. It gave her something concrete to focus on, something professional. She could finally breathe.

There was a problem, though. His range of motion was not good. In fact, he was regressing. The flexion in his knee was noticeably reduced. Maybe it was just stiffness from their workout yesterday, but the sinking feeling in her chest told her it wasn't that simple.

"Have you taken any anti-inflammatories today?" she asked.

"I took a couple this morning," Theo replied, changing his position on the mat. "I must have overdone it yesterday. It was pretty stiff when I got up."

Mallory tried to hide her growing concern. She went through some therapist-assisted stretches, carefully flexing and extending his knee, paying attention to any resistance he gave her or any pain he might be experiencing. Theo's face told her what she needed to know without asking. He wasn't going to give her an accurate measure of how bad his pain was, but his face couldn't hide it.

"No bike today. I think we're going to stick with stretching and mobility work today."

"It's not that bad," Theo argued. His voice no longer had that soft and flirtatious tone to it. "If I want to get on skates again, I'm gonna have to be able to push myself. When Erikson tore his ACL, he was running on a treadmill by this point in his recovery. He was lifting, rebuilding muscle. You sure didn't force him to do any of this light stretching stuff day in and day out."

Mallory let out a frustrated laugh. "Erikson is twenty-two years old and that was his first knee injury that I'm aware of. He didn't have scar tissue or a meniscus tear to deal with. You, on the other hand, have a much bigger battle to wage here." She needed to control her emotions. She was getting mad at him, even though the passion in her voice came from a place of concern. She softened her approach. "I know you're not an old man, but your body is at that point where it doesn't bounce back as easily anymore. That's just reality."

Theo clenched his jaw so hard she thought he was going to crack a tooth. "I get that Erikson and I aren't the same. I'm just saying you can't coddle me and think I'm going to get better. I need to be pushed. *Hard*."

"Lie down on the floor," she said, her tone making it clear she wasn't asking.

He glared at her for a couple seconds but did as he was told, muttering under his breath as he stretched out on the mat. Mallory took hold of his bad leg by the ankle. She pushed it until it was perpendicular with the ground. Slowly, she pushed against his leg, guiding it past the midline. His hamstrings were tight.

"Hold your leg just below your knee and pull it toward you," she instructed. "You should feel the stretch."

He grumbled but did what she said. His face twisting with discomfort as she helped bend his knee. The strain on his face once again answered the questions she hadn't asked yet. To drive home her concern, she let go of his leg and held his foot, twisting his leg slightly to the right.

Theo let go of his leg and yelped. "What was that?"

"That," she said sadly, "was me pushing you." She held his gaze. "That was just stretching, Theo, and your pain was so bad you couldn't hold on. If I let you do more, if I let you lift weights or get on the balance board or even run on a treadmill, you would reinjure your knee so badly that you'd never play hockey again."

That was not what he wanted to hear. He sat up slowly, grimacing as he leaned back on his hands, his legs straight out in front of him. "That's such baloney."

It pained her to see him like that. "We made a promise to be honest in here, Theo. About who we are to each other and about how you were doing in therapy. I would not be doing my job if I let you do more than your body can handle."

It was silent while he mulled over her words. The only sound was the hum of the heat kicking on. Mallory didn't want there to be tension between them when there had already been so much nonsense today. He had been so happy at breakfast. Spoiling his mood was worse than spoiling Brady's proposal.

"Hockey is *my* job. I made a promise to get back on the ice. What about that promise I made to myself and my team to fight hard and play again?"

"You are fighting," she said, trying to assure

him that no one was letting him give up. "But you must do it the right way or you could lose the thing you're fighting for. I know you don't want to risk that."

Theo's chest rose and fell with heavy breaths. Mallory fought the urge to reach out to him, to comfort him. She was his physical therapist, not his girlfriend. They needed to be on the same page about his workouts even if it made him sad.

"Fine, no weights, no bike. Just stretching. I want my range of motion back," he said, pushing himself to his feet.

"Good," she said. If she could keep him focused on a goal, even a small one, maybe he would feel better. "Let's work on that."

Theo took a step into her personal space. His eyes dropped to her lips for just a second and snapped back up. "Since we're being honest, I have a question."

Mallory swallowed hard. "What's that?" she asked, her throat tight.

"What was running through your head today when I pulled that ring out of my pocket?"

His unexpected shift from brooding athlete who was mad at his physical therapist to flirtatious friend gave her whiplash. "I… I—" She wasn't sure how to answer. Her heart was pounding so hard she thought for sure he'd know exactly what she had been thinking because he'd be able to hear it. "I don't know. I was confused why you had the ring when I was sure it was Brady who was going to propose."

"How sure were you?"

Heat crept up her neck. "I was a hundred percent sure until you were holding the box in your hand. Then it dropped to ninety-nine."

Theo's eyebrows shot up. "Only one percent less?"

"Why would you propose to your fake girlfriend? I knew there had to be another explanation."

"We must be extremely talented actors if your sisters believed it so much so that they sent your dad to talk me out of it." He took a step back, and Mallory fought the urge to move in his direction to maintain their proximity to one another.

"Honestly, I don't have to work too hard to pretend that I'm having a good time with you." She tipped her chin up, hoping to fake a little confidence. "You're a fun person to be around when you aren't fighting with me about your therapy."

He nodded, the corners of his lips curving upward. "Honestly, I think I pretend to not like you more than I pretend to be falling for you. I probably like you more than I should. I'm not sure what we should do about that if you were feeling the same way."

Mallory's mind was racing and she struggled to

keep her breathing even. His words hung in the air, daring her to respond. If she wasn't careful, she could flip her world upside down. It was unclear if that would be good or bad anymore.

"We should—" she began, but Theo took a step closer and she lost her train of thought.

"Should what?" His eyes searched hers.

Her body was overheating. She wanted to run out of the room, out of the inn and jump in the snow until freezing to death was all she had to worry about.

"We should stay focused on improving your range of motion," she finally managed, though her voice was unsteady. Any false confidence was long gone.

Theo didn't say anything. He stood so close that if she moved even an inch, their bodies would be pressed together. She took a small step back, needing to put some space between them.

"I think we both know you aren't thinking about my range of motion right this second," he challenged.

The air between them seemed to crackle. She opened her mouth to remind him of those boundaries they had both promised to keep, but no words came. She was caught between the overwhelming urge to kiss him and the voice in her head telling her there was no way this could be real.

"We must be such good actors that not only

have we convinced our families, but we're deluding ourselves into thinking this is something that could hold up against the world of trouble that would be waiting for us back in Boston."

Theo tilted his head slightly. "Too much trouble, huh?"

"Much too much," she replied, her voice firmer this time. But she didn't move. Neither did he.

For a moment, it felt as if time had stopped. She wasn't sure who leaned in first, but the distance between them seemed to shrink with every breath. Just as his lips hovered dangerously close to hers, Theo paused. His eyes locked on hers, and she could see the war waging inside him.

She was in the midst of the same internal battle. This would be so much trouble, but what if it was worth it? She remembered how it felt to kiss him the first night they were here. It had been the best kiss she had ever had. Maybe this was him telling her he felt the same. For a second, she thought he might close the gap and kiss her again. An unusual mix of panic and anticipation shot through her.

Theo let out a resigned breath and stepped back. "Right. Neither one of us needs any trouble." His voice was strained like it physically pained him to pull away. "Lord knows I have enough of that."

Mallory felt a strange mix of relief and disappointment in her chest. She had been the one to say no first, but his agreement felt more like a rejection.

Running a hand through his hair, Theo's jaw tightened as he got back down on the mat, ready to stretch. "Let's get back to work," he said.

Mallory nodded, wishing she hadn't been so quick to turn him away. "Okay, let's start with your legs extended in a V. Reach forward with your hands, first in the center and then we'll have to lean to the right and left."

She got right back into work mode, but she couldn't shake the lingering tension in the air or the nagging feeling that trouble was coming whether they acted on these feelings or not.

CHAPTER THIRTEEN

MONDAY MORNING, Theo decided to join his brother, who needed to run errands in town. The winter edition of Seasons at the Lake was two days away and there was a lot to do in a little time.

"When you fell in love with Alexa, did you know it was happening?" he asked Brady as he stared out the passenger side window at the snowy hills.

"She was a guest at the inn. I thought she was leaving for good in a few days. I had no idea what I was doing."

"You fell in love with her in one week? How is that possible?" Theo needed to know because there was no way that was what was happening between him and Mallory. He could not be falling for this woman. Although he had known her longer than a few days, he only got to *know* her over the weekend.

"That's a great question, but I don't have any answers for you," Brady replied. "Alexa and I just clicked. She instantly became someone I wanted to be around."

"You like being around people in general. That's your personality. Why was she different from everyone else?"

Brady gave him a side-eyed glance. "Why are you so interested in my relationship with Alexa? Are you trying to say something about how quickly we got engaged? Because if that's why you came along, I am happy to take you back to the inn and run all these errands by myself."

Theo hadn't meant to make Brady defensive, but he wanted to be careful about how he cleared up this little misunderstanding. He didn't need his brother wondering why he was so confused about his feelings for the woman who was supposed to be his girlfriend.

"That's not it." He held up his hands to show he meant no harm. "If you think you're ready to settle down, good for you. I'm just asking because you seem so sure. The only thing I've ever been that sure about is that I wanted to play hockey."

Brady's whole body seemed to relax. His smile was back. "Are you questioning if what you and Mallory have is moving in the same direction as me and Alexa?"

"No, no, no, I'm not ready to settle down like you. I'm not even thinking about that."

"Mallory is pretty awesome. Not gonna lie, I

was not expecting you to bring someone home, but especially not someone so…"

"So what?" It was Theo's turn to be defensive. Mallory was an amazing person. He would be lucky to have someone like her in his life.

"So normal. So down-to-earth. So easy for the whole family to get along with. You've tended to date girls who cared more about what you do for a living than who you are as a person."

Theo rolled his eyes. "You sound just like Nora. And for the record, I haven't dated that many people for you guys to think that all I ever do is let women take advantage of me."

"I'm sure no one takes advantage of you, brother. You've never dated anyone long enough for that to happen." Brady turned on to the main road in town. "Mallory just seems like the kind of woman you bring home to meet the parents. And you did, which means you must really like her."

He did really like her, only he hadn't known that he felt that way until *after* he brought her home. How was he going to explain that to his family someday? Mallory wasn't on board with pursuing anything further than this week, though, so it didn't matter how he felt. How would they explain this to Icemen management? She was right; it was too messy.

Main Street was bustling with last-minute Christmas shoppers. It was amazing to Theo that he could be away for so long yet come back and everything was exactly the way he remembered it. Cooper's Pharmacy and Soda Fountain, a popular spot, had its windows decorated for the holidays.

There were festive lights strung across the street and wreaths with red bows hung from the top of every lamppost. The town green was blanketed in a layer of snow. The green was the heart of Apple Hollow and in the center of it was where they displayed the giant Christmas tree covered in colored lights. Theo and his family used to come to town the Saturday after Thanksgiving for the annual tree-lighting ceremony.

"I'll park around the corner," Brady said, nodding toward the print shop. "We can grab the order and be out in five minutes."

"Fine by me," Theo replied, though his mind was still churning over their conversation.

As they climbed out of the car, Theo heard a familiar laugh. When they turned the corner to get back on Main Street, there was Mallory, standing in front of the bookstore with her mom and sisters, all of them loaded down with shopping bags.

"Mallory?"

"Look who it is," Savannah said with a knowing grin, nudging Mallory with her elbow.

Mallory's laughter faded as she spotted him, her eyes widening slightly before she plastered on a smile. She adjusted the bags in her arms. "Hey. What are you doing in town?" she asked.

"Errands," he replied, stepping closer. "Brady's making me his unpaid assistant."

"Well, aren't you the sweetest," Selene said with a warm smile. "And, Brady, can I just apologize one more time for whatever part my family played in interfering with your proposal yesterday."

Mallory's cheeks turned pink as she spoke through clenched teeth. "Why are you bringing that up? We don't need to rehash anything from yesterday."

Brady chuckled, his easygoing personality taking some of the tension out of the air. "All that matters is that Alexa said yes. I understand there were several misunderstandings. No one needs to apologize."

Erica stepped forward. "I'm the one who jumped to conclusions and got everyone else worked up. You know that Hayden and I just got engaged, and I think I freaked out thinking that Mallory was going to get engaged before we even had my engagement dinner."

Theo pressed his lips together so he didn't laugh out loud. Mallory had told him that Erica hated sharing the limelight. He hadn't realized how true that was.

Mallory shared a look with Theo before glancing at Erica. "The fact that you have no qualms about saying that aloud is mind-boggling to me."

Savannah couldn't hold in her laughter and Avery shook her head.

Erica, unfazed, continued. "You and Alexa should join us for our engagement dinner tomorrow night to make it up to you. Theo is going to be there, right?"

Theo and Mallory hadn't discussed their plans for today. Things had gotten awkward yesterday, and they ended up doing their own things after they finished his workout.

"I go where Mallory tells me."

Avery raised an eyebrow, her expression amused. "Oh, you two are already like an old married couple."

Mallory's face turned a deep shade of crimson as she glared at her sister.

"What?" Avery asked innocently.

"Leave your sister alone," Selene said. She turned back to Theo and Brady. "We hope you both can join us for dinner. Alexa, too."

"That's very sweet of you," Brady said. "But we are setting up for Wednesday's big event, and I have a feeling that Alexa and I will be working all day tomorrow on it. I appreciate the invite, though."

"Well, then it will just be Theo," Selene said.

"Don't you have hockey practice tomorrow?" Mallory asked.

Theo wasn't sure if she was trying to discourage him from coming or not. "That's tonight. I was hoping you'd come with me."

"Oh." Mallory seemed surprised by his request.

With a quick flick of her wrist, Selene said, "There you have it. Sounds like these two lovebirds will be able to make it to the engagement dinner."

"We should let you guys get back to your errands. We need to finish our shopping," Mallory said.

"I thought we were done now that you finally found something for Theo," Savannah said.

Theo blinked, his curiosity instantly piqued. "You got me a gift?"

"No," Mallory said quickly, her voice a little too high. She glanced at her sisters, her mom and then back at Theo. "I mean, not really. It's nothing. Just something small."

"Stop it," Selene said. "It's a lovely gift. I'm sure he'll love it."

Savannah grinned. "Small? You spent, like, twenty minutes deciding between—"

"Let's not," Mallory interrupted, her eyes narrowing like she wished she could shoot lasers out of them and incinerate her sister. "Theo and Brady have a lot to do for the event on Wednesday. We should let them go."

As Selene and her daughters said their goodbyes and turned to go, Theo couldn't help but smirk at Mallory who lingered a moment. "Twenty minutes, huh?"

She shook her head. "Don't get too excited. Just because I'm an indecisive shopper doesn't mean I'm a good one."

"Theo's a very good gift-giver," Brady said. "You should prepare yourself."

The smirk was wiped from Theo's face. He was teasing her about the gift she bought when he hadn't thought about getting her a gift at all. Clearly, both sides of the family would be expecting him to get her something.

It was Mallory's turn to relish in *his* discomfort. "Oh, I know. I hope he doesn't embarrass me with his generosity. Surely, he remembered I'm a simple girl with simple tastes."

Great. They weren't going to be able to rush back to the inn. Theo needed to go shopping and he wasn't leaving until he found the perfect gift.

MALLORY SPENT THE whole day wondering what Theo was going to get her for Christmas. When he asked her to come to hockey practice with him, she decided to do him a favor and let him off the hook.

"I just want you to know that you do *not* have

to buy me a Christmas present," she said as they pulled into the ice rink parking lot. "I got something today for my sister that I thought she'd like better than what I had sent to my mom's back when I thought we weren't going to be celebrating together. I can wrap that up and say it's from you."

Theo put the car in Park and looked at her with a furrowed brow. "I'm not doing that. I got you a gift. Well, a few gifts."

A few? She felt her heart rate pick up. "You can take them back. I don't want you to feel pressured to get me something when that was not part of the deal."

"Too late," he said casually, getting out of the car.

Mallory fumbled with her seat belt and stumbled out after him. "I'm serious, Theo."

He stopped walking, letting her catch up to him. There was a stubborn glint in his eyes. "So am I. I should have thought about getting something before I found out you got something for me. But it doesn't matter. When you like someone, you get them Christmas presents. I like you, Mallory."

His words stole her breath away. Every time she thought they were back on track with keeping things professional, he would do or say something to make her consider being reckless. It would be reckless to fall for Theo Seasons.

He held the door to the arena open for her. "I

think you like me, too. That's why you got me a gift."

"I never said I didn't like you," she muttered, stepping inside. She just didn't want him to mess up her life.

"Good," he said in a way that she knew there was a giant grin on his face, but she refused to turn around to be sure.

Hank was manning the front desk again. He greeted Theo like he was his own son, coming out from behind the counter and giving him a big hug. "It's mighty nice of you to work with these kids while you're home on break. It means so much to them."

Theo shrugged. "We can't lose to the Snow Tigers, Hank. You know how it is. I remember what it was like to play against them back in the day."

"I think the game you scored your record number of goals was against the Snow Tigers."

Theo grinned. "Of course it was. Who else would motivate me that much to score six goals in one game?"

Mallory tilted her head. "Is that a lot for one game?"

"Is that a lot? Oh!" Hank nearly fell over, clutching his chest dramatically. "That's a double hat trick! It's almost unheard of. The record in professional hockey is seven."

Mallory held her hands up in defense. "I work

with hockey players, but I'm just learning about the game. I knew Theo was impressive. I didn't realize he was *that* impressive."

Theo nodded toward the door. "Banner. Outside. Side of building. Remember?"

Mallory nodded. "Right. Big deal. Huge." She laughed when he rolled his eyes at her.

"Well, you better get in there. Those kids are ready and waiting for you. Their parents are excited as well. I told them they can't be bothering you for things like autographs. Let me know if anyone causes you any trouble."

"Thanks, Hank."

Mallory followed Theo into the rink. The whole place needed a makeover, but it also had a certain charm to it. She liked knowing this was the place that Theo first learned to love hockey. Being there made her feel like she had been let in on a secret part of him that he didn't let others see.

"How come you wanted me to come to practice with you?" she asked. "You seemed pretty frustrated with me yesterday during therapy, and then you didn't want to spend any part of the rest of the day with me."

"I was a little annoyed by PT Mallory and Fake Girlfriend Mallory gave me the clear message that she needed some space from her fake boyfriend or she was going to cross those lines she likes so much." He reached into his pocket and took out a whistle on a string, putting it around his neck.

There were two things Mallory was a sucker for—one was a man who was honest about his feelings and the other was a man who acknowledged the feelings of others. Theo was of course doing both those things.

"I do appreciate the break from all that togetherness with my family. That was very considerate of you."

He took off his jacket and sat down to tighten the laces on his boots. "I should probably admit that there was a little bit of selfish intent mixed in there."

Mallory tipped her head. "How was having me come with you selfish?"

"When I brought you here the last time, I think that was when you really started to like me," he explained. "Maybe I just wanted to see if I can get you to like me even *more*."

This last reason warmed her cheeks. Theo gave her a wink and stepped onto the ice in his boots. Mallory had to sit down thanks to her knees getting weak. More? If she liked him any more than she already did, he would end up being the person she liked the most.

He grabbed a hockey stick and slung it over his shoulder. The dads who had been helping coach, immediately deferred to him. As if they would be able to keep the team's attention now that Theo was there. The kids were already buzzing with excitement, swarming around Theo like he was a superstar. Probably because he *was*.

He had them go around and tell him their names. If he remembered all twenty kids' names when this was all over, he was beyond impressive. Once introductions were done, he had them get to work, putting them through a series of drills.

After a couple drills, one of the boys asked, "Coach Theo, how come you're not skating with us?"

Theo put his arm around the boy's shoulder. "Because that lady on the end of the bench over there," he said, nodding toward Mallory. "She's trying to help me get back on the ice for the Icemen. If I do something that could hurt my knee, she'll rat me out to the doctor and they won't let me do anything fun anymore."

"It's not nice to be a snitch," one of the boys standing by the board said to her.

Mallory raised her eyebrows. "I am not a snitch," she said defensively.

"She's not a snitch…*yet*," Theo said, moving closer to where she sat.

"Let's not forget that I'm here because you invited me. If you were afraid of me telling the doctor on you, you wouldn't have brought me."

Theo smirked. "That is true." He nudged the

kid who had called her a snitch and peeked over his shoulder at her. "We need to be nice to her. I hear she bought me a cool gift for Christmas and I don't want to get on her bad side."

Mallory shook her head. He was too much.

Grabbing a puck, he began showing off. He might not have been on skates but he still had some tricks he could do with a puck and a stick. He flipped the puck effortlessly from one side of the blade to the other, bounced it off the toe of the stick, and sent it spinning like a top before flicking it up and catching it mid-air.

"Whoa!" one of the boys said.

"Do it again," begged another one while the biggest kid out there tried to imitate him unsuccessfully.

Mallory couldn't tear her eyes away. Watching Theo with the kids was like seeing someone in their element. He was radiating confidence. He showed the kids a few more tricks before getting back to coaching. He offered tips and encouragement to each kid as they practiced passing drills. His patience was impressive as he helped one boy adjust his grip on the stick and then clapped another on the shoulder after a decent shot on goal. It was truly impossible not to fall for him more than she already was.

She reminded herself this wasn't real, that their relationship was an act. But as Theo glanced over his shoulder and caught her watching, smiling just for her, Mallory felt herself losing the will to care about what would happen when they returned to Boston if they stopped holding back.

"You okay over there?" he called, his voice echoing across the rink.

"Fine," she replied as she looked away, afraid he would see just how much she cared about him.

"Good," he said, carefully moving closer to her. "Because we've got one more drill to run. You in?"

Mallory pointed to her chest. "Me? Do a drill?"

"You won't be doing the drill. You will be an obstacle for kids to skate around in the drill. You will be holding a stick, though. You think you can handle that?"

Mallory bit her lip, her heart pounding. She was not prepared to be on the ice, but what the heck. She had sat on the sidelines long enough. "Show me what to do," she said, getting off the bench.

Theo set Mallory up on the ice with a stick and instructions to pretend she was trying to steal the puck without moving anything but the stick. The kids were told to skate around some cones and then around Mallory before taking a shot.

The lone girl on the team, number forty-four, who Mallory learned was named Kayla, moved with such ease across the ice. She was the one Theo had taken note of at the last game, and she was still impressing him today. She darted around the cones and Mallory with more agility than everyone else on the team.

Theo noticed, too. "Kayla!" he called, motioning her over to where he was standing with the dads who helped coach.

Kayla skated up to him, her stick tucked under one arm. "Yeah?"

"How are you feeling about playing center?"

Kayla hesitated, glancing at the boys practicing nearby. "It's a lot of pressure," she admitted. "Everyone will be counting on me."

"Griffin and Tommy usually play center," one of the dads said. Mallory guessed he was Griffin's dad.

"I'm pretty sure Kayla showed everyone the other day why she should be center. Besides the goals she scored, her face-off was textbook."

"I don't think we can afford not to play her at center," another dad said. The third dad nodded in agreement.

"What if it's not the same when we play the Snow Tigers?" Kayla asked, looking right at Theo.

He crouched down to be at her level. "I know exactly how you feel. I play center, too, and it's a lot of pressure. But you've got something not everyone does."

"What's that?"

"Grit," Theo said, standing to his full height.

"You stay focused under pressure, you recover quickly from a mistake and you are always in there making a second effort. Your toughness and determination, your *grit*, are why you can make plays that most players can't."

Kayla blinked up at him. Mallory could only imagine what it would be like to have someone she idolized tell her she was special.

"You really think so?" Kayla finally asked, her expression hopeful and full of pride.

"I know so," Theo said with a definitive nod of his head.

"Even though I'm not as big as some of the guys?"

He tapped the blade of her stick with his own. "You can use your size to your advantage, especially against bigger guys on defense. If you get low and use your center of gravity, you'll have the advantage going to the net."

Kayla's face lit up with understanding. "Okay. Got it."

"And one more thing," Theo added, his voice lowering conspiratorially. "You're good, but you can't win games on your own. Trust your wings. Let them help you make the play."

Kayla nodded. "Thanks."

"You're welcome," Theo said, standing and patting her helmet. "Why don't you call everyone in for my last lecture."

Kayla skated off, calling for her teammates to gather up at center ice. Mallory felt her heart squeeze. Watching Theo mentor these kids had the exact effect he had been hoping for. Not only did the kids adore him, but she also wasn't far behind.

Theo caught her watching again and raised an eyebrow. "What?" he called out, smirking.

"Nothing," Mallory replied, trying to escape back to the bench.

"Nope," Theo said, coming up beside her as she carefully shuffled across the ice in her tennis shoes. "You have to come to center ice since you're part of the team now."

"I was basically a human cone. I don't think that makes me part of the team."

He laughed and it hit her right in the chest. Her heart stuttered and then raced. "You are hilarious. And you're coming to center ice with me." He wouldn't take no for an answer and held onto her arm to help her turn around and go where he wanted her.

At center ice, Theo gave the team one last pep talk. He told them if they played the way they'd practiced tonight, the Snow Tigers wouldn't know what hit them. The boys and Kayla were fired up. Theo expected to hear that they left everything on the ice on Friday. He led them in a final cheer.

"I wish you could be here for the game," Kayla said to Theo as everyone began to disperse.

"Me, too. But the Icemen have a game on Saturday, and I'm trying to get back for it. That means I have to leave on Friday."

"Even though you can't skate because of—" She nodded at Mallory.

Great, now all the kids thought she was the reason he couldn't play hockey.

Theo scoffed. "I wish it was as simple as getting Mallory to tell me I could skate, and yes, it's strongly encouraged that I do as much with the team as possible even though I'm injured."

"Bummer," Kayla said in a heavy sigh. "Well, thanks for helping us. I hope we make you proud."

Mallory saw the shock on Theo's face. He couldn't even respond before Kayla skated off.

She took his hand in hers. "Are you okay?"

Theo blew out a long breath. "I wasn't expecting her to say that." He rubbed his closely cropped beard and cleared his throat. "I don't think these kids realize that I hope I make them proud, too."

Mallory gave his hand a reassuring squeeze like he had done to her this weekend. "You have already made this whole town proud."

"I don't want it to be over. I'm so afraid it's going to be over."

She wanted to tell him his career wasn't over, but she knew better than to make promises. "Maybe you should try not to spend too much time worrying about what's ending," she said softly, "and focus on what new things could be coming your way. Those things could be even better than what's already been."

Theo's gaze dropped to her hand. Was her touch grounding him in the way his did when she needed it? "You make it sound easy," he said.

"It's not," she admitted. "But if anyone can do it, it's you."

Mallory could see the tension in the line of his jaw. He pressed his lips together like he wasn't willing to share what he was thinking.

His eyes met hers, and for a moment she forgot how to breathe. "I don't know if I can do it alone."

Mallory's heart stuttered in her chest. She wanted to tell him he didn't have to, that she was here, but she couldn't trust her voice to hold steady.

Before she could respond, Theo tugged on her hand. "We should go. Hank's probably ready to lock up."

Mallory nodded, her throat tight as she followed him toward the exit. Walking side by side, her thoughts kept circling back to the look in his eyes, the weight of his words. She swore she wouldn't do this, but she was falling in love with Theo Seasons. This fake relationship was taking an unexpected turn.

CHAPTER FOURTEEN

THEO WAS FALLING in love with his fake girlfriend. It was ridiculous. It was scary. It was the best feeling in the world. By Tuesday night, he couldn't stop smiling when he thought about seeing her in a few minutes.

When there was a knock on his door, he assumed it was her and he pulled it open with a little extra enthusiasm.

"Whoa, careful with my doors," Quinn said, inspecting the hinges as if Theo did damage by whipping it open.

"This isn't your door. None of the doors in the inn are *your* doors. They're soon to be *our* doors, but they'll never just be yours."

"Who will be the one fixing the doors that break when Dad retires? Me."

"Wade," Theo countered. Wade Kramer was the inn's handyman. If anyone was fixing things around there, it was Wade.

Quinn scowled at his younger brother. "You have no idea what it's like to live here, work here."

"If you came up here to lecture me on what a disappointment I am because I have a life outside of this place, you can head right back downstairs to your little check-in desk."

"I didn't come up here to fight with you. I came up to see if you can help me with something."

Theo carefully drew the door back and stepped aside so Quinn could come inside. "I would love to."

His brother stepped past him and stopped when he noticed the furniture had been moved. "You turned the suite into a gym? Where did you get that exercise bike?"

"I bought it and had it shipped here," he replied, wondering why that wasn't obvious.

"You bought an exercise bike for your week-long vacation?"

"Yes."

Quinn shook his head. "The fact that Dad takes on all this debt while you buy thousand-dollar exercise bikes for your vacation is the most ridiculous thing I have ever heard."

"Do you want me to be your boss, brother? I'll happily buy everyone out and you can answer to me." Their dad would *never* allow it and he wouldn't ever overstep like that, but it was fun to watch Quinn's expression change at the thought of having Theo own the inn.

"No, thank you. I don't ever want to work for

you. I just can't imagine making all that money for playing a game a few times a year."

Theo's jaw dropped. "Playing a game a few times a year? Is that what you think my life is like? If it is, you do not understand what being a professional athlete entails."

Quinn held up his hands. "Like I said, I didn't come up here to fight."

"Could have fooled me." His eldest brother believed he was the hardest working man around. He had no clue because he basically spent his whole life behind that front desk.

"I wanted to know if you would look over my speech for the retirement celebration tomorrow." Quinn had a notebook in his hand. "I don't do a lot of public speaking, but I know you have to stand in front of reporters and do press conferences all the time."

Oh, so he did realize that Theo's job was more than simply *playing a game*.

"Okay. I'd be happy to look it over. Are we all speaking at this thing or only you?"

"Do you want to say something?"

Theo hadn't thought about it. He probably should say something. "Shouldn't we all say a little something?"

"You're going to have to talk to Nora and Brady about that. All I know is that I am saying something and right now, this is what I've got and I need someone to look it over and offer me some suggestions so I don't make a fool of myself."

There was another knock at the door. Theo opened it with much less vigor than the last time. Mallory was on the other side in a red dress that made him want to cancel all their plans tonight and stay in with her instead.

"Hi." The light caught the soft waves of her hair as she tucked a strand behind her ear, her cheeks faintly flushed.

He really did love when she wore her hair down. "Hi," he replied, smiling at her like an idiot. The air between them seemed charged. He could feel it. Being around her was different than being around anyone else.

"Hello," Quinn called from behind him, breaking the spell.

"Hi, Quinn. I'm sorry." The rosy flush of her cheeks deepened. "I didn't mean to interrupt. I should have texted you to see if you were ready."

"No, you're not interrupting. Quinn just stopped by to drop something off. I was waiting for you. Come in, please." Theo stepped back, motioning for her to come in.

"Nora's right. Sometimes it seems like you two have been dating forever and other times, you act like you're on your first date. I can't figure this relationship out," Quinn said, stepping around them both to leave. "If you could give me some feedback before you go to bed tonight, I would appreciate it."

"You got it."

"Good to see you again, Mallory," Quinn said on his way out. "Have a good night."

"Good night."

Theo closed the door behind his brother and turned to face a panicked-looking Mallory.

"Your sister and brother have been talking about us? Are we that bad at being normal around them?"

"Normal?" Theo laughed, tilting his head slightly. "Nothing about us is normal, so I don't know how anyone could watch us together and think that."

She let her pretty brown eyes close for a second. "I seriously can't believe no one has figured it out yet. Sometimes, I think Avery is on to us, but then she's distracted by the boys, and she forgets to confront me."

"I think we're doing just fine." He stepped closer and reached up to tuck the same strand of hair behind her ear that she had moments ago but had fallen forward again. "We're giving first-date vibes because maybe these are like first dates."

"First date implies there will be more dates," she said, giving nothing away with her expression.

If he told her that he was falling in love with her, she might bolt right out of this room. She might run downstairs and confess to her family right before Christmas that this was all a lie. He was having too much fun to let that happen.

"Like I told your family the other day, I do what you tell me. If you tell me I can have more dates, I will go on more dates. Happily."

She bit down on her lip and he had to force himself to stay rooted in his spot. If he did what he wanted, she would already be in his arms.

Mallory cleared her throat. "You make it almost impossible to say no to."

"*Almost* impossible but not impossible, huh?"

"Are you ready to go to my sister's engagement party?" Mallory asked, dodging the question. "Because if we're late, she won't forgive me."

She wasn't ready to do more than play her part, but she was considering it. He could tell she was straddling that line she had drawn and it might not take much to get her to cross over.

"I am ready if you are," he said, offering his arm. She took it and let him lead her out into the hall. "You look beautiful, by the way."

Mallory glanced down at her dress. "I've been borrowing my sisters' clothes because I brought a lot of spandex and oversized sweaters and zero dresses."

"Well, they should just give you all the outfits you've borrowed because there's no way anyone can look as good as you have looked in all the dresses I've seen you in."

She ducked her head so her hair fell like a shield, covering her face. "Stop saying all the right things. I don't know if I can handle it."

"Then my plan is working perfectly."

Her gaze snapped to his. "You were the one who thought this plan of mine was a terrible idea or have you forgotten?"

"It was a terrible idea. Still is a terrible idea. It doesn't mean that I can't like you. Stop being so likeable, and maybe I won't like you." Confessing his like for her had to be less scary than the word *love*.

"I'm not that likeable," she protested as he hit the button to call the elevator. "You also promised to not try to make me fall in love with you, but that's all you seem to be doing lately."

Theo's body went rigid. "Say again?"

"I don't know what I'm saying anymore. You and that shirt, looking all…" She huffed. "And that watch on your wrist and the way your hair is perfect and you smell like something I want to spray on everything I own so I can smell it all the time. You're so distracting, so let's just not talk until we get downstairs and we're around my family."

The elevator dinged and Mallory let go of his arm and marched inside the moment the doors opened. Confusion furrowed his brow as he joined her in the elevator. He glanced down at what he was wearing. His button-down shirt was nice, but nothing too fancy. His cologne was expensive. She might think twice about spraying it everywhere if she knew how much it cost, and he had spent quite a bit of time on his hair. It was nice to know it was appreciated. He was unsure what his watch had to do with anything.

The right side of his mouth quirked up in a crooked smile. She was falling for him like he was falling for her. She could talk around it all she wanted. She crossed her arms, her posture determined despite the way her petite frame made her look like someone he needed to protect. This was not the way the two of them had thought this was going to go, but here they were.

THEO STOOD THERE smirking the whole way down to dinner. Mallory wanted to torture him with some squats or wall sits, something to wipe that smile off his face. She also wanted to kiss him. Actually, she wanted *him* to kiss *her*. There was part of her that wanted to relinquish control and let him take the lead.

Kissing was a bad idea, though. Mainly because she was fairly certain he wanted that, too. He would probably gloat all night if she caved.

The elevator opened on the main level, and Theo waited for her to exit first. As she entered the lobby, she felt the pressure of his hand on her lower back as he came up beside her. He leaned in close. "Your family isn't going to doubt that we're together tonight. Not for one second."

His words sent an unexpected shiver down her spine. Asking him to play the part of her boyfriend had been one thing; truly being wooed by him was another. Mallory had no idea how to navigate something real.

Nora had seen to it that they could have the smaller private dining room again for the engagement dinner. Mallory's mom greeted them at the door when they arrived.

"Theo," she said, throwing her arms open. She wasn't kidding when she had told him she was a hugger. "We're glad you could join us."

"Thanks for inviting me." Her mother released him and his hand immediately returned to the small of Mallory's back. "We were just talking about how nice it's been that we get to spend the holiday with both families. Your surprise was a real gift."

Mallory watched as her mother was swept off her feet by his charm. He knew exactly what she wanted to hear.

"Oh, thank you for saying that. William was so afraid I was overstepping with this idea, but I'm so glad you two think it was a good idea."

A good idea? That would never be how Mallory classified it.

Erica and Hayden came over, making sure everyone was aware they were the guests of honor this evening. "We sat you two over there between Avery and Savannah," Erica said, pointing to the two empty chairs. "Mom made a crossword puzzle for you to fill out while we wait for dinner to start. All the words have to do with me and Hayden."

"Fun," Mallory said, trying to be as nice as Theo.

"And your sister was so great," Erica said to Theo. "She helped me put together a slideshow we're going to play after dinner."

"Nora is the best. I'm glad she could help." Theo's hand slid from Mallory's back to her waist. He pulled her against him. "Our families work so well together. Isn't that awesome?"

Mallory glanced up at him. His cologne smelled so good she wanted to bury her face in the crook of his neck and just inhale. "*So* awesome."

"Just wait 'til you see the menu for tonight. Laura let me and Hayden talk to the chef and we got to help create the menu. He's also amazing. And Gavin gave us two bottles of champagne to toast at dinner. Wasn't that so nice?"

"He was very generous," Mallory said. The way Theo's family had embraced the whole Moore clan was too kind. They were doing all these nice things because they thought Mallory's relationship with Theo was real.

The wooden walls and beams gave the room a

rustic charm. An inviting fireplace adorned with a garland of greenery and red berries was lit on one side of the room. There was a Christmas tree in one corner and a ball of mistletoe hanging above the doorway where they stood. Mallory and Theo had been the last to arrive.

They sat down and Mallory scanned the crossword. The clue for one across was—this is where Hayden and Erica met. That one was easy. Based on the number of letters, it had to be *college*.

Erica asked for everyone's attention. "When you guys finish the crossword, I have prizes, so you have to do it."

Mallory and Savannah gave each other a knowing look. Their little sister was smart. The only way to get everyone to participate was bribery.

"We need to work together," Theo said, grabbing one of the pens that her mom had left in the middle of the table. "We need to win, but I don't know any of these."

She grabbed her own pen, feeling mischievous. "I don't think we're supposed to do this as teams. I want my own prize," she said, covering her crossword so he couldn't take her answers.

"Stop." He laughed. "For real, you need to tell me the answers."

"I'll help you, Theo," Greg offered.

"Thank you." Theo glared at Mallory before scooting his chair closer to Greg.

"First one done wins," she said, already halfway finished.

Theo growled but kept his head close to Greg as he tried to help her brother-in-law think of the right word that fit the spaces.

"They met at UMass. That doesn't fit, though," Greg complained.

Mallory got stumped on five across which asked where they went on their first date. Why would any of them know that? She would have to use the down questions to answer that one. She knew Erica's middle name. Hayden's middle name must have been Edward given the letters she already had.

The waitstaff came in and took everyone's drink orders, but that didn't slow Mallory down.

"What's your favorite Christmas movie, Erica?" Theo asked. They were catching up. "Give us a hint, at least."

Mallory knew it was *The Grinch*. A minute later, she was entering the last answer. "Done!" she shouted, waving her paper over her head.

Theo's wide shoulders slumped as he accepted defeat. "What's her middle name?"

"Sloane with an *E* at the end."

"An *E*?" Greg tossed his pen down. "I knew it was Sloane, I didn't realize you could spell that with an *E*."

"We're done now, too," Theo said. He slid his

chair closer to Mallory. "You win." As he looked over his shoulder, his mouth was close to her ear. "Just know that for refusing to team up with me, I'm going to have to corner you under that mistletoe later so your mom doesn't get suspicious because you weren't being nice to me."

Mallory swallowed hard. He was threatening to kiss her later? Heat crawled up her neck. "I dare you," she said, a little more breathless than she would have liked.

"Of course you do." He laughed quietly and faced forward with that smirk back on his face.

The drinks arrived, and Mallory was quick to take a sip of her cocktail to cool herself down. Erica and Hayden came around and handed all the sisters and their partners their own box.

"Avery didn't do the crossword. Why does she get a prize and Theo doesn't?" Mallory asked as Hayden set down a box in front of Greg.

"Um, I don't have a box for him, but we do have something. You'll understand when everyone opens their boxes. Trust me, if I knew who your boyfriend was before we got here, I would have a box for him, too."

Hayden went back to his seat and pulled a gift bag out from under the table, quickly bringing it back to Theo. Theo tossed the tissue paper on the table and slid out a bottle of champagne.

"You can pop that open on New Year's," Hayden

said. "Or whenever you have something to celebrate."

Mallory unwrapped her gift, curious what everyone else got. As soon as she opened the box, she knew what was happening. Inside the lid of the box, there was a sign asking her to be Erica's bridesmaid. The box contained a travel wine glass that had Mallory's name on it, a bunch of hair scrunchies with a card that said Help Me Tie the Knot and a jewelry box with the letter *M* monogrammed on it.

Avery got the same thing and Savannah's asked if she would be the Matron of Honor. The guys opened theirs, asking Greg and Chance to be Hayden's groomsmen. Inside was an engraved flask, a mini bottle of whiskey and a cigar.

The sisters all came together for a group hug, everyone accepting the responsibility of standing beside their baby sister when she got married next year. Greg and Chance got up and shook hands with Hayden, happy to stand up for him.

Mallory sat back down next to Theo. She put a hand on his knee. "Thank goodness they didn't know who my boyfriend was before they got here. He's a big enough hockey fan that he would have asked you."

Theo was unbothered. "Guess I'll just have to be your plus-one."

The way he said it made it seem like he meant it.

As if they would still be playing this game when Erica got married.

"I'm very fun at weddings," he added.

"I'm sure you are," Mallory said with a giggle. He couldn't be serious, but he showed no signs of joking. Ten months from now, there was no way they would even be working together on his knee. He'd be playing or… She didn't even want to think about the other option. Thinking it put it out there in the universe.

Dinner was as delicious as Erica had claimed it would be. The kitchen staff at the Seasons Inn had gone all out for this dinner, making it extra special for Mallory's little sister. Theo socialized with her family like they were part of his. Everyone toasted Erica and Hayden, and then they sat through a ten-minute long photo montage of pictures of the two of them over the last four years, ending with their engagement photos.

As the night came to a close, Theo got up to talk to Mallory's dad. Avery and Chance said goodnight and took the boys to bed. Savannah, once again, looked like she was ready to hibernate for the rest of winter.

Theo returned, offering a hand to help Mallory up. Their gazes locked as she slipped her hand in his.

"Ready?" he asked.

She was ready for this dinner to be over but not ready for her time with Theo to be done. "I think I'm the only Moore sister who isn't dead on her feet."

Theo pulled her close and wrapped his other arm around her waist. He swayed to music that wasn't playing.

"What are you doing?" she giggled.

"Dancing," Theo said with a crooked grin. "Don't tell me you don't know how to dance, Mallory."

Her cheeks flushed. "Of course I do, but—"

"No buts." He spun her, and she laughed despite feeling self-conscious. His hand settled firmly on the small of her back. There was something about that spot contact that sent the butterflies in her stomach into overdrive.

Mallory felt her heart stutter when Theo leaned closer, his lips brushing her ear as he murmured, "Should we find somewhere to do a little dancing so the night doesn't have to be over?"

Her breath hitched, but before she could answer, Theo stopped. He glanced up and she followed his gaze. They had danced all the way to the spot under the mistletoe. His brown eyes locked onto hers with an intensity that made her head woozy.

"Well, would you look at that," he said, his voice low and teasing. "Looks like I took your dare, after all."

Mallory's lips parted, her pulse racing as he cupped her face gently, his thumb brushing her cheek. "You better make this good," he whispered, leaning in. "What's left of your family is watching."

The kiss was soft at first, a sweet brush of lips that deepened into something more. Mallory quickly forgot there was anyone else in the room, her hands sliding up to rest on his chest. When they finally broke apart, Theo rested his forehead against hers, a smile tugging at the corners of his mouth.

"Perfect," he said, his voice a little rough like he was affected by that kiss as much as she was.

"Remind me to dare you to do things more often."

CHAPTER FIFTEEN

CHRISTMAS EVE DAY at the Seasons Inn was a whole new experience thanks to Brady's big idea. By the look of things, Theo's brother was expecting the whole town of Apple Hollow as well as all the guests to be hanging out at the inn today.

"Thank you so much for offering to help," Alexa said, handing Theo and Mallory each their own clipboard.

"Of course! We're happy to do it," Mallory said, cheerfully.

Happy was not exactly how Theo felt about being given several jobs today. He also hadn't exactly offered as much as his brother had begged for his assistance.

The first activity of the day was checking in the people who were registered as vendors for the holiday craft bazaar that would be happening in the Four Seasons Room later today. Brady had local artisans and small businesses lined up to sell handmade ornaments, candles, baked goods, scarves and other seasonal items according to the flyer Theo was staring down at.

After that was done, he was supposed to be the surprise judge in the Ugly Sweater Parade and then the referee for the broomball game between the high school junior and senior classes, taking place on the frozen lake.

"Are we doing the same things?" he asked Mallory as she flipped through the papers on her clipboard.

"You both are going to get the vendors set up in the Four Seasons Room. Then I have you splitting up for a bit but coming back together later. Is that okay?"

"We'll be fine," Mallory assured her. "He likes to act as though he can't live without me, but he can."

Maybe not as easy as it would have been before that kiss last night. Once again, he was pretty sure she had changed his brain chemistry with those lips. Kissing Mallory was not like anything he'd experienced before. It was better in every way.

Mallory elbowed him in the ribs.

Ow. "You can count on us, Alexa," he said to avoid further violence.

Alexa smiled and started to walk away but swung back around. "Don't forget that before the fireworks at the end of the night, that's when Brady is going to announce the retirement, and we'll bring out the cake and champagne. Quinn is going to make a toast, and if you want to say something, you can as well."

Theo had looked over Quinn's speech and it was extremely heartfelt and everything that all four Seasons siblings would want to say to their parents. He only had a couple notes for his brother last night. There wasn't going to be a need for anything else to be said.

"Quinn's speech is amazing. I'm not going to try to go before or after that."

"Okay, then we're all set. Thanks again!" And Alexa was off.

It was all-hands-on-deck. There wasn't a room or a common area that wasn't being used for something related to Seasons at the Lake. They had as many employees working today as they could as well as some volunteers from the community helping out. Still, they were short, hence Theo and Mallory being put to work.

The lobby was where people picked up a list of activities and a map of the inn. They were going to have Story Time with Mrs. Claus by the fireplace before lunch. The main dining room had an area sectioned off for a hot cocoa and cookie-decorating station.

"You're the only one they need to thank for helping out," Theo said, brushing some hair out of Mallory's face. She had it half up today with some loose strands framing her face. "You're a guest here. You shouldn't be forced to man registration desks and run reindeer games."

"No one is forcing me to do anything. This is awesome. I get to be part of making the magic happen. My nephews are going to love all of this."

"Well, no doubt Erica will be excited about Christmas Karaoke and your dad is very intrigued by the ice sculpture contest. We were talking about it after dinner last night."

Mallory's head tipped slightly to the right as she narrowed her eyes. She didn't say anything for a couple seconds and then looked away.

"What?" he asked, wondering what was going on in that head of hers.

"Nothing." She shook her head.

"That look is never nothing."

She let out a breath. "I don't know. I can't get over that you know things about my family and I know things about your family. A week ago, all we really knew about each other was what we did for a living."

"I knew that you had terrible taste in music. I had to listen to it in the physical therapy room for too many hours."

She laughed and playfully punched him in the arm. "My music is good. You must be the one with bad taste."

Theo shook his head and reached for her hand.

He wasn't sure at what point that had become automatic when they were together, but he liked the physical contact. It was comfortable in a way it hadn't been just a few days ago. If he wasn't holding her hand, he was touching her back, her leg, her shoulder.

"Let's go register some crafters," he said, leading the way to the Four Seasons Room.

There were thirty vendors signed up for the bazaar. Many were shop owners from Main Street. The Apple Hollow Bakery brought a variety of goodies—cookies wrapped in cellophane and tied with colorful ribbons, mini pies decorated with Christmas-shaped piecrust cutouts and boxes of the most delicious chocolate fudge.

The Apple Hollow Knitting Club showed up with a variety of holiday-inspired blankets and crocheted pillows in the shape of Christmas trees, gingerbread men and friendly snowmen.

"I'm going to help the lady with the handmade soaps. She's all by herself, and Avery loves that kind of stuff. I want to text her some pictures of all the cute stuff she brought," Mallory said, getting up from her chair.

Theo didn't want her to go, but knew he wasn't going to stop her from being helpful. "Don't be gone too long. I loathe being all by myself."

She rolled her eyes as she tugged on the sleeves of her ivory sweater. Her sweater and dark jeans looked good on her. Getting to see her in something other than black pants and light blue Icemen polos was an added perk of bringing her along on this trip. What if he could get it put in his new contract that he could date whoever he wanted even if they worked for the organization? Would they give her grief for being with him? He would have to talk to his agent about the possibility of putting that kind of language in a new contract. *If* he got a new contract. Theo shook his head. That kind of thinking wasn't helpful.

"Hi, we're here to set up for the bazaar," someone said. As soon as Theo looked up to greet the new vendor, the woman's eyes went wide. "Oh, my gosh, are you Theo Seasons? You are, aren't you?"

"I am. And you are?"

"I am such a fan. My husband and my sons are also huge fans. We love the Icemen and we love watching you. We always tell everyone we know outside of Apple Hollow that you are from here. It's like our six degrees of separation from someone famous."

Theo smiled. Fan encounters were not something to take for granted these days. Being injured and having the future of his career up in the air meant there might not be fans soon.

"Well, I appreciate the support and I'm sure the team does as well."

"Do you think we could get a picture? Our sons

are never going to believe that we saw you. I told them that we were coming to your family's inn and maybe we would get lucky, but they thought I was just trying to get them to help me sell my ornaments."

"How old are your boys?" Theo asked.

"They're twins and they're twenty-year-olds who don't get out of bed until noon," her husband chimed in. "Having them home from college always makes me wonder if they ever make it to their morning classes."

Theo chuckled. He had skipped college, getting signed right out of high school, but he could imagine some kids weren't as disciplined as a guy getting paid to be on the ice at whatever ungodly time the coaches wanted him there.

"Maybe we should call them and tell them to get their butts out of bed. There's going to be so many cool things going on here all day long and into the night. They'll be missing out if they sleep the day away."

"You would talk to them? On the phone?" the woman said, looking like she might pass out.

Her husband noticed the same thing and held onto her to keep her steady. "We could FaceTime them. Get your phone out."

The woman started tapping on her phone. "Okay, it's ringing."

"You guys start talking and then I'll jump in," Theo said.

He heard someone answering. "What time is it?" the person asked.

"I think you and your brother should get up and come over to the Seasons Inn as soon as possible."

"Mom, come on. We're on break. Don't make us sit at a craft fair all day."

"A craft fair? This is Seasons at the Lake!" Theo said, jumping into the frame. "I heard you and your brother were big Icemen fans and you didn't even want to come and wish me a Merry Christmas?"

The kid on the screen had eyeballs the size of golf balls. "Theo Seasons?"

"The one and only. Where's your brother?"

Twin #1 scrambled out of bed and started yelling for his brother. The screen got blurry as he ran out of his room and into another one. "Isaac, get up! Mom and Dad are hanging out with Theo Seasons from the Icemen."

"Yeah, right," Twin #2, aka Isaac mumbled.

"Does your brother's word mean nothing to you, Isaac? Why would he lie?"

Said brother must have handed him the phone so he could see for himself. He threw his covers off and put on his glasses before peering at the screen like he was struggling to believe his own eyes.

"Theo Seasons? For real? Oh, my gosh! This is insane. Why are you with my parents right now?"

Theo chatted with the boys for a minute, explaining the event that was going on at his family's inn. It didn't take much convincing to get them to get out of bed and drive over to help their mom and enjoy the activities.

As he pointed out where they should set up, he spotted Mallory taking pictures of his little phone fan encounter. She had returned from the far side of the room where she'd been helping the soap lady. Her cheeks were flushed, probably from the warmth of the room and thickness of her sweater. She wore a smile that could outshine any star in the sky.

"WOULD YOU LIKE me to get a picture of you guys with Theo?" she asked the couple as she approached the table.

"That would be so awesome. Thank you." The woman took her phone back from Theo and handed it to Mallory.

There were about a million more thank-yous before they headed off to set up their booth. Mallory thought she couldn't be more smitten and then Theo made this the best Christmas ever for some fans.

"You are too cute," she admitted, sitting back down at the check-in table.

"Me? Cute?" He frowned.

That wasn't the reaction she was expecting. "What's wrong with being cute?"

"That's not the word a guy wants to be called. It's how you describe puppies and babies."

"What would you prefer I call you when you're being adorably sweet to a nice couple and their children?"

"Anything but cute," he said, squeezing her inner thigh with that giant hand of his. It wasn't cute… It was hot. It was also making her feel like she was losing her mind. Theo was a famous hockey player with fans who wanted to take his picture and get his autograph. It was unrealistic to think that they would go back to Boston and he would want to pursue something real with her.

"How's it going in here?" Theo's dad asked.

"It's going. Everyone should be set up by the time the doors open for the shoppers," Theo replied.

"Mallory, it's so nice of you to take time out of your day to help us out." Gavin Seasons looked like an older version of Theo, except a little balder and a little grayer. If that was what Theo had to look forward to looking like when he was older, he was a lucky guy. Although she kind of hoped Theo kept all his thick brown hair.

"I'm happy to do it."

"Good, because I was wondering if I could drag

you away and have you help me for a little bit. It looks like Theo has this under control."

"This is the only thing we get to do together," Theo whined. Not cute or hot, but it was a little funny. Since when did he need to be attached at the hip? "Why can't someone else help you?"

Mallory patted the hand on her leg. "You'll be okay. I bet we meet back up after the Ugly Sweater Parade and before the Broomball."

"If there was anyone else, I would have taken them, son."

Mallory said goodbye to Theo, giving him a chaste peck on the cheek before she left. It seemed like something a girlfriend would do to her boy-friend in front of his dad. They were trying to keep up pretenses. As unrealistic as this relation-ship was in Boston, they were doing well at mak-ing it look real here.

"I think I've been more surprised by Theo this visit than all the visits combined in the past. He is just absolutely a different person with you around."

"This isn't the real Theo?" she asked cautiously, not sure she wanted to hear the answer. It would make sense that he was acting out of character. It would justify all the doubts rolling around in her head day and night.

"Oh, this is the realest Theo I've seen in years!" he assured her. "You have to understand, the boy who would drop in for a hot minute and be gone the next day, that was not the real Theo. I actually started to hope he wouldn't come at all because it was so hard on his mom to see him for such a short time."

"He has said this is the longest he's been home in a while."

"As much as it makes me sad that his injury prevents him from doing what he loves, I selfishly love his company, and yours, so much more."

She couldn't hide how happy it made her to hear him say that. "Someday, hockey won't be an excuse to be gone any longer, and maybe that will make coming home easier and easier for him. He says he's having fun this year."

"Oh, he's having fun. I see it on his face every time I see you two! That boy isn't much of a smiler. He never has been, but he smiles whenever he looks at you. I'm really happy you two have found each other. He is going to need a strong partner when playing hockey is no longer an option. You seem to fit that bill."

The knot in her stomach pulled tight. She hated that it was more likely not going to be her at his side when he stepped away from the ice for good. Lying to his parents had made them believe that Theo was returning to the version of himself that they had been missing. Would he still be that person when this trip was over?

"Here we are!" Gavin said. She hadn't been paying attention to where he had been leading her. They were standing outside his office. He opened the door and flipped on the lights. "So, the person we had coming to read to the children in a half hour called and said she's unable to make it due to eating some bad tacos last night. I need someone to put on this." He grabbed the garment bag that was draped over the back of his chair. "And be Mrs. Claus for me. Are you game?"

Mallory stared at him for a moment as she processed his request. "You want me to be Mrs. Claus and read to the children?"

"Unless you know someone else who would be willing," he said with an apologetic grin.

Actually, Mallory knew the perfect person. She didn't take the garment bag but held up a finger to signal to him to give her one minute. She pulled out her phone and dialed her mom's number.

"AND I DON'T think the boys realized it was my mom. They sat there, listening to every word she read out of that book and never once said anything about Mrs. Claus being their grandmother."

The joy on Mallory's face was worth every second they had been apart. Theo's dad had pulled her away without telling her what he needed, but she had solved his problem in the best way possible. It sounded like her mom had the time of her life being Mrs. Claus during story time.

"Your mom is amazing, but how could they not know?"

"If I hadn't known, I'm not sure I would have picked up on it right away. She wore a wig with a cute bonnet and she even changed her voice. Maybe it was the glasses. She had these little round wire-rimmed glasses. Maybe Superman was onto something using glasses as a disguise."

Theo laughed as they walked through the ice sculpture displays. "Your mom Clark Kented everyone?"

Mallory's laughter mixed with his. "I think so!"

She fixed the beanie on her head and slipped her gloved hand back in his. They were using some down time to check out the ice sculptures. There were some talented people in and around Apple Hollow. The weather was perfect. Brady had lucked out—it was sunny and welcoming but cold enough that the ice sculptures held their sharp edges, and the lake remained a perfect sheet of glass for skating.

He tried not to think about how much he wanted to skate on the lake, skate anywhere actually. Growing up, he wore skates more than shoes. His knee ached as if he needed the reminder of what was keeping him off the ice.

"What's wrong?" Mallory tugged on his hand.

He shook his head. "I was trying to decide between the candy cane with the bow and the sleigh full of presents. Which one do you think is best?" he asked, steering them away from anything that had to do with his injury.

"I know they've been working on these for a few days, but all of these are incredible," Mallory replied. All week, the artists carving the ice sculptures had had access to a tent on the grounds where they could start their works of art that went on display today. "I don't know which one I would say is the best. I do like the dinosaur wearing a Santa hat."

"That is one of the better ones."

"Mallory, Theo!" Avery shouted from over by the angel ice sculpture. She carried Sebastian and Chance had a strong grip on Xavier's hand.

"Are you guys having the best time today or what?" Mallory asked Xavier when they got close enough.

"I want to come here every Christmas," the little boy said in reply.

"I will say, I don't think that Grandma and Grandpa's house will ever top Mr. Theo's inn," Avery said. "Don't tell Mom I said that, though."

Theo put his hand over his heart. "Your secret is safe with me."

"No, it's not," Mallory said to his surprise. "He's

the secret spiller. His sister told me he can't help it. It's sort of like a disorder."

"Don't you start. I will not have that lie spread about me. I can keep secrets just fine," he said, narrowing his eyes at her. She of all people should know that.

Avery took a step away from the ice sculpture that Sebastian was trying to get his little hands on. She bounced him on her hip to distract him. "This really is a lot of fun. I am truly jealous that my sister gets to come here whenever she wants. Your family knows how to make someone's vacation special."

Theo nodded. "I will pass along the compliment."

"The boys want to go play some of the reindeer games. I told them they could do the ring toss on Rudolph's nose. You two smitten kittens want to join us?" Avery asked.

Mallory released Theo's hand the moment her sister called them kittens. Wasn't that what they wanted? Didn't she need her family to believe they were in love?

"I have to go inside to judge the Ugly Sweater contest," Theo said, checking his watch. This was where he and Mallory were going to part ways again. He was truly sad about that. These feelings he had for her were making him a lovestruck fool.

"I'll meet you over there," Mallory said as he'd expected. "I'm going to walk Theo up."

They said their goodbyes and headed toward the inn. "Are you okay?" he asked her as she rubbed her arms like she'd caught a sudden chill.

"I'm sad that I actually won't get to come up here whenever I want. This place is growing on me."

Was the inn the only thing growing on her? "You're welcome anytime. My family would love it if they could entertain you all four seasons of the year."

"It won't be the same when we *break up*. No one wants to host their brother's ex. It would be awkward."

"What if you weren't my ex?" Theo said, stopping his ascent up the hill.

Mallory shook her head. "You don't really mean that. I think I've not only tricked my family, but I've tricked you into thinking you like me. Once we get back to Boston, you'll realize it was all pretend."

"What if it's not pretend, Mallory?" He was done listening to her tell him what he could or couldn't feel. It was one thing when she strong-armed him about his workouts. That was her job, to tell him what he could do. But when it came to his heart and his feelings, he was the only one who decided what he wanted.

She looked up at him with those big brown eyes. He wanted nothing more than to wipe the sadness from them. "What about the Icemen?"

"I get it. I understand that it makes this feel impossible, but what's the worst they're going to do? Fine us? I'll pay your fine and mine. They aren't going to fire two people who contribute to the organization just because they fell in love."

Her eyes were as wide as saucers. "They what?"

He didn't mean to spring feelings that strong on her. He was still trying to give what he felt a name. "You know what I mean. They aren't going to fire people because they started having feelings for one another. That doesn't happen."

"I don't know. I think that we both signed contracts that say it can."

"If they try to fire you, I'll threaten to quit. They won't let that happen. I just think that there's something pushing us together that's bigger than both of us. I can't fight it off anymore. I like you. I like you a lot. So much I don't want you to go play reindeer games with your sister and her family. I want you to stay with me and judge ugly sweaters. I want to be with you. There, I said it."

Mallory bit down on her bottom lip. She seemed to be wrestling against those feelings a little bit more than he was willing to. He was just about to tell her it was okay if she wasn't ready when she wrapped her arms around his neck and kissed him like it was the only thing she wanted to do for the rest of the day.

"I can't believe this is happening," she said, breathless. She loosened her hold on him, but that only encouraged him to tighten his. "I want to be with you, too. You told me you weren't going to make me fall in love with you. I hope that's the last time you lie to me."

Theo kissed her lips one more time. "Last one."

Mallory's smile lit up her whole face. It felt amazing to be the one who helped put it there. She took his hand and tugged him back up the hill to the inn. "Let's go judge some ugly sweaters."

THE REST OF the day went by in a blur of Christmas cheer. Mallory had eaten one too many cookies and drank her fill of hot chocolate. She and Theo had gone inside and outside and inside again.

Mallory didn't know Brady very well, but based on seeing how happy he was when Alexa accepted his proposal, today had to be the second best day of his life. This event had been his idea according to his brother, and he was clearly proud of what he had accomplished.

Theo's whole family had been gleeful busy bees all day. Maybe that was because the whole town and all the guests at the Seasons Inn were having a ball. Mallory's family had been completely entertained.

Everyone was gathered back outside for the grand finale. It was time to toast Theo's parents and shoot off some fireworks. The temperature had fallen a bit with the sun having set, but bundled up in her goose-down jacket, hat and gloves, Mallory was very comfortable. It might have helped to have a muscular professional hockey player wrapped around her as well.

They were doing this. They were going to stop pretending and do this dating thing for real. It felt a little less stressful to only have to lie about when they started dating and not that they were. Theo promised they would try to talk to the powers that be within the Icemen organization when they returned to Boston.

"Okay, we need the family to all be on the patio in five minutes," Alexa said, as she fluttered around the lawn, making sure everyone was where they were supposed to be.

Mallory spun around to face her *real* boyfriend. "You should go. I'll find my family," she said.

"You can come up with me on the patio."

"I know we're doing this, but I don't think we're at the standing-up-with-the-family-during-a-momentous-event stage yet."

He rested his forehead on hers. Their breaths were visible and mingled together. "Fine. But as soon as this part of the evening is over, maybe you and I can find somewhere we can go to be alone?

I feel like we've been surrounded by a hundred people all day."

Mallory laughed. "Maybe because we have been." He wanted to spend some time with her alone. How was this real life? "I am picturing the couch in your suite, soft blankets and a Christmas movie on the television."

"It's a date." He kissed her lips and let her go. "Find me after the toast."

She promised she would and watched him go join his family on the patio. She pulled out her phone and used her teeth to tug off her glove so she could text her sisters to see where they were.

"Right behind you!" Savannah called out, making Mallory jump. The whole gang was with her. "Where did Theo run off to?"

"They are going to announce their parents' retirement and do a toast before the fireworks."

The Moores all huddled together and couldn't stop talking about how much fun they'd had. It was the most exciting Christmas Eve in history. Mallory had her arms linked with Savannah and Erica, and they were all bouncing on the balls of their feet to stay warm.

"I was so mad at you for ditching us for Christmas." Savannah leaned into her sister. "But I am so glad you did and that we crashed your party. This has been the best. Mom is ready to move here."

Mallory tipped her head and scrunched her face. "I don't know about moving here, but I am sure the Seasons would love to see her again." Now that she and Theo were going to try to be serious, there was a possibility of coming back. "Maybe we can vacation up here in the summer. Alexa was telling me all about the fun things there are to do that time of year."

"And to think you thought she was faking it," Erica said to Savannah.

Mallory stopped bouncing and her heart stuttered in her chest. "What?"

Erica continued, "Savannah thought you were just trying to get out of Christmas with the family. She thought there was no boyfriend, and then when you introduced us to Theo, she thought he was pretending to be your boyfriend so Mom didn't disown you."

"So I didn't do what?" asked their mom, coming up behind them.

Mallory was still spinning from the fact that Savannah knew exactly what she had done without knowing she had been right. Erica was right, too. Mom would disown her if she knew the truth.

"We were just saying that we didn't think you were going to get out of that costume today," Mallory said to deflect. "You are the best Mrs. Claus I have ever seen."

Their mom wore a megawatt smile. "I had the best time. Did Avery show you the pictures?"

"They were priceless," Mallory said, feeling this weird mixture of guilt and gratitude. Lying was wrong, but she was so thankful that everything she'd done had led her to this moment.

Her family had been allowed to have experiences they never would have gotten had she not taken Theo up on his offer to come home with him. Everything about this vacation had been magical. Maybe no one would have to know that it started out the way it had if what Mallory and Theo had now could stay real.

Their mom was quickly distracted by Sebastian asking for Nana to hold him just as Brady came over a loudspeaker.

"Good evening, Apple Hollow and our fine guests here at the Seasons Inn!"

Savannah nudged Mallory. "Don't be mad that I didn't believe you. You have to know it was kind of an unbelievable story."

Unbelievable because it wasn't true. Mallory felt the guilt climb back up her spine and lay heavy on her shoulders. "You don't have to apologize, Sav. I wouldn't have believed me, either."

Savannah's eyes narrowed before she offered her a tight-lipped smile. Brady was thanking all the people who helped make today a possibility.

They'd had sponsors from local businesses and lots of volunteers.

"Most importantly, I want to thank the two people who, without them, none of this would be possible. My parents, Gavin and Laura Seasons!"

The crowd clapped and cheered. It reminded Mallory of the applause Theo got at the rink. Everyone in the Seasons family was beloved by this community. Laura looked embarrassed by all the attention. She was shielding herself with Gavin's larger frame.

"Some of you might be aware and some of you may not, but at the end of the year, my parents are going to be stepping away from the family business. They have decided to retire while they are still young. What they don't know is that we couldn't have them leave without giving them a little goodbye party."

The expressions on Gavin and Laura's faces meant that the surprise had been successful. They'd had no idea they were about to get celebrated. Nora and Alexa brought two chairs out and had the guests of honor take a seat.

Brady's grin said he was pleased with himself. "We have some people who would like to say a few things before we really get this party going with some fireworks."

Brady invited two people to come up along with Quinn, who was going to speak on behalf of the family. The first person to speak was the mayor of Apple Hollow. She let everyone know that the Seasons Inn was a treasured part of the town, and a lot of that had to do with Laura and Gavin. She spoke of the ways they gave back to the community and how the inn provided jobs to locals and brought in guests from all over so they could experience everything that Apple Hollow had to offer.

Next up was Maureen, the very first person Mallory had met when she arrived at the inn. Maureen had worked at the inn for the longest. She spoke about the kind of employers the Seasonses were. How humble and understanding they were. She relayed a few examples of how they went above and beyond to make sure the people who worked there knew they were the reason the Seasons Inn was the best hotel in all of New Hampshire, all of New England if Maureen had anything to say about it.

Last up was Quinn. He accepted a hug from Maureen before taking the microphone from her. While Gavin and Laura gave her a hug, thanking her for her kind words, Quinn spoke to the crowd first. "My name is Quinn, and I am the oldest child of Gavin and Laura. My siblings and I would like to thank everyone for their kind words today and for the love you have always shown our parents and this inn."

The crowd once again whooped and hollered.

Quinn continued, "This was a hard speech to write. On one hand, I know how important it is that we're celebrating your retirement. This is the long-awaited moment when you finally get to take some time for yourselves. On the other hand, we're marking the end of an era, an era shaped by your incredible dedication, your amazing vision and your overwhelming love for this place."

Nora gave her mom some tissues. Poor Laura was already crying. Mallory tried to catch Theo's eye, but he was focused on Quinn.

"This inn isn't just a building or a business. It's your legacy. It's a place where families have gathered, some love stories have started and countless memories have been made. It's a home, not just for me, Brady, Theo and Nora, but for everyone who's ever walked through those doors. We all have you two to thank for that. I also want to thank you for teaching us how to do what you do. You didn't just teach us how to run an inn, though. You taught us about hard work, about kindness, about perseverance. You set standards, not just for this place but for us as people. Standards we're proud to live by."

That was the moment that Theo's gaze landed on Mallory. She smiled at him and he smiled back.

"I speak for all your children when I say that we hope you thoroughly enjoy this next phase of your life. I promise, *we* promise, to maintain the integrity of what you've built here."

A giant cake that was a replica of the Seasons Inn was wheeled out. There were lit sparklers on top. The waitstaff from the dining room were roaming the lawn, passing out little glasses of champagne to the guests. Brady handed Quinn one at the same time Theo gave his parents each one.

"If everyone could please raise your glasses. Here's to you, Mom and Dad. To the love you've poured into this place, to the memories you've created and to the new chapter you're about to begin. Thank you for everything. We hope to make you as proud as you have made us. To Laura and Gavin!"

Everyone who had a glass held it up. Mallory and her sisters clinked glasses before taking a sip. The whole Seasons family was hugging. That had been such a lovely tribute to them. Snow started to fall like confetti as if on cue. It was coming down in fat fluffy flakes.

Brady took the microphone back. "Let's celebrate!" And with that, the fireworks went off over the lake. Everyone turned around so they could watch, but Mallory's eyes were still glued to the family on the patio.

Could she be so lucky to be welcomed into that family someday? The Seasonses were everything she could hope for in a second family. There was part of her that worried she was being set up for something that was going to leave her sadder than she could imagine. The way they did this, meeting each other's family before they ever realized they liked one another, changed the stakes of this relationship. If it didn't work out, it wasn't just Theo she would lose. It was the possibility of being part of something more.

She turned around and watched the beautiful bursts of colored lights flash above the frozen lake. For now, she would enjoy the view. The worry and anxiety would still be there tomorrow.

CHAPTER SIXTEEN

THE RINGING OF Theo's phone pulled him from his restful slumber. When he opened his eyes to silence the stupid thing, he realized he was not in his bed. The warm body pressed against him also clued him into the fact that he wasn't alone. He was on the couch in his suite and Mallory was cuddled up with him fast asleep. She was a heavy sleeper if neither his phone's ringtone nor the television was having any impact on her snooze.

They had stayed up and watched a movie last night after all the Seasons at the Lake activities finally ended for the day. Apparently, they had both been more exhausted than they thought they were and had fallen asleep. His phone stopped ringing, the call going to voicemail. He had moved enough, though, to rouse Mallory.

As soon as she realized what had happened, she bolted upright. Her questions coming in quick succession. "What happened? What time is it? Why did you let me fall asleep?"

Theo rubbed his eyes and began the search for

the phone under the blankets. His phone had been in his hand. It probably fell when he sunk into a dreamless sleep. He found it between the couch cushions.

"Nine in the morning," he reported.

"Nine? I'm supposed to meet my family to open presents right now." She was up and moving, looking for her own phone and then trying to get her boots on. "I can't believe this happened. It's Christmas. We should have been more aware of what was happening."

Theo furrowed his brow. "I don't think you can blame us for not being aware that we fell asleep. That's how sleep works, you aren't aware it's happening until you wake up."

She pulled one of her boots on and started tying the laces. Her hair was an adorable mess and she had sleep lines on her cheek. "You know what I mean. We should have been careful about not letting ourselves drift off. I should have gotten up as soon as I felt my eyes getting heavy."

Theo got up and stretched his arms above his head, yawning. "I promise that no one is going to be mad at you for sleeping a little later than you were supposed to. Why don't you text them and apologize. Let them know we'll be there in less than a half hour."

"We?"

"Am I not invited to present opening? I have

presents for you and your family to open. I also know that you have a present for me to open. One that took you…what was it…twenty minutes to pick out?"

He loved the way her scowl made her even cuter than she was. "Do not tease me before I've had some coffee, Santa. Of course, you're invited. I thought you might want to spend Christmas morning with *your* family."

His family were the ones calling him this morning—Brady to be exact. "I think they might also be looking for us."

"Us?"

"You know you are always welcome to anything my family does together. They basically expect it." He walked over to the closed curtains and drew them open. He was met with a view of a winter apocalypse. "Oh, boy, looks like it's a blizzard out there."

It started to snow during the fireworks and must not have stopped. Snow was swirling and there were inches upon inches of fresh snow on the ground.

Mallory came up beside him. "Holy moly. Good thing this wasn't in the forecast yesterday."

"Hope you were dreaming about a white Christmas."

She smiled up at him. He loved her smile more than her scowl now that she was wearing it.

"Well, *we* have two Christmases to go to. What should we do?" she asked, looping her arm with his.

Theo kissed her on the forehead. "I think I have an idea."

Thirty minutes later, Mallory's and Theo's families were all gathered in the cozy dining room where they'd had dinner to celebrate Erica and Hayden's engagement. The fireplace was roaring and everyone was mingling.

Sebastian and Xavier were busy playing with the toys that Santa had brought to their room overnight. They thought it was pretty cool that Santa had figured out how to find them when they weren't at a house.

Theo's family had been paying better attention to the weather reports than he had. They had all stayed at the inn last night instead of going back to the house. The whole county was under a blizzard warning, so no one was coming to or leaving the inn today.

"So, we just got up early and made a breakfast buffet for the guests," his mom was explaining to Selene. "We're going to have to get creative for lunch and dinner. I don't think we can expect anyone from town to travel in this storm to come in for work."

"Please know that we are all willing to help in whatever way we can. I miss cooking for a crowd, and nobody loads a dishwasher quite like William."

"That's so very kind of you."

"It's Christmas," Selene said. "And *a blizzard*. I think people are going to be understanding that things might have to be done a little differently and we're all going to need to chip in."

Theo's mom squeezed Selene's hand appreciatively. He knew both his parents were going to struggle with not being able to provide guests with the best of the best. As Quinn said last night, they set high standards for themselves.

"Are we opening presents before or after I deliver this baby?" Savannah asked, earning a laugh from many around the room.

Selene suggested that due to the size of the group they all open at the same time. Everyone was on board with that idea. Mallory and Nora worked together to sort all the gifts by person. Theo checked the gift label every time one was put in front of him. As soon as he saw Mallory's name, he was surprised by how big it was. The box was over two feet wide and almost two feet tall. Its width was slim, though. He gave it a little shake.

"You will not be able to guess, so don't even try," Mallory said as she continued playing Santa's elf.

He was going to save that gift for last. Once they finished sorting all the gifts, there was a flurry of

unwrapping. Ribbon and paper littered the ground.
Oohs and ahhs were quickly followed by thank-
yous and you're-welcomes. Avery clapped when
she opened something she liked. Nora cried when
she opened the gift from their parents. Hayden
laughed when he got the same shirt Greg and
Chance had both gotten when they joined the family, which said I'm My Mother-In-Law's Favorite
Child.

Mallory did the same thing Theo did. She saved
his gifts for last. "Looks like we're down to the
final gifts."

"Looks like it. You go first since you have more
than one to open from me."

Theo had gotten her three things. He hoped
she understood his sense of humor for the first
one. Mallory picked up the smallest box first and
unwrapped it. It was a book about the greatest
hockey stories ever told. He had found the only
copy they had at the local bookstore.

She raised an eyebrow. "Will I find you in this
book, Mr. Seasons?"

"Although I am quite the superstar, I have not
yet been memorialized in the greatest hockey stories ever. Maybe when they come out with vol-
ume two, I'll have a shot. I just wanted you to
learn more about the game, since you work for
a hockey team and are dating a hockey player. A
little knowledge can go a long way."

The second gift was a bit more on the practical side but still hockey-related. He had noticed that she didn't have a scarf when they had spent time outside. One of the little shops in town had hand-knit ones in all different colors.

"I am picking up on a theme. Teal, white and gray. These are the Icemen colors." She wrapped it around her neck and threw the last bit over her shoulder with flair. "I love it. Now, you open yours before I open my last one."

He was excited to see what she'd gotten him, so he didn't argue. He ripped off the paper to find an unmarked box inside. No hints that would tell him what it was holding. When he opened one end of the box, he could see the frame first. It was a picture of something. Theo slid it out of the box and was speechless.

"What is it?" someone asked from across the room.

Theo smiled as he took it all in. He had lived in Apple Hollow for the first eighteen years of his life and had never seen anything like this.

"It's an artist's rendition of a map of Apple Hollow," Mallory explained. "It includes the Seasons Inn and the ice arena. It's got Main Street and all the fun shops. The green, the town hall."

Brady came up behind Theo and so did Quinn. "Look, there's the high school," Brady said, pointing to it on the map.

"I struggled with what to get the guy who can buy anything he wants whenever he wants. After listening to your stories about the ice arena and growing up around here, it dawned on me that home was something you can't usually get your hands on. I thought this would be a sweet reminder of the real thing."

No one outside of his family had ever been so thoughtful. "I love it," he said, setting it down so he could give Mallory a hug.

He suddenly felt self-conscious about the last gift she had to open from him. The map should have been the last gift since it was the best. Everyone else was finished, so they were all watching.

Mallory peeled back the wrapping paper on the gift. Under the paper was a box that read Apple Hollow Sporting Goods. She lifted the lid and pulled out the teal jersey with the number seventeen on the back and arms. It helped being the hometown guy. The small sporting goods store in town luckily carried a bunch of merchandise with his name and number on it.

"So when a guy wants to go out exclusively with a certain girl, he gives her his number to wear. It means he belongs to her."

"Aw, that's sweet. He wants to go steady with you," Selene said. "Wait, weren't you already exclusive?"

Mallory held Theo's gaze. "Don't overthink it, Mom," she said with a crooked smile.

MALLORY LOVED THAT Theo gave her his jersey, asking her to be his girlfriend officially. No one else understood how significant it was except for the two of them. She would proudly wear his number and let the world know he was hers.

The whole group turned into every dad on Christmas morning and started picking up the discarded wrapping paper, bows and ribbons. The inn was already short-staffed thanks to the weather; there was no way they were going to leave this room before they cleaned it all up.

Quinn's phone chimed with an incoming text. His brow furrowed as he read it. "Sounds like the storm is causing some trouble. Jonah just texted me that the highway into this area is completely shut down. There are some downed trees blocking everything coming in and going out. He wanted us to have a heads-up in case we have guests who are checking out tomorrow. There's no way anyone can go south."

"Who's Jonah?" Mallory asked Theo.

"He's a friend of Quinn's. He's a state trooper, I think." Theo moved closer to his brother. "What do you mean no one can go south? They'll have it cleared by tomorrow, right?"

"It's a blizzard out there, Theo. How could they

clear it in the middle of a blizzard? Hate to break it to you but looks like you're stuck in Apple Hollow a little longer than you planned. Since it's an act of God, I'll give you a hefty discount on your rooms for the extra days."

"You better not be charging him for their rooms," Gavin said. "That better be a joke."

It looked like Theo was hoping all of this was a joke. "Days? I need to be back in Boston for the game on Saturday."

"There's no way out of here other than the highway, Theo," Brady chimed in. "If you went north and tried to cut east or west on some of those rural roads, you'd just run into trouble. No way any of those are going to get cleared anytime soon. You're going to have to wait it out."

"Great." Theo pulled out his phone and started texting someone. Mallory's guess was someone at the Icemen organization.

They were snowed in, and no one was sure for how long. Quinn's phone chimed again. "Oh, boy," he said, reading and replying. "Jonah said good thing we got that new roof this fall. He heard on the police radio that the arena's roof collapsed. Major damage. No one was in there at that time, but it was so loud people nearby thought there was an avalanche."

"The arena?" Theo looked up from his phone. "I better call Hank."

"Thank goodness it's Christmas and he wasn't there," Mallory said. Given the condition of the arena, it wasn't a surprise that something like this could do some damage to it. That's going to be a huge mess to clean up and an even more expensive one to fix. Poor Hank.

"We should figure out a way to pass along some information to the guests throughout the day. We need to make sure people know about the road being out," Gavin said, snapping into action. He apologized for having to break up the celebration, but he and his family needed to take care of inn business.

"So much for the poor guy's last few days before retirement being peaceful and quiet," Alexa said to Mallory after Brady kissed her goodbye.

Mallory shook her head. "Nothing like a blizzard, a lockdown and no staff to help keep this place running."

"Well, we're not going to sit here and do nothing," Mallory's mom said. "We are all capable of helping out. Why should those five be left to manage everything alone? Who is with me?"

The four sisters exchanged glances. Their mother was not going to let them out of this one. Today, they would offer up their able bodies and pitch in wherever Gavin and Laura needed them.

"We're in," the four of them said at the same time.

CHAPTER SEVENTEEN

CHRISTMAS DAY WAS full of ups and downs. As frustrated as Theo was that they were stuck in Apple Hollow for another couple days, there were worse things than getting to spend time with Mallory. By noon, the storm had passed and everything was eerily still outside. The whole town was blanketed in a thick layer of new snow. It was strange that something that could appear so beautifully serene could also be so angry and dangerous under certain circumstances.

It was easy to feel helpless in these situations. People couldn't control the weather. Theo decided that he liked the way Selene looked at things. When there was a problem, be part of the solution. It was as simple as that. The Moores had pitched in and helped the Seasons family keep the inn's dining room up and running, which allowed for Quinn and Nora to man the front desk.

Theo's mind was on a different problem. He was focused on how to be part of the solution to some of Hank's problems. He'd immediately decided that he was going to make a substantial contribution to the renovation fund. Theo was going to make sure Hank had everything he needed to make Apple Hollow's Ice Arena the greatest facility in New England.

Of course, the old man's biggest worry was that games and practices wouldn't be able to go on. There certainly was no way the game against the Snow Tigers could take place tomorrow as planned. Theo had a vested interest in seeing that at least this one game was played at home instead of at the Snow Tiger's rink.

"What about having the game here?" Theo asked his dad as he followed him around the dining room while Gavin refilled guests' water glasses.

"Having it here, where?" his dad asked, heading back to the kitchen to get more water.

"On the ice where we had the broomball game on Christmas Eve. We can clear the snow and smooth out the surface like we did before. We can make a snow barrier and they can play pond hockey."

"Theo, that's a big job, son. I don't know."

"I've got Hayden, Greg and Chance ready to help me. Brady and Wade have already started clearing the parking lot and walkways of snow. It'll be like when the NHL does the Winter Classic. It'll be fun."

His dad chuckled. "Your idea of fun and my idea of fun are very different. It's cold out there and people are buried under all this snow."

"More reason for them to want something positive to look forward to. Everyone from Belmont should be able to drive down here. The roads will be clear between here and there by tomorrow."

That caught his dad's attention. "I thought you were hoping to be back in Boston by Saturday?"

"With the highway closed south of here, it's unlikely I'll get out of here before the weekend is over. Might as well just plan on staying. If I'm staying, I want to see this through."

"If you think you can make it work, you should try to make it work," his dad said. "But can you go get busy with that or else I'm going to put you to work in here."

Theo showed his palms and backed away. He was not built to work at the inn like his siblings. Turning the lake into an ice rink was way more his style. That was what he was going to do.

They finished with clearing enough space for a rink and smoothing it out before dark. Mallory and Erica brought them hot chocolate as they were wrapping up. Mallory had her red jacket on along with her new teal, white and gray scarf. He liked having such a helpful girlfriend.

"Can I keep you?" he asked as he took the cup from her.

"I think it's more like you're stuck with me. Literally. We can't leave."

He gave her a kiss on the cheek, which felt

warm against his lips. He had been outside for so long that he was having flashbacks to being in the ice bath back at the Icemen training facility. "I'm ready to go sit by a fire all night or at least until I defrost."

"Let's get you inside. You really outdid yourself. The kids are going to be so excited about this. As if you didn't already have hero status—this is going to make you a hockey god."

Theo shook his head. All he wanted was for the kids on the Howlers to have fun and give it their best against the Snow Tigers tomorrow. He didn't need any of this to be about him.

They got inside and peeled off their jackets and gloves. The men had worked up an appetite. Staff for the inn had arrived for the dinner shift, so it was almost business as usual in the main dining room. Greg, Chance and Hayden had been a huge help. He owed them dinner and drinks. Mallory's sisters had chosen well. Hopefully, they felt the same way about him and Mallory.

Chance was the first to head up. He needed to go help get the boys ready for bed. Greg was soon to follow. Hayden and Erica hung around.

"Well, after everything you did to help today, I think the least I can do is get you two seats on the glass the next time you come to Boston," Theo said. "I can even get you VIP and you can come see the locker room, meet some of the players."

Hayden's eyes went wide. "Seriously? That is so awesome. Mallory has helped us get tickets before but front row on the glass with access to the locker room. That's incredible."

"Sorry my position with the organization isn't quite as prestigious as his," Mallory teased her soon-to-be brother-in-law. "To think you *only* got to go to a game."

"Stop," Erica said, tossing a balled-up napkin at her sister. "You know we appreciated what you did, but you can't deny your boyfriend gets the awesome perks."

Mallory leaned into Theo. "My boyfriend gets the best perks."

Boyfriend. He was someone's boyfriend. A little ball of anxiety rolled around his stomach. He didn't have a good track record of being a good boyfriend. There had never been a woman who inspired him to be one. Mallory was different. Her family was different. What if he didn't live up to their expectations?

Mallory smiled at him and it was electric. She believed in him now. He'd have to make sure he didn't blow it.

MALLORY WAS CERTAIN there was nothing that would ever top this year's Christmas. It had been a wild ride, and the thrill of it continued into the next day. Theo and her family had done an amazing job prepping the ice for this hockey game. She was feeling nervous for the team, but excited to be a part of it all. The kids were already warming up, their laughter and the scrape of blades echoed across the winter air.

She wasn't the only one who was battling some nerves. She glanced over at Theo, who stood near the sideline. His brown hair was ruffled slightly by the breeze and his brows furrowed in concentration. He'd been stressing about the game all morning, determined to make everything perfect. From working with Brady and Hayden to resurface the ice to giving the kids tips on how to adjust to playing on a lake, he'd been hyper-focused on making today a success.

"I think this is going to be their day," Mallory said, sidling up beside him. "I mean, Apple Hollow deserves a win, don't you think? Mother Nature owes us one for trashing the rink."

Theo chuckled, the tension visibly leaving his body. "You might be right. But if they're going to win, they need to remember the basics. This isn't like playing on an arena surface. No boards to save you if you overshoot, and the ice is a little less forgiving."

Or a lot less. As if to prove his point, one of the kids skated past the puck and tumbled onto the ice with a loud thump when he tried to correct himself. He popped up quickly, brushing snow off his pants.

Theo cupped his hands around his mouth to call out, "Heads-up, Tyler! Keep your knees bent and your weight forward!"

Mallory's heart was so full, seeing him like this, in his element. It was why she had fallen for him so fast. The kids respected him and took every bit of advice he offered. Just like at the practice before Christmas, he balanced authority with encouragement so perfectly, making each of those kids feel like they could contribute to the team's success.

The game began with a whistle, and the tension in the air shifted. Mallory's family and Theo's family were all standing with her in the viewing area on the lake's shoreline. Her eyes tried to follow the puck as it skittered across the ice. The Snow Tigers came out strong, pushing the Howlers into defensive mode. The kids from Belmont weren't undefeated because of luck. They were big and fast.

"Come on, Kayla," Theo called out as number forty-four skated after the puck. She may have been the only girl on the team, but she had taken to her new position as center like she had been playing it her entire hockey life. However, even Kayla was struggling to adjust to the lake's quirks. She overshot her passes and misjudged her angles without being able to play off the boards. Theo was right; pond hockey wasn't the same.

"They all look a little nervous," Hayden said as Kayla hesitated before making her next move.

"Don't overthink it!" Theo's brown eyes were fixed on the ice. "Find that grit!"

His words had an immediate impact; Kayla snapped out of her hesitation and intercepted a pass. She maneuvered around two defenders before firing a shot at the net. The Snow Tigers' goalie blocked it and the Howlers' side of the crowd groaned.

Theo clapped his hands and shouted, "There it is, Kayla! Keep that up!"

Mallory watched as the Howlers began to find their rhythm. Theo's pregame advice seemed to sink in, and the kids started using the open ice to their advantage. Tyler redeemed himself with a clean steal, passing the puck to Kayla, who set up an assist that tied the game.

By the final minutes of the third period, the score was tied 2–2. The crowd of parents and hotel guests cheered from the sidelines, bundled up in scarves and mittens, their excitement helping the players dig deep for that last bit of energy.

Kayla had the puck again. She used her skills with her stick to weave through the other team's defense. Mallory held her breath as Kayla faked left, then right, leaving the two boys trying to stop her confused and beat. She raced toward the net, nothing but pure determination on her face.

"Come on, Kayla," Mallory whispered, gripping her sister's hand tightly.

With a flick of her wrist, Kayla sent the puck sailing past the goalie and into the back of the net. The crowd erupted in cheers as Kayla raised her stick and her teammates circled her in celebration.

Mallory and her sisters jumped up and down, hugging and cheering for these kids they didn't even know. When she glanced over at Theo, he was staring right at her. His face split into a grin that made her stomach flip.

She ran over to where he was. "They did it!"

"They sure did," Theo said, and before she could process what was happening, he grabbed her by the waist and pulled her close.

Her heart skipped a beat as his hand came up to cup her cheek. "Mallory," he said a bit breathlessly.

"What?" she asked, her voice barely above a whisper.

He didn't answer. Instead, his lips met hers in a kiss that was as sweet as it was unexpected. The world around them seemed to disappear, the cheers of the crowd fading into the background as she kissed him back with the same level of adoration.

When they finally broke apart, Theo's hand lingered on her cheek, his eyes searching hers. Mallory felt heat creeping up her neck, but she couldn't bring herself to look away.

"You helped them do that, you know. I saw how they responded to your coaching today."

"That was the most fun I have had in a long time," Theo replied, his smile a bit more vulnerable than before.

"Coach Theo, we did it!" one of the kids shouted, as they all skated over to where the two of them were standing. Theo released her so he could greet the team. He high-fived kids left and right, telling them all what an amazing job they had done. Parents took pictures of the team with their special guest star coach. Mallory took out her phone so Theo would always have this memory to look back on.

As the ice cleared and the kids went off with their smiling parents, Theo went to retrieve a puck that had skidded off into the deep snow. He jogged toward the edge of the lake, but Mallory's stomach dropped as he lost his footing for a second and had to catch himself. Almost instantly, he bent over with his hands on his knee.

"Theo!" She hurried over to him.

He tried to wave her off, his jaw clenched. "I'm fine," he said, though the strain in his voice told a different story. He was crouched in the snow, gripping his bad knee.

"You're not fine," she said, kneeling beside him. "You slipped and I saw it bend when you caught yourself."

"It's fine," he snapped, pulling away. "It's just a little stiff."

Mallory's heart pounded in her chest. "If you did something to it, we need to address it right—"

"I said I'm fine," he interrupted, his tone sharper than ever. He stood, wincing as he put weight on his leg.

He was trying so hard to mask his pain. This was not the way she wanted to end this day. This huge win should not be overshadowed by the reminder that his knee could be the end of his career. "Do you want me to ask Brady to come help you?"

He looked at her and she saw the fear hiding behind the frustration. "Just give me a second. I don't need anyone to make a big deal about this. There are people looking. Please, stop fussing over me."

She let him limp away from her. The physical therapist in her said that this wasn't just a flare up. She had seen it, the way his foot came down and how he was a little twisted trying to keep his balance. Limping was not his style. He would only do that if it was bad.

Mallory stayed frozen in place, the warmth of their kiss now a distant memory as a knot settled in her stomach. The girlfriend she had only just become told her that a reinjured Theo was going to be very different from the one she had been falling for. Hopefully, he would let her in and not continue to push her away.

CHAPTER EIGHTEEN

THE PAIN IN his knee was excruciating. There was something very wrong. He could lie to Mallory all he wanted, but he couldn't lie to himself. He had jogged across the ice to get that puck like there was no reason to be cautious. One second later, he was off balance and about to fall. He probably should have let himself fall over. If he had done that, he wouldn't have come down on his knee in that awkward position.

He iced it when he got back to his room. He did everything Mallory would have told him to do if he had let her in instead of pushing her away. He hadn't meant to snap at her. His pride got in the way and his fear made him flustered. She didn't deserve any of his ire, though.

There was a knock at his door on Saturday morning. Mallory had given him the space he had asked for, and now he was hoping she was out there forcing him to let her in. He would let her.

He hobbled over to the door only to find Nora

on the other side. "What's going on?" she asked as he backed away and limped over to the couch.

"I slipped on the ice yesterday and now I'm paying for it."

"I know what happened to your knee, Theo. I was there. We all were. I'm talking about why I just talked to Mallory and she told me you've been hiding in here since yesterday. Do not let this injury ruin things for you. I was super suspicious about this relationship you sprung on us when you first got here, but Mallory is one of the nicest people I have ever met. You do not want to scare this woman away by being your cantankerous self."

"I thought that was a word we only used to describe Quinn," he tried to joke.

Nora crossed her arms over her chest. She was dressed in her uniform, so she must have left her post by the front desk to scold him. "Exactly. Don't be bitter like him. I can only take one brother with that kind of attitude."

Theo rubbed his head with his hand, mussing his hair in the process. "I know. I'll do better. I just need my knee to not blow up my life right now. I need to get better and get back on the ice. I miss it so much, Nora. I can't even put it in words. It's like if Mom and Dad told you they were selling the inn and you had to find a new job somewhere else. What would you do? Just go work at a different hotel? Can you imagine not being the concierge of the Seasons Inn?"

Indignation turned to understanding. His sister came to sit next to him on the couch. "I can't imagine that. I don't want to work anywhere but here. I know that hockey means something more to you than a job. It always has."

"I don't know who I am if I am not a hockey player. That's who Theo Seasons is. He's a hockey player."

"Theo Seasons is also a brother and a son. He's a friend. He's Mallory's boyfriend. I can see how she feels about you by the way she looks at you. She has fallen for you, and it doesn't have anything to do with Theo Seasons, the hockey player. It's about Theo, the man."

He let out a deep sigh. He wanted to believe everything she said was true. For the first time, he had a woman who wanted to be with him for a lot of reasons that had nothing to do with how he played hockey. In fact, being a hockey player was why she hadn't wanted to get together in real life.

"Can I ask you something and can you be totally honest with me?" Nora asked. Her eyes were gentle like their mom's. It made it impossible to refuse her sometimes.

"Sure…"

"You and Mallory didn't come here as a couple, did you?"

"What makes you ask that?" He figured answering her question with a question was a better plan than risking a lie or the truth.

"Your face when she first introduced you to her family. Actually, your face pretty much the whole first day you were here. The way you look at her now tells me something has changed. In a good way for you," she added quickly "but there was something that first day."

"You cannot tell anyone else anything I'm about to tell you."

As soon as the words left his mouth, she was on her feet celebrating that she was right. "I knew it!"

"I'm serious, Nora. Mallory would be so embarrassed."

His sister sat back down, still bouncing with excitement. "I promise. I won't say a word. I'm not the secret spiller in the family."

Her little dig almost stopped him from telling her. His expression must have darkened because she immediately started apologizing. "I'm sorry. I didn't mean that. You have done a really good job keeping this secret. I promise if you confide in me, I'll keep it to myself."

"Fine. Mallory was trying to avoid the chaos at her parents' house this Christmas. She was feeling a little overwhelmed, so she told her mom that she had a boyfriend and was meeting his parents up here at the inn. That was the only excuse Selene would accept since she's kind of obsessed with getting Mallory married off."

Nora nodded. "I can believe that about Selene. She wants her girls to be happy and I bet she thinks happily married is the best version of happy."

"That's my understanding. All I knew at the beginning of December was that Mallory was free to continue my PT over the holidays. I got her a room, and the plan was I would pay for her room and board and she would help me stay on track with therapy."

"But the Moores thought she was meeting her boyfriend and decided to surprise her by booking rooms here as well. Ah…that's why you looked absolutely confused."

Theo chuckled. "Yeah, confused is one way to put it. I had no clue what was going on and I felt really bad about lying to you and the rest of the family, especially Mom. She was so hurt that I didn't tell her I was bringing my girlfriend home."

Nora scrunched her nose. "Yeah, she said something to me about it. She couldn't believe none of us knew."

There was a part of him that wished he could go back in time and do things differently. The only reason he wouldn't was because they might not have gotten together for real if they hadn't had to pretend.

"I can't believe you didn't call me out earlier. I was waiting for you to corner me," he said, wincing as he adjusted his position on the couch.

"Do you need to go to a doctor?"

Her concern made him irrationally angry. He refused to believe this was as bad as her face implied she thought it was. "It's fine."

"Will you please talk to Mallory? Let her know you're *fine*. Don't let your fear mess this thing up." Nora stood up and started for the door. "I haven't seen you smile as much as you have the last couple days around her."

"I will find her and apologize for being cantankerous like Quinn."

Nora smiled. "See ya later, secret spiller."

Theo threw one of the pillows on the couch at her, hitting the door as she hurried out, laughing.

"I DESERVE THIS," Avery said with a sigh as her massage chair vibrated in tandem with Mallory's. Mallory sank deeper into her chair, letting whatever was inside it work out all the tension in her back.

"You and me both," Erica said, switching hands for the nail tech.

Savannah admired her freshly finished nails; the French tips looked beautiful from where Mallory was sitting. "Why did we wait until the last full day to do this? We should have been coming to the spa every single day."

"Chance would have loved that," Avery said sarcastically.

"We should do a mother-daughters spa weekend here in the spring," their mom suggested with a blissed-out sigh and closed eyes. "That would be fun."

Mallory wasn't sure she would be coming back. Not after Theo had given her the cold shoulder following the hockey game. The image of him limping off the ice replayed in her mind. His denial was going to cause permanent damage if he wasn't careful.

She knew that there was something really wrong because he was hiding from her. If he couldn't let her in when things got tough, what were the chances this relationship was going to last? Things were bound to get tough—that was how life worked.

"Brady was telling me about how gorgeous the leaves were in the fall," Erica said, pulling Mallory from her frustrated thoughts. "He takes guests out on ATV trails in some national park nearby. He said the views are so beautiful that photos can't even do them justice. Hayden totally wants to do that."

"Greg wants to come back in the summer after Quinn told him they have kayaks and paddle boards," Savannah chimed in. "Apparently you can rent a boat, go water skiing. It sounds like Greg's perfect lake getaway."

Great. The whole family was in love with this place. Meanwhile, Mallory felt like she was still standing on the outdoor ice rink with her heart in her hands, waiting for Theo to come back.

Mallory's phone vibrated with a text and her stomach fluttered when Theo's name appeared on the screen. *Now* he wanted to talk. The stubborn part of her considered ignoring his text and letting him sit there waiting for her. The part that wanted him to be vulnerable and let her in was begging her to respond immediately.

She opted for somewhere in the middle. She didn't ignore him, but she wasn't overly friendly either.

Can't right now.

It was polite but firm. Hopefully, it was enough to remind him she wasn't at his beck and call while leaving the door open.

"Was that Theo?" Savannah asked, too observant for Mallory's liking.

"It was."

"Is everything good?"

"*I'm* good," she replied, trying to appear relaxed even though her chest was tight.

Another buzz of her phone. When would you be available? Theo texted back.

Mallory had no answer for him. She wasn't on a schedule. She was trying to enjoy being pampered.

Erica's phone chimed with a text. Her brows pinched together as she tapped on her phone screen with the pads of her fingers, careful not to mess up her nails.

"What in the world?" she said, pinching her fingers together against the screen like she was trying to zoom in. "Ah, Mallory, I think you went viral."

"What?" Avery sat up a little straighter and pulled out her phone. "On what?"

"My friend from work texted me a screenshot asking if the person in the video is my sister," Erica explained.

Mallory took her feet out of the water and dried them on the towel that was sitting nearby. Barefoot, she padded over to her sister to see what she saw. "How did she know it was me? What am I doing?"

"Well, it's not just you. Theo might be featured as well."

Mallory looked over her shoulder and saw a picture of her and Theo kissing at the end of the hockey game yesterday.

Erica showed Mallory the posted video with the caption: Help me find Theo Seasons's mystery woman. They're in LOVE!

There were already over five hundred comments. Mallory's stomach dropped. "Did anyone identify me?"

"From what I saw, not yet," Erica said. "I did tell my friend that it was you, so maybe she commented."

"It's been reposted a lot of times," Avery said as Mallory tried to find anything that said her name.

"Welcome to your relationship reveal," Savannah said, her eyes glued to her phone as well.

Theo was going to freak out. Mallory handed Erica her phone back. "You need to tell your friend to delete the comment with my name in it if she posted it."

"Too late," Savannah reported. "Someone else said it was you and other people are repeating your name and that you work for the Icemen."

Mallory felt a chill down her spine. "What? How?"

Avery added, "It's all over the comments further down. Looks like someone googled you and really did their research."

"This can't be happening," Mallory said, feeling nauseous. "I need to show this to Theo. We were planning on talking to HR when we got back to Boston. Looks like we're going to be approaching them a little sooner than we thought."

"You'd better hurry," Erica said. "Before it spreads further."

Mallory grabbed her shoes and her phone, apologizing to the spa attendants as she hurried out. Her heart was racing as she made her way to Theo's room, her mind spinning with worst-case scenarios.

When she knocked on his door, Theo answered almost immediately, his brow furrowed in concern. "Mallory?"

"I need to show you something," she said, stepping past him into the room.

"I know you're mad at me, and I deserve—"

"It's not about that," she interrupted, thrusting her phone toward him. She played the video, and Theo's expression shifted from confusion to dread.

"Okay, well, this can't be that big."

Mallory's phone buzzed again, and she glanced at the screen. This time it was a message from Avery, who had forwarded a link. Her stomach flipped when she saw the headline: "Theo Seasons Skips Icemen Game to Step Out With New Girlfriend"

"Oh, my gosh," Mallory said, her voice shaking. "That's a terrible spin."

Theo frowned, sitting back down on the couch and pulling out his own phone. "Okay, maybe it's a bigger deal than I thought."

He fired off a text to his PR manager and another to his agent, summarizing the situation. "Let me see what they think before we freak out."

Mallory paced the room, her arms crossed. "I'm not freaking out. I just think we need to have a plan. HR is going to find out sooner rather than later, and it's going to look worse if they hear about it from a tabloid."

Theo's phone buzzed, and he read the messages from his PR manager and agent. His jaw tightened, and he set the phone down with a soft thud on the couch.

"What did they say?" Mallory asked, her voice tight with apprehension.

"They think I need to get ahead of it," Theo said, rubbing a hand over his closely cropped beard. He looked up at her, his expression pained. "But this couldn't have come at a worse time."

"What do you mean?" she asked, stepping closer.

"I'm injured," he admitted. "I wasn't able to skate when I got here and I might have made it worse yesterday. That puts me in a terrible position to beg the organization to bend the rules for me. This is the wrong time for me to be making demands."

Her heart sank. She hadn't expected him to fold so quickly. "What are you saying? The fact that you might have hurt your knee again means this relationship is dead in the water?"

He shook his head, sighing heavily. "In professional sports, your value is tied directly to what you can do right now, not what you did last season. Right now, I'm just an injured player whose personal life is splashed all over the internet. A personal life I'm not supposed to have with someone who works for the same organization that I do."

She could see the pain and the fear he was trying so hard to keep hidden. She sat down next to him but a respectable distance away. "Then we tell the Icemen it was a misunderstanding. No relationship to see here. All of that was taken out of context."

Theo turned to face her, his brown eyes filled with worry. "I'm messing this up." He reached for her hand, but she didn't want his touch right now, so she put her hands in her lap. She needed to hear that he wasn't giving up before they even gave it a go. "I need to figure out how to manage this," he explained. "I have to figure out how to make it look like I'm still valuable to them."

Mallory frowned. "I'm valuable to them as well. I have worked hard to gain the positive reputation I have earned there. This impacts my career, too."

He ran a hand through his hair. "Absolutely. I don't want to mess things up for you, either. I'm just not as confident as I was the other day when I said I would threaten to quit. They might let me."

As frustrated as she was, she reached out to place a hand on his arm. "We'll figure it out."

His seemed to relax under her touch. His eyes

found hers and she saw his determination had returned. "First, get our story straight. Then, we contact the organization and try to get ahead of all this internet stuff. Maybe if we're upfront and honest, they'll make an exception. It's not like you have anything to do with whether they give me a new contract. You don't negotiate with my agent about anything. Why would it matter if we're dating?"

Mallory's heart pitter-pattered a little stronger. He didn't want to roll over and give up. She nodded. "Okay. Let's start making sure we're on the same page about how this all started."

Theo gave her a small tired smile. "I'm sorry for running away yesterday."

She let out a small laugh. "I'm not sure I would call that running."

Theo dipped his head. When his eyes lifted, she saw the humility there. "I don't want to walk away from you."

It wasn't a promise that he wouldn't leave, but at least he didn't want to. Mallory would have to take what she could get at this point. They needed to take accountability. At least they'd be doing it together.

CHAPTER NINETEEN

"WHAT WERE YOU THINKING?" Olive, his PR manager, sounded exasperated. The conference call was not going as well as Theo had hoped. Olive wasn't accustomed to handling these kinds of fires since Theo typically kept out of trouble.

"Listen, I'm being completely honest here," Theo said, trying to steady his tone. "There was no plan for this to turn into a relationship. It just…happened."

"Given the state of things," his agent chimed in. Darren was as levelheaded as they got. He was careful with his words, but his tone was firm. "I don't think now is the time to publicly defy the Icemen's rules, Theo. If this just happened, it can just as easily unhappen."

"I agree," Olive added bluntly.

Theo ran a hand over his beard, frustration gnawing at him. Mallory had gone off to have lunch with her sisters and mom. This viral video had already disrupted her spa day, and the last thing he wanted was for her to give up anything else for this. He had promised to fill her in once the call was over because he believed these two were going to come up with the perfect plan.

It was a good thing she wasn't here to hear this, though. Both Olive and his agent were firmly against doing anything that might jeopardize his career. Their suggestion to end it didn't sit well with him, though.

"What if I can't do that?" Theo said, his voice quieter but tinged with defiance. "What if I don't *want* to do that?"

Olive sighed. "If you had picked anyone else for a holiday fling, I could have spun this a million different ways that all would have ended with you looking like you were starting the New Year off fresh and having fun." She paused, clearly gearing up for the blow she was about to deliver. "But this? This looks like you paid for the team's physical therapist to come to New Hampshire, then seduced her, using your influence and celebrity to manipulate a romance out of her."

"I did *not* manipulate anyone! She's the one who asked me to pretend we were dating. And I didn't pay her to come here—I only covered her room."

"That almost sounds worse," Darren said. "Listen, I get it. She's cute. You like her. Fine. Let's refocus on your recovery and get you back on the ice. Mallory can't be part of that any longer. You're going to have to work with a different PT. Preferably someone you have no interest in dating. Once you're off injured reserve and we secure that contract extension, you can dip your toe back into the dating pool. Maybe it's with Mallory, maybe it's with someone else."

He wanted to tell Darren that there was no *someone else*. He could feel the heat rising, creeping up his neck.

"What he's trying to say is we have to switch the narrative," Olive said, tagging back in. "We can't let fans focus on how you blatantly ignored the team's rules and skipped a game to make out with your physical therapist at some posh resort somewhere. We need to shift the story to your recovery and how far you've come. We need to build excitement about your return to the ice, not this mess."

Theo dropped his head into his hands, trying to keep his frustration in check. He struggled to put the right words together to get them to understand. "I didn't skip a game on purpose. There was a blizzard. The highway back to Boston was shut down," he said, frustrated that he had agreed to go to that game in the first place. He clenched his jaw, anger simmering as he thought about the situation he'd ended up in. "And for the record, we're *not* at some posh resort. This is my family's inn. I grew up here. My *family* lives here."

"That's perfect," Olive exclaimed. "Let's go with the family angle. I need pictures of you celebrating the holidays with your family. I want you with your arms around your mom. I want you and your brothers laughing at some hilarious joke you made. Whatever you can get me, I can use it."

Theo exhaled slowly, pinching the bridge of his nose. "Sure."

"Why were you two at a youth hockey game, anyway?" Darren asked.

"The local arena I grew up playing at suffered some damage because of the blizzard. The kids were playing their biggest rivals, so I gave them a place to play hockey."

"Also amazing," Olive said, sounding like she was multitasking. It was clear that she was typing something up. "Send me some names so we can push that hometown hero returns to help underprivileged youth and save the day after a blizzard."

"They aren't underprivileged," Theo corrected her. "And I didn't do it alone. If it wasn't for Mallory's family, I don't know if we would have got it done."

"Fine, fine," Olive said, breezing past his protest. "We'll scratch underprivileged. Maybe misplaced. No, wait." She was clearly typing. "Displaced. That works better."

Theo gritted his teeth, his patience wearing thin. "Sure, whatever." He leaned forward, resting his elbows on his knees. At least they weren't focusing on breaking up with Mallory, but they still needed a strategy for talking to the organization. "Maybe if the team sees how much good

Mallory and I accomplished this week, they'll be okay with us being together."

"Changing the narrative was step one," Darren said. "Step two is telling the organization you are so sorry and will never let that kind of thing happen again. It was a momentary lapse in judgment. You're dedicated to getting back on the ice and helping the team win a championship."

Theo's head fell back against the couch, staring up at the ceiling. His chest tightened with guilt, frustration and a deep gnawing fear. "Why can't we spin it like there's no possibility of our relationship ever being a harm to the organization?"

Neither Darren nor Olive spoke immediately, and Theo's thoughts churned in the silence. His knee throbbed, a cruel reminder of the lies he'd been telling about how bad the pain was, about how much progress he *wasn't* making. He could barely walk right now. Skating again was beginning to feel like a fantasy. What kind of leverage did he have to make demands or plead his case?

Finally, Darren answered him, "You can call the front office after we change the narrative. Tell them you and Mallory got caught up in something and see what they say. My opinion is that there are reasons they put those clauses in contracts. People taking advantage of people with less power in an organization like that. Also, if you two break up and things end badly, they don't want to deal with lawsuits or claims of an unsafe work environment. They aren't going to believe you when you both think everything is rainbows and sunshine that there isn't the potential for harm."

His words hit him like a punch to the gut. Theo clenched his jaw, fighting to keep his emotions from spilling over. It wasn't fair. But fairness had nothing to do with the game he was playing.

He swallowed hard and sat up straight. "Fine. I'll send you the photos and whatever details you need so you can plant the other stories."

"Thank you," Olive said.

"Theo," Darren added, his voice softer this time, "You are a hockey player. It's what you were born to do. Don't lose it because of some woman. There are a lot of women out there."

Theo didn't respond as he ended the call. There were lots of women, but there was only one Mallory. That mattered to him. She mattered to him.

He stared at his phone for a moment before tossing it onto the table in front of him. For the first time in a long while, Theo didn't feel like the determined, unstoppable center he'd always been. He felt like a man standing on cracked ice, trying desperately not to fall through.

"You are a hockey player. It's what you were born to do. Don't lose it because of some woman. There are a lot of women out there," a voice told Theo.

Mallory froze outside Theo's door, her forehead resting on it. The words filtered through, muffled but clear enough to make her stomach drop. She waited, her pulse pounding in her ears, hoping Theo would say something, anything to defend her.

That she wasn't just some woman.

That she mattered to him.

That he wanted her in his life, no matter what.

But the silence on his end was deafening.

His silence was an answer in itself.

Mallory's throat tightened, the ache filling her chest. She had overheard enough of the conversation to piece it together. He was choosing his career, protecting what little of it remained. And maybe he was right to do so. His hockey career, built on years of sweat and sacrifice, was literally hanging by a thread.

And their relationship? It wasn't even built on solid ground. It had started as a lie, an arrangement designed to get her out of her family's endless nagging and to make his holiday easier. She wanted to laugh at the absurdity of it all, but the urge to cry was stronger.

Why would Theo fight for something so fragile? So fleeting? They'd been together for days, not years. She was kidding herself if she thought she mattered enough for him to risk his future.

She took a shaky breath, willing herself to push

the emotions down where they couldn't choke her. The only way to get through this was to go back to pretending it didn't matter. It was all just pretend, wasn't it?

Her fingers curled into fists at her sides, her nails digging into her palms. She needed to stop being naive. What she should be worried about now wasn't Theo or whatever mess of feelings she had for him. She needed to focus on damage control with the Icemen. When someone in the organization heard about this little tryst, her entire career could be on the line.

Mallory tried to calm her racing thoughts. The plan was simple. She'd call the front office and tell them the truth. The whole truth. She'd tell them there was no real relationship, only a charade that had somehow become public knowledge. She'd own it before it spiraled further out of control.

Her stomach twisted as she thought about what she'd say to her family. Her mom wouldn't be nearly as forgiving as the Icemen might be. The disappointment in her mother's eyes was going to crush her.

Mallory glanced at the door one last time. She wanted to knock, to walk in and demand answers. But what good would it do? Theo had already made his choice. It wasn't her.

She pushed off the wall, her chin lifting even as her heart sank. She had survived worse than this.

She'd survive this, too. Forcing her feet to move, Mallory walked away, leaving Theo's silence and all her ridiculous hopes that she had finally found someone who cared about her enough to make the sacrifices.

She knocked on her parents' door without the hesitation she had had at Theo's. She knew her mom was downstairs having lunch with her sisters. It wasn't her mom who she wanted to talk to first, though.

Her dad opened the door, and Mallory immediately fell into his arms. She let all the emotion that had been pushing its way to the surface out in one good cry.

"Come in here and calm yourself down, sweetheart," her dad said, gently guiding her into the room and closing the door. "What's got you so upset?"

"I lied," she blurted out. It felt good to say it out loud. "I lied about everything because I didn't want to go to Christmas at your house."

Her dad pulled back to get a look at her. "You lied about everything? What does that mean?"

"Theo and I weren't dating," she admitted. "When I told Mom that I couldn't come because I was meeting my boyfriend's parents, I didn't even have a fake boyfriend. I made Theo play along because I thought if Mom knew the truth, she would never forgive me." The tears were back in full force. "She's never going to forgive me."

"Oh, honey." Her dad pulled her back in for a hug. "Your mother is many things but unforgiving is not one of them."

Mallory took a shaky breath and began to tell him everything—how she'd made up the fake relationship, how her real feelings for Theo had developed, how they'd tried to make it work and how the Icemen's strict no-fraternization policy had complicated everything. She explained the viral video, Theo's conference call and how he'd ultimately chosen his hockey career over their budding relationship.

"He's choosing hockey. Honestly, I get it. You'd be mad if I chose someone I had been dating for a hot minute over my career."

Her dad chuckled softly. "I wouldn't be mad at you. I'd ask you to explain why dating someone was more important, so I could understand why you were making such an impulsive decision. But mad? No."

The two of them stood there in silence for a minute.

"We can tell your mother together if you want."

Mallory nodded. That was exactly what she wanted. Her dad was so good at this kind of stuff.

She washed her tears off her face while her dad texted the rest of the family that they were needed up in his room. Before long, the door opened, and her mom and siblings entered, their faces filled with worry.

"Why didn't you answer me?" her mom asked, her tone sharp with concern. "What's going on?"

"There's nothing to worry about, Selene," her dad said, his voice calm and reassuring. "Sit down. Your daughter has something to tell you."

Mallory's stomach twisted as she sat down with her family. She managed to get through the whole confession without breaking down, although tears welled in her eyes when her mom stopped making eye contact and she stared at her clasped hands instead.

"I'm so sorry, Mom. I know I shouldn't have lied. I know I shouldn't have asked him to lie to you. That wasn't right."

Her mom remained quiet, her face unreadable, which only made Mallory's chest tighten further.

"I knew it," Savannah said, her tone unsurprised. Of course, she had been suspicious. Savannah always questioned everything.

Avery, however, looked aghast. "I can't believe you made us hang out with his family. Did they know?"

"No!" Mallory said quickly. "They had no idea."

Her dad reached over to pat her mom's hand. "Selene?" he asked gently, prompting her to say something.

Selene finally looked up, her expression softer

than Mallory expected. "I'm not mad," she said slowly. "But I am disappointed."

Mallory winced at the words, which somehow stung more than anger.

"I wish you'd just told us how you were feeling," her mom continued. "I would've understood if you needed space this Christmas. You didn't have to make up a whole story to avoid us."

Mallory's heart cracked at the sadness in her mother's voice. "I'm sorry," she whispered. "I thought it was easier this way."

Her mom reached over, taking Mallory's hand in hers. "Next time, just talk to me, okay? I'm your mom. I'd rather know the truth, even if it's hard to hear."

"You're not going to let it end like this are you?" Avery asked.

"There's not much I can do other than come clean with the Icemen and hope they let me keep my job."

"Um, do you forget where you came from?" Avery asked. "Moores do not roll over when things get tough. We fight."

"If Theo's PR manager thinks he needs to change the narrative, we can help change the narrative," Savannah said, pulling out her phone.

"What are you talking about?" Mallory wasn't sure there should be any interference with the PR.

Erica had her phone in hand already. "How can

the Icemen ask the cutest couple in the world to break up?"

"I'm not sure Theo and I are the cutest couple in the world."

Avery kept tapping on her phone. "Oh, but you're about to be. Everyone loves a love story, and no one wants the bad press that would come along with forcing them to break up. We're going to use your sudden viral moment to your advantage."

Mallory wasn't sure how to do that, but if anyone could figure it out, it was her sisters and her parents. In that moment, surrounded by her family, Mallory felt a small flicker of hope.

CHAPTER TWENTY

THEO HAD ONE thing to do before he talked to Mallory about the new PR plan and they made the call to the Icemen together. He had to tell his parents the truth about his relationship with Mallory.

He found them in the inn's kitchen, his mom busy putting together the desserts for dinner while his dad fulfilled the "difficult" role of taste tester.

"I'm glad I found you," he said, stepping into the room. "I need to talk to both of you."

His parents exchanged a quick look before turning their attention back to him. "What's up, dear?" his mom asked, not pausing in her careful chopping of walnuts.

"It's about me and Mallory."

"I love Mallory," his mom said with a bright smile. "I'm glad you didn't keep her a secret forever. She is so sweet and her family, well, they were just so helpful and kind. I don't think we would have managed Christmas as smoothly as we did without them."

Theo winced. This was going to be harder than

he thought. "That's kind of what I wanted to clear up with you." He rubbed the back of his neck. "The thing is, I know I told you Mallory and I were dating before we got here, but that wasn't true."

His mom stopped chopping. His dad's fork paused halfway to his mouth.

"When she came to Apple Hollow, she was just my PT, here to help me work on my recovery. I didn't want to waste any time, not even for Christmas."

The confusion on his parents' faces was why he had managed to play along for as long as he had. He hadn't wanted them to feel foolish. He told them everything, especially making it clear that he actually began to have real feelings for Mallory.

His dad set his fork down carefully, leaning back in his chair. "So, where do you stand now?"

"That's the problem," Theo admitted, running a hand through his hair. "My PR manager wants me to say the whole thing was a mistake, apologize to the Icemen for breaking their rules and promise it won't happen again. Darren had the nerve to tell me I'll find someone else because there are plenty of women in the world and I'm a hockey player."

His mom gasped. "But there's only one Mallory."

Theo gave his mom a crooked smile. "That's how I feel."

"What's the plan, then?" his dad asked, crossing his arms over his chest. "You can't let her go, but you can't risk her job, either."

Theo let out a long breath, bracing his hands against the edge of the counter. "That's the question I've been sitting in my room trying to answer."

He hesitated. Saying it out loud was going to make it real, but it was time to be honest about one more thing.

"My knee is shot," he admitted with a sigh of resignation. "There is no chance I'll ever regain the range of motion I need to be on the ice with the world's best hockey players." There was no shame in telling the truth, no matter how much the truth broke his heart. "I am going to have to retire at the end of this season."

His mom's eyes glistened, and his dad's jaw tightened as he processed the words.

"Theo," his mom whispered, coming around the counter to wrap him in a hug. "I'm so sorry."

He hugged her back. It had been a long time since he had sought this kind of comfort from her. "It's not the end of the world," he said quietly, though the crack in his voice betrayed the ache in his chest. "It's just not how I thought it would end."

His dad stepped forward, resting a hand on Theo's shoulder. "You've had an incredible career. No one can take that away from you, son."

Theo nodded, his throat tight. "I just want to figure out how to make this right with Mallory. If I have to choose between her and hockey, the choice is already made."

His phone rang in his pocket. It was Olive. "I have to answer this," he explained to his parents. "What's up, Olive?"

"This thing is blowing up so big I don't know if we can shift the narrative before the Icemen catch wind of it. People really want you to be in love, Theo."

He wasn't sure what she meant, but it was nice to have the support because he was falling in love and the Icemen weren't going to be able to tell him he couldn't be.

"OPERATION MAKE THE World Love the Love Story is in full effect," Avery said in full boss-lady mode.

Mallory chuckled despite the knot of nerves in her neck and shoulders. "I don't know what that means exactly, but I think I like it."

Still there was this inkling of doubt. Even if they could convince the Icemen organization that it would be a bad look to keep Mallory and Theo apart, she wasn't sure Theo was on board with being together. After all, he'd had nothing to say when his agent essentially told him there were other fish in the sea.

"Why the face?" Savannah asked from her spot on the bed.

Mallory sighed, glancing around at her family. Savannah and Mallory were perched on the bed; Erica leaned against the desk, and Avery had claimed the desk chair. Their parents were snuggled together on the small loveseat. It was cozy and warm, the kind of moment that usually made her feel safe, but not today.

"I don't know. What if you do all this and he doesn't want to be with me?"

"That would be the next phase of the operation," Avery replied. "You need to go find your man and convince him to fight."

That would be a lot easier if the dread that had nestled into her stomach wasn't reminding her how horrible rejection would be. "I don't know what to say."

"Here's what you say," Erica said with all the dramatic flair she possessed. "Listen, Theo. I'm awesome and you like me and we are amazing together and we shouldn't let anything get in the way of that, especially some silly policy at work."

"Should I write that down?" Mallory asked, her laughter breaking through the nerves. Without her family, she would not have been handling this as well. She was grateful they were here.

"All you have to do is speak from the heart,"

her dad suggested. "Hopefully, your honesty will give him the courage to be honest back."

It was good advice but still terrifying to think about putting her feelings out there and not have them reciprocated. "Okay, I'm going to go talk to him."

"You got this, Mal," Savannah said, giving her shoulder a squeeze. Avery and Erica also offered their encouragement. Her mom smiled.

She glanced around the room at these people, her people, who had supported her every step of the way. "I appreciate that you all don't hate me for running away this Christmas and lying about why. I'm also really glad that you didn't know I was running away and that you followed me because I would be lost without you."

Her mom stood, pulling her into a tight hug. "We love you, Mallory. Now go get your guy," her mom said, nudging her toward the door.

Mallory opened the door to find Theo standing on the other side, his fist raised like he was just about to knock.

"I was coming to look for you," he said, his voice low and steady unlike her heart at the moment. "And here you are."

"Here I am," she repeated softly.

"You know what?" her mom said, glancing between them. "There are way too many bodies in here. I think we should all go down to the lobby and see what's going on for activities the rest of the afternoon." She ushered everyone out, pausing at the door to give Mallory a wink. "Feel free to use our room to talk."

One second they were all there and the next the room was empty. Mallory gestured for Theo to join her inside. His limp was still visible, raising more than a few concerns. "I was just about to go looking for you. Guess we both had the same idea."

Theo slid his hands in his pockets. "Guess so."

"Do you want to go first or should I?" Mallory asked, praying he would take the lead.

"Ladies first, of course."

She cursed the rules of politeness. Taking a deep breath, she spoke her truth. "I told my family everything. No more pretending, no more lying under the excuse of not wanting to hurt people's feelings." She fidgeted with the sleeves of her sweater. "I came back to your room while you were on the phone with your agent and PR person. I heard what they were saying and what you... weren't saying."

Theo winced. "Oh, Mallory. I wish I had known you were there."

She shook her head and held a hand out to tell him to stop. "I get that their job is to protect your career and public image. It makes sense that they'd encourage you to end things with me."

Theo stepped forward, resting his hands firmly on her shoulders. "I am not ending things with you. I know what my team was trying to do, too. The thing they just weren't understanding was the nonnegotiable piece to this is you. I want to be with you."

"Me?" It was hard to believe him after everything they had talked about and everything she heard him talk about on that conference call.

"Yes, you." His voice was soft and sincere. "I know I've been difficult the last twenty-four hours. I wanted to have it all because I'm used to getting what I want if I want it enough. Hockey is the only job I've ever had. But there's a reality I haven't wanted to face, and that's the one that includes me stepping away from playing hockey and finding out what the next stage of my life is going to bring. I don't know what that's going to be, maybe coaching, maybe running my own hockey program, but I want you to be part of it."

Tears welled in her eyes. "Are you serious? Because if you made me fall in love with you and this is all a lie, I will *never* forgive you."

Theo pulled her against him. "I have never been more serious. You are the one, Mallory. I know it, my family knows it—"

"My family knows it," she added.

They both laughed. Theo leaned back just enough

to look into her eyes, his voice dropping to a whisper. "I love you."

Her breath caught, and before she could respond, Theo leaned down, pressing his lips to hers in a kiss that left no room for doubt. It was tender and filled with all the promises she hoped someday he'd put into words.

When they finally pulled apart, Mallory smiled, her hands resting on his chest. "I love you, too."

Theo grinned. "Good. Because we've got a lot to figure out, but I'm not letting you go."

Neither of them knew what the future held, but in that moment, it didn't matter. They had each other, and for now, that was enough.

EPILOGUE

WHY HE HAD ever agreed to wear a tux was beyond him. Theo tugged at the collar, trying to loosen the bow tie that felt more like a noose. Whoever invented men's dress clothes clearly harbored a grudge against men. He felt like he was being strangled every time he had to suit up like this.

"Can I get two glasses of champagne?" he asked the bartender. While she got his drinks, he checked his watch. He had five minutes to get back to where he belonged.

Anywhere Mallory stood was where he belonged.

Another week had passed and every moment with her simply confirmed what they knew to be true—this was the real thing. True love, unexpected and extraordinary. It had started as a ruse, but now, nothing felt more genuine than what they shared.

"Here's your champagne." The bartender slid the two glasses his way.

Theo tipped her generously. "Happy New Year in a couple minutes," he said to her.

She laughed. "Happy New Year to you, too. And tell Mallory the same. Team Love forever!"

Theo chuckled as he grabbed the glasses. Somehow, he and Mallory had become a sensation, the internet's favorite couple. People were rooting for them like they were the underdog team in a playoff game. Online petitions flooded the Icemen's inbox, begging the organization to let them be together. Mallory's sisters spearheaded a social media campaign that could rival the most expensive PR firms in effectiveness.

By some miracle it worked.

The Icemen relented. Whether it was because they didn't want to be the villains breaking up Team Love or they genuinely saw no harm in bending the rules, Theo didn't care. All that mattered was that Mallory was his, and he was hers, no matter what the world threw at them.

He turned the corner, and there she was.

Mallory stood near the ballroom's grand windows, her hair falling in loose waves around her shoulders, the sequins on her black dress catching the light and sparkling like stars. She was breathtaking.

"For you, my dear," he said, handing her the champagne flute.

She gave him a chaste kiss in return. "Thank you."

"What if we kiss during the countdown *and* at midnight?" he asked, wrapping one arm around her waist so he could pull her tighter.

"I think that's against the rules."

"What rules?"

"The make-a-wish-at-midnight rule. If you kiss your true love at midnight and make a wish, it's supposed to come true," she replied.

"That's a new one," he said, narrowing his eyes as if trying to figure out if she was serious. He'd have to google it later to see if she was pulling his leg. There wasn't any time now as the countdown had begun.

"Ten! Nine! Eight!" the crowd roared, the energy in the room electric.

Theo's heart raced as he looked down at Mallory. She was smiling up at him, her eyes shining with happiness.

"Seven! Six! Five!"

He tilted her chin up gently with his fingers.

"Four! Three! Two!"

Her arms slid around his neck, pulling him even closer.

"One! Happy New Year!"

Theo didn't hesitate. He leaned down and kissed her, his other hand pressing against the small of her back to hold her against him. The world around them dissolved. The noise of the crowd, the clinking of glasses, the cheers, all melted away.

It was just them.

The kiss was everything—sweet, passionate, full of promises for the year ahead. It was the kind of kiss that said this is forever.

When they finally pulled apart, Mallory looked up at him, her cheeks flushed. "Did you make your wish?"

Theo shook his head. "I didn't have to. It already came true."

She smiled, her fingers brushing against his jawline. "Good, because so did mine."

* * * * *

Get up to 4 Free Books!

We'll send you 2 free books from each series you try PLUS a free Mystery Gift.

FREE Value Over **$25**

Both the **Harlequin® Special Edition** and **Harlequin® Heartwarming™** series feature compelling novels filled with stories of love and strength where the bonds of friendship, family and community unite.